DEFINITELY, *maybe*, YOURS

DEFINITELY, *maybe*, YOURS

LISSA REED

interlude ✦✦ **press**

ISBN 13 (trade): 978-1-941530-40-5

ISBN-13 (ebook): 978-1-941530-41-2

Published by INTERLUDE PRESS, New York

http://interludepress.com

BOOK DESIGN by Lex Huffman

COVER PHOTOGRAPHY by LaToya Conward

COVER DESIGN by Buckeyegrrl Designs

CHAPTER HEADER ART @depositphotos.com/sonya_illustration

10 9 8 7 6 5 4 3 2 1

To Jess:
You have always been my Buffy.
Thank you.

When all is said and done, the weather and love are the two elements about which one can never be sure.

❧ ALICE HOFFMAN

Chapter One

I COULD JUST GO HOME. I REALLY COULD.

Craig props his chin on his hand and stares through the plate glass window, through the large, swooping white and gold letters that spell out *Sucre Coeur*—backwards of course, from his safely indoors perspective—as a tiny red Toyota goes careening down Queen Anne Avenue. The car's tires slide over the ice-sheened asphalt in front of the bakery, and Craig winces as it squeals through the intersection. *Assuming I would make it home. The odds look good for neither pedestrian nor driver.*

A decade of Januaries in Seattle and he has still not quite come to grips with the danger factor of winter here. Not that his native England hasn't got its share of dangerous cold weather, but he'd had eighteen years to get used to that before he took off for the States. By similar reckoning, he'll acclimate himself to Seattle nicely by his thirty-sixth birthday.

Then he'll move somewhere else. With a beach.

Craig observes how very, very far the sugary sprinkle of snowfall is from warm white sand, and sighs.

"Don't worry," says a voice, bright with amusement. "It could snow ten feet, and you'd still find a way to make it to the pub."

Adrenaline sends Craig spinning to face the voice while simultaneously jumping what must be a good foot into the air: not his most graceful moment. Heart racing, he collapses against the register stand. "Don't sneak around like that!"

Laughter, light and airy and free of any remorse or contrition whatever, floats from the depths of the bakery kitchen before the owner of the voice emerges and pools of shadow resolve into the diminutive shape of Sucre Coeur's best decorator. "Right," Sarita says, dropping the pink plastic trays she's carrying onto the marble top of the display case with a crash, "because when I'm wearing Docs and carrying a stack of trays, I am totally a sneaky ninja. Not my fault you weren't paying attention."

This is not an argument he will win with any dignity or grace, Craig understands—best not to try. "I didn't realize you were still here. Thought you'd gone out the back entrance when you started the dishwasher. I heard the door."

"I did go out the back entrance, to take the garbage out to the dumpster. As is part of my duties when closing, much like washing the display trays and putting them back." With exaggerated care, she pulls open the display cases and starts returning the trays, widening her already large dark eyes in mock astonishment. "Ooh, look, doing my job, ooh, I'm a freaky quiet ninja-slash-decorator."

"All right, you've made your point; I wasn't paying attention, shut it." He sticks his tongue out at her as he tugs at one of his dreads, willing himself to calm down, already.

"Weren't doing your job, either," Sarita observes, arching one delicate black eyebrow. "Register count? Inventory? Time off slips?"

Craig snorts and reaches beneath the counter for a zip bag and a manila envelope. "Done and dusted, thank you very much."

"Because you have to get to the pub, because it's Thursday." Again the mock innocence as Sarita closes the display case. She pretends to dust her thin hands together and hold them out for his inspection. "Yes?"

"Because our esteemed employer is coming to pick up the money and paperwork on her way to the airport; she's got a red-eye to Brussels." He draws himself up to his full five feet, eleven inches, more out of a reach for dignity than any attempt to intimidate Sarita, who is possessed of the impressive implacability of a Galápagos tortoise. "I always have the paperwork done early for Theodora anyway, whether she's off on holiday or not. I think I resent the implication you're making."

"That you go to the pub every Thursday, rain or shine or snow, because you have a routine and you like your routine?" She pokes at the messy bun of black curls piled atop her head, a pile that adds a good three inches to her height. Her attitude adds another foot at least. "What's to imply?"

"You make me sound dull." Craig pulls his coat and hat from the cupboard below the register and stacks them next to the zip bag and envelope. He checks the pockets of the puffy blue anorak, making sure the wax paper bundles he stashed away earlier are still there, and slides a glare at Sarita and her amused eyes. "I like things a certain way. Nothing wrong with that. That pub's got good microbrews and decent food. Not a bad place to spend a couple of hours before I go home."

"Alone, because you don't pick up anyone at the pub." Sarita rolls her eyes as she tugs her own winter gear from the cupboard and slips into a bright pink coat. She yanks a bright rainbow-knit cap down over her hair and tucks her stray curls under the wool. "Don't you—"

"Alone, because I usually have work to do when I get home *from* the pub," he retorts, raising his voice to carry over whatever lecture she is about to deliver about the human condition. His human condition, specifically. In the four years they've worked together, he's heard a thousand of these lectures, and they've only gotten worse since Sarita decided to enter the University of Washington's graduate philosophy program. *God spare me the philosophy grad student's view of the world.* "Which, tonight, includes a review of that blues band we saw last week. The arts district wants it for the debut issue of their new quarterly. I've got a deadline." He raises an eyebrow at her. "See? I don't only ever go to the pub. And I am not always alone. Took you with me that time."

"I didn't say you only ever go to the pub, I said you never deviate from routine, and your routine is that you go to the pub on Thursdays and you never go home with anyone," she corrects, her irritation and stern tone at distinctly stark odds with the fuzzy pink mohair mittens she's pulling on. "And that's—"

"A perfectly acceptable way to live, for me and a thousand other people in this world," he says, feeling no guilt or shame over interrupting her twice. Well. Perhaps some guilt. His mother would have shot him for being so rude. "It's nice. It's quiet. I like nice and quiet. My life is perfectly satisfactory by my standards, which is a good thing, as it's my life and all." Craig pauses and takes a closer look at Sarita. Tonight, at close range, her implacability seems more like a veneer than second nature. "Hey. What's your problem? You're giving me more shit than usual this week."

She knots a rainbow scarf at her throat with more aggression than is generally required for the task. "Nothing."

But Craig Oliver is the middle-ish child of a rambunctious, English, Caribbean *and* Scottish family, with all the patience such a position in life has forced him to develop, and so he stands and waits while putting on his own cap and gloves and he keeps a steady eye on her.

She gives in with a sigh and another of her expert eye-rolls but doesn't look at him, seeming to prefer instead the apparently fascinating sight of her mittened hand stroking the black and white marble top of the display case. "Sengupta family dinner tonight."

That is not usually something that upsets her to this degree, so Craig casts about for something that might. *Ah. There.* "So your sister and her husband are in town," he guesses—correctly, if the tight, flat line of Sarita's mouth is anything to go by.

Craig has never met Anjali Bhattacharyya, but watching the aftermath of clashes between Sarita and her enormously homophobic elder sister over the last several years has made him strongly question his pacifist tendencies. *There's someone who'd benefit from a long dunk in Puget Sound. Repeated ones, perhaps.*

Sarita's mouth is still compressed into that thin line. Her tan face is a bit paler than usual, which makes her eyes stand out and appear even more dark and enormous. Craig puts his hand over hers, stilling the swish of wool over marble.

"Hey," he says, tilting his head to try to catch her evasive gaze. "Hey. Come on. Skip it, hey? Come out to the pub with me. Have a pint, split a basket of chips. We'll go back to my place and listen to the CD that band gave me. You can help me with the review. Yeah?"

She shakes her head. "Can't." Her voice is hoarse, almost too soft to hear. "Devesh is out of town, that *rat*, so I have to go. I've skipped too many anyway. Damn it." The deep breath she takes in seems to go all the way down to her toes. It must give her the boost she needs, because when she looks up at Craig, her eyes are bright again. "It's fine. I'll be fine. Really. Mama always speaks up when Anjali gets too stupid anyway. I mean, Devesh is better at it, but 'Oh no, sorry, Reeti, Sunil and I just can't miss this Yorkie breeders' meet-up.'" The contempt in her snort could power a small car engine. "What good are big brothers if they're not there when you need them?"

"I can fill in," Craig offers, winding his scarf around his neck. "Go with you to dinner. I like your mother's cooking. Is it biryani tonight? With the mutton? Love it when she does that."

Sarita's laughter as she swats at him is heartening. "Oh, God, because a gay black Englishman at the dinner table wouldn't be more shocking to Anjali than any of the girls I've brought home!" She lets out a hoot. "No thanks, Craig. I appreciate the offer, seriously, but I've got to learn to deal with her one of these days." She gets up on her tiptoes and is only just able to plant a kiss on his cheek; she has to tug him down by a loop of his scarf to do it. "Nah, I can do it. You go to the pub. Find someone else to rescue."

"I could go home," he says, feathers ruffled again. "You know I could."

Sarita pats his coat sleeve. "You won't."

I bloody well will. "I'm going to."

She's just starting to tilt her head and smile when the bakery door crashes open, its cranberry-painted frame smashing into the white tiles of the wall and making the jingle bells on the knob shriek in cacophony. "Sorry I'm late," Theodora gasps. She motors into the bakery on impractically high-heeled suede boots, a swirl of blonde shag and pashmina and Opium. "Quick, hand over the deposit; I'm going to be late to the airport as it is and I know you're going to want to get to the pub, Craig."

"Oh, for fuck's sake," Craig groans.

CRAIG CAN'T FIGURE OUT IF HE'S PROVING A POINT BY GOING to the pub or not. It's too late, of course.

He's already here, standing outside and glaring up at the sign.

"There's nothing wrong with a routine," he grumbles and brushes a flake of ice from his face, where it has been numbing a pinpoint-sized spot on his face for five minutes. "Nothing wrong with peace and quiet. I get by. I like it."

He really does, so why is he so annoyed by Sarita's needling? He's got the solitary life down to an art form, a thing of beauty. He's got his work managing the bakery; that pays the bills. He's starting to get a decent amount of freelance work writing for publications around Seattle; that feeds his soul. He doesn't like going to clubs all the time; he's happy to go home to the cozy third-floor apartment he rents from Theodora, have a cup of tea and listen to music or watch a movie.

Here and there, when he wants it or needs it, he can find someone to spend a night with. Sex is just another need to fill. He's got enough to do looking out for himself, and he's content with it; no need for anything longer-term.

So why, again, is he standing outside The Order of the Garter, glaring up at its blameless blue-lettered heraldic sign and arguing with himself?

"Because I'm right, and there's nothing wrong with routine," he snaps aloud, startling a pair of rugby-jerseyed fellows who have just shoved the mahogany and glass door of the pub open into his face. His cheeks go hot and he ducks their glances as he shoves past them into the warmth of the pub. What the hell. He's cold, it's warm inside and he has earned a pint, blast it.

"Craig!" The wave of a hand catches his attention, and he has to smile as he unwinds his scarf and skirts the crowd that's watching and betting on the boxing match on the big-screen television. The hand belongs to Katie, his favorite of the Garter's many bartenders and the reason he prefers to come here on Thursdays. He likes her constant parade of changing hair colors—a return to last autumn's red-streaked black this time—and elaborate facial jewelry, not to mention her relentlessly cheerful demeanor and the way it contrasts with her vast wardrobe of fishnets and black lace. Certainly not the usual girl you find behind the bar at a sports pub.

It helps that she's the only bartender there who remembers what he likes and pulls a glass whenever she spots him coming through the door. Craig likes the look of the pint glass she's got in her hand. He pushes his way through the heaving, murmuring crowd of UDub students clogging the tables in the middle of the pub—law students, from the sound of it, and all of them about three happy sheets to the wind if his judgment is any good—and aims for a spot as far from them as he can manage. He stops near the end of the bar, a couple of spaces short of a limp, possibly unconscious fellow in a gray woolen pullover who has collapsed in a precarious pile on top of the very last stool, and shrugs off his coat. "Tell me that's something good, Katie love. It looks good."

"Does it look like your favorite oatmeal stout?" she asks, green eyes bright, as she slides the glass down the length of the polished bar. She's clearly pleased with herself; she sticks her beringed hands into the pockets of her apron and rocks back on her heels, watching him. "Because it is. Paul got it back on tap this morning. Said he knew you'd be in tonight."

Score a point—no, make it ten points—for routine. Excellent. Just excellent. "God, yes, Paul's timing on getting this one back on tap is perfect. Thanks." It's all the goodness of an oatmeal cookie in an alcoholic beverage, with hints of chocolate and black currant under the warm, roasted flavor of the malt, and it's his favorite microbrew that the pub offers. "Christ, that's amazing, even better than last year."

"I'll be sure to tell him you said so; he was hoping he'd improved on the last batch, and you know yours is the opinion he trusts most on this one." Katie wiggles her eyebrows and beams a hopeful little smile back at him, shoulders twitching with her eagerness. It never fails to amuse Craig that Katie is the most cheerful punk-Goth-whatever in the free world. "Got my payment?"

"'Course I have." With a wink, Craig pulls a ten-dollar bill out of his left coat pocket and a carefully bagged almond and raspberry-lemon croissant, Katie's all-time favorite baked good, out of the right. He passes them across the bar as if he's James Bond—if a very cheeky and cheery sort of 007. "You know I'll always look out for you. Keep the change."

Katie squeals and flops across the bar to squeeze him breathless, and her ponytail slaps him in the nose. She bounces off with her treat in hand and Craig shakes his head and pulls long black and red hairs from his face, as he does every time this happens. Katie really is his favorite bartender at The Order of the Garter, hell, his favorite bartender in Seattle and maybe even the world. Much too good to be working at a grotty little pub, fending off unsavory advances and spilled drinks four nights a week; that's why Craig will bring her any bakery treat she wants, anytime she wants it, until she finally wises up and gets the hell out of this place.

Time for another sip of this excellent, excellent stout. Craig reaches forward. It's a good Thursday.

Of course, that's when it takes quite the sharp turn, leaving every Seattle-pub-Thursday Craig's ever known in the dust.

"Well, aren't you a hit with the ladies," comes a surly drawl from his left, startling Craig just as he's got his fingers around his glass. "Was that a croissant in your pocket, or were you actually happy to see her?"

"Both," Craig replies, shifting around to lean on his elbow and survey the formerly silent pile of misery hunched over two stools down, the limp guy at the end of the bar that Craig had spotted on his way in. He is not unconscious after all, much to Craig's surprise; judging by the row of empty shot glasses upside down in front of him and the distinct aroma of tequila emanating a good four-foot radius from his person, he *should* be. Craig winces and turns away as the fumes burn his nose.

"Baked goods. That's a new one. Never saw anyone use baking to hit on the ladies before." Mr. Misery sways his head upright, pushes a wild flop of brown hair out of his eyes and swings around until he locates Craig. He blinks. "Does it work?"

Surprised by the color of the eyes meeting his—an unusual shade, gray, not blue-gray or blue, but the gray of a sky covered in early storm clouds—Craig answers without thinking. "I wouldn't know. I don't hit on girls. Katie's my friend, not my type."

Those eyes, compelling even when bloodshot, spark with something that might be interest. "Huh. Well. Wouldn't have figured." He squints in a clear attempt to try to focus on Craig. "You know, if you were looking to hit on guys using baked goods, though, I can tell you right now that I bet it would work. Wanna try it?"

With effort, Craig holds in his startled laugh. This proposition is definitely going to rank among the most unusual ones he's ever received, maybe even blasting to number one with a bullet. He tilts his head to take a closer look at his new friend, he of the bloodshot gray eyes and five o'clock shadow and thick brown hair—the sort of rat's nest that can only be caused by anxious fingers running through it. The guy is white; not just generally speaking, but white as the proverbial sheet, probably several shades lighter than his usual tone, and a dusting of freckles across his cheeks stands out in sharp contrast.

And the smell of tequila. Oh, honestly. He might as well have dipped himself in that tequila.

But. But...

Whoever this guy is, he's a poster child for sadness, and that is the sort of character Craig's heartstrings have never been able to resist. He remembers the other package in his coat, the one in the breast pocket that he'd been saving for himself. His hand moves of its own volition in response to the hurt radiating from the guy, and he extracts the wax paper-wrapped bundle from the inner pocket of his discarded coat and sends it sliding down the bar with a flick of his finger. "You look like you need this more than I do."

"What, is it a roofie cookie?" It's a surly snap, accompanied by a glare of equal surliness, but the guy picks up the package and plucks the wax paper from the treat inside with surprisingly delicate fingers. Suspicion clouds his eyes. "Is it going to knock me out; are you going to drag me into some gross apartment upstairs and kill me? Is the little Goth bar girl in on it? She looks like she'd get a kick out of murder."

"Get fucked. That happens to be a rum and fruit biscuit made from my Nan Oliver's recipe for Christmas cakes, I'll have you know." Craig snorts into his stout and shakes his head. *The nerve of you!* "I made that with my own two hands this morning. I was saving it for myself, and I had to arm-wrestle a little old Jamaican lady at my bakery for it, too, because it was the last one. I'll have it back if you don't want it."

"I didn't say I didn't want it." The man leans away, holding the treat out of Craig's reach. "I didn't know."

"So much for being a Good Samaritan." He's out his dessert, and he can't drink his stout in peace. Craig mentally moves five points from the pro column for his Thursday routine to the con. "I don't usually get accused of being a serial killer when I offer people snacks."

"Oh." The cookie is set gently down on top of its erstwhile wrapper, and the man casts Craig a sidelong glance. "So you're not taking me up on the offer to hit on me, either. Was I not clear?"

The next sip of beer goes down the wrong pipe entirely. "Jesus." Craig coughs. "You meant that? Is that what it's like in your world? People use baked goods either as instruments to lure murder victims into their web or as tools of seduction?"

Uncertainty and stubborn pique are a strange combination, but they work; at least they do on this guy's face. "Well. People do like cookies. I like cookies."

"It's a fair point, but no, right now I just meant to be nice, and I am regretting it, slightly." Craig scoots onto the bar stool next to the tipsy fellow and pulls his glass over. Extending his index finger, he nudges the cookie closer to the other man. "Come on, eat up." If the guy's mouth is full, he can't talk, and maybe Craig can get in a few sips of his pint.

The other man handles the sweet like a relic. He takes a nibbly bite out of it, then a bigger one, and with the next bite takes a full quarter of it into his mouth. A huge smile spreads across his face as he chews. "Oh, my God. What is this?"

"Told you. Fruit spiked with rum, baked into a black cake biscuit, straight from my Nan's recipe box. Well, mostly." Craig says, "It's a bit like your fruitcake, I suppose. Glad you like it."

"I love it. Christ, that's good." A sigh escapes the guy as he sets what's left of the sweet down once more and glances at Craig; his gaze is a little steadier now. "Are you *sure* you're not at least hitting on me a little? Because I was serious. If you wanted to, it would work, especially with this." He looks— rather temptingly—as if he's about two seconds from orgasm, eyes hooded and dark, cheeks flushed. "God, that's amazing." He brushes his hands off on his jeans and extends the right one to Craig. "Alex Scheff."

"Craig Oliver." Craig accepts the handshake, unsure if he should be laughing or... interested? The fellow is nothing if not persistent.

Should be or not, he's surprised to find that his interest is already there. It has taken a while to identify it, it being something Craig's not felt in a while, but—yes. This is definitely interest he's feeling.

Really?

In response to an offer from a drunk, disheveled, mildly hostile white guy? Definitely not Craig's usual in any way, shape or form?

And yet...

"You serious?" he asks, propping his chin on his hand. "You're for real?"

He can't quite believe that *he* might be for real. Lord help him.

Alex shrugs; his mouth curves into a hesitant smile. "Yeah, actually. If you're game." And it's still a surprise, but Craig finds that he is in fact game. Is it the misery he can't stand not to try to help? Or is it the fact that the guy's good-looking, if rumpled? Or hey, maybe it's the fact that this Alex fellow has the best arse he's seen wrapped in designer jeans in a while.

Maybe it's all of it. Or none of it.

"Find someone else to rescue," Sarita had said. This can't be at all what she meant, but—in for a penny.

I can break routine just fine.

He'll get the guy a glass of water, some coffee, sober him up a bit and see what's really lurking beneath the tequila and the gloom. Then he'll decide. Craig raises his hand and flags Katie down before turning back to Alex with his most winning smile. Crossing his arms, he leans on the bar. "Come here often?"

"So you work in a bakery, and you were born near London." A frown furrows Alex's brow as he counts off points on his fingers. "Your mom is from Scotland, and your dad's family is from the British Virgin Islands?"

The alcohol-sodden pile of near-doom has sobered into something vaguely resembling a human, thanks to the undiluted cup of Costa Rican and two big tumblers of water Katie has supplied, but he still seems to be in that phase of drunkenness that centers around deep concentration and the repetition of what one has just heard in order to be sure one *understands* what one has just heard. It's cute. Tragically comic, but cute.

"All correct, except, to clarify, I manage the bakery. And I'm head baker." Craig's cheeks flush with heat, and he ducks his head at the rush of embarrassment, glad that his dark skin covers the blush. "Sorry. That sounds like I'm bragging. I'm really not." *Unless it helps.* Craig is not without his own tragic comedy, it would seem, which is terrible, given that his mild interest has definitely given way to marked desire in the last hour.

But Alex's responding chuckle is warm, a short burst of throaty baritone that resonates in Craig's stomach like a shot of good whiskey. From the base of his spine, it sends butterflies winging out along the lines of his nerves. "It's not bragging if it's the truth," Alex says, wiping a thumb over the condensation on his glass. From beneath unfairly long lashes, his gaze sweeps up, the clearer whites of his eyes in breathtaking contrast to the startling gray of his irises. "Right? I mean, you bake a mean rum cookie, so if you say you're the top dog at your bakery, I'll believe you. No question."

Craig is sincerely out of practice with this flirting thing and still not sure it's a good idea. He cannot cope, not even a little bit. "Back to you. Please. You're from here in Seattle, and you started university in Portland, but then you moved back home to finish? And you work in advertising now." Craig nods toward the row of inverted shot glasses. "Hence the alcohol abuse and the general air of discontent, one assumes, if *Mad Men* is to be believed. Right?"

It's a calculated shot in the dark. Over the course of their brief time together, Craig has learned quite a lot about his handsome new friend's life in general; however, said handsome new friend has been deeply unforthcoming about the circumstances that brought his unlikely self to the Garter, and Craig has determined to sort out this mystery before he decides whether he will drag the man into his bed.

Oh, all right. He's decided to do that regardless. Just... not immediately. Not until his curiosity is satisfied.

Unfortunately, his opening shot has missed. Alex's face closes off and his eyes go darker than resting storm clouds and into the charcoal skies of an oncoming hurricane. "Not really." He doesn't elaborate, doesn't volunteer further information; but that only piques Craig's need to know into overdrive. Oh, the mystery of this man! It is as irresistible as those eyes. And that arse.

Craig's English, so of course there's a tiny part of him that fancies he might have been Sherlock Holmes in a past life. Never mind the fictional status of the world's greatest consulting detective. Taking a sip of his second beer, he considers the evidence at hand. Mysterious, morose young gay male in a pub, paying no attention to the sporting match and drinking some very serious alcohol by himself... it does make one curious.

"It's a little early in the evening to be getting sincerely, seriously drunk, isn't it?" Craig eventually asks. This is what he knows thus far: Alex is twenty-five, only a short while out of college with his advertising degree, and one half of a creative team at one of the top advertising agencies in Seattle. From what hasn't been said, Craig imagines he knows this: None of that has contributed to the state in which Craig found him. "That is to say, your purpose in coming here was absolutely to get drunk, and not necessarily to enjoy it. Have I got it right?"

Alex doesn't answer, and he isn't looking at Craig, which leaves Craig to carry on with what may now be the right track. He clears his throat. "Quite apart from your peculiarly excessive drinking," he goes on, with a weather eye on his taciturn companion, "you don't really seem the pub type."

This is very, very true, the truest of all true things. Alex's jeans have a designer label; what can be seen of his casual blue button-down is a little too well cut, his carefully scuffed boots a little too deliberate. The gray pullover he wears over his shirt is a cabled Aran knit that Craig would lay money was imported from Ireland. Under the hair combed by anxious fingers is a style with its roots in an expensive salon, and now that the tequila aura is lifting a bit, Craig smells a cologne of excellent quality on that well-tended skin.

In short, Alex shrieks *money* from every angle. Taking into account the advertising career, Craig could buy Alex as the type to drink to excess quite easily—but he can't quite reconcile the location in which Alex has chosen to do so. Gay bar, wine bar, nice clean hotel bar, absolutely and yes. Dark little hole in the wall, divey sports bar sort of place down in Queen Anne? When careful probing reveals that he lives a few minutes away in Capitol Hill, quite near its own wide array of legendary gay bars and more than decent restaurants? Not so much.

Craig waits and fiddles with his drink, and eventually his patience wins out. "I was having dinner a few blocks away, and it didn't go well, and when I finally stopped walking I was here," Alex finally admits, rolling his eyes. "Simple as that."

And I'm the Duke of Cornwall. Craig claps Alex on the shoulder, sympathy in his very soul. He knows well enough what it's like to get dumped, even if it has been a few years, and the signs are clear as calligraphy. "Tell you this much, whoever the guy is, he's clearly an idiot for letting you get away." This statement, far from pulling a chuckle and blush out of Alex, makes him recoil and snort. Craig can only blink and take a second guess. "All right, he's... *not* an idiot?"

Another snort, another eye-roll, and Alex downs half of his third glass of water. "No, he is, it's just... it's complicated," he grumbles, mouth twisting. It's a little heartbreaking to see this one small gesture completely belie his distinctly thorny facade. It's clear that Alex thinks he is being very strong, that he is a fortress, impenetrable and immovable.

He is wrong, very wrong, of course. Craig can see right through him. And while he is, on the one hand, quite interested in unraveling Alex in bed—oh, he has *such* a weakness for the high-strung, for poking and prodding and cheerily teasing them into relaxation—he is also rather concerned with banishing the unhappiness from Alex's handsome face.

It takes only a moment to come to a final decision.

"Right. That's it." Tossing another ten on the bar as a tip for Katie, Craig slips off his bar stool and takes Alex's arm, enjoying the look of surprise this elicits. "You're coming back to mine. It's not far."

Alex wobbles to his feet, warily surprised. "I am?"

"You are," Craig confirms.

This doesn't seem to alleviate Alex's bafflement at what must seem one hell of a non sequitur. He rallies, though, and it's just so cute, how he's trying to make sense of things. "Okay. You're really good-looking and God knows I'm seriously into your accent, but are we actually doing this?"

"Going to my place? Yes," Craig assures him, picking up their jackets and carefully guiding his new friend back through the crowd of men by the television. "We have to."

"Have to?"

"Mm hmm." Out on the street, he drops Alex's arm long enough to wind his scarf around his neck and beams. "That's where the tea is."

Chapter Two

ALEX PEEKS AROUND THE TINY APARTMENT WHENEVER
English Guy—*Craig, he has a name*—turns around to mess
with the plastic kettle thing and urge it to heat up, already.

Brown brick walls on two sides, deep blue plaster on the
others. The plaster walls are hung with framed black and white
prints of various world landmarks: Kilimanjaro, a temple in
some place that might be Nepal, the Sagrada Familia cathedral.
Low-wattage lamps cast warm golden light throughout the
single room; there's no television, but a big laptop sits on
the table over by the floor-level, comfortably rumpled futon
mounded with pillows.

Alex had thought they'd tumble right into that bed as soon
as they got through the door, but to his surprise, Craig seems
to have been serious about the tea thing. The tea thing really
is a thing. Who knew?

It's cute, though. *Craig* is cute. Very, very cute. Hot and
cute. As in, could model for any ad campaign Alex has worked
on this year. Just about six feet, broad shoulders tapering
to a trim waist, *nice* ass, skin like deep brown velvet, neatly
trimmed facial hair around a mouth that surely knows the
art of kissing, and oh, those eyes. Those dark coffee bedroom

eyes sparkle with laughter and tempt so seductively. They should be outlawed.

He should be photographed. The long-quiet voice in the back of Alex's mind hisses, and he pushes it away.

He doesn't disagree with it, though.

A heavy ceramic mug clunks down onto the postage stamp-sized table in front of him, and when Alex starts and looks up, Craig is casting him a broad and very sexy grin while he pours hot water over the teabags; steam plumes up between the two of them. Craig's smile is infectious, his hospitality is heartwarming, and the fact that the guy works in a fucking *bakery* and carries *cookies* in his pockets is absolutely goddamn adorable.

He doesn't usually do adorable. Adorable leads to attachment and Alex Scheff definitely absolutely no way *ever* does attachment. Boy, has he learned that lesson the hard way.

But he is not thinking of Jeff right now.

"What are you thinking about right now?" Craig puts a tiny pitcher and a sugar bowl in the center of the table and plops down into the other wicker-seated chair with his own mug of steeping tea.

Okay, maybe Alex *is* thinking of Jeff right now. *In a cautionary tale sort of way.*

He really would rather not. "Do you do this often?" Diverting the conversation seems like a much safer path. "Bring strange men you meet in bars back to your apartment for... tea?"

"As opposed to murder, I assume you mean?" Craig's lopsided grin really is very appealing, and very cheeky, and Alex likes the way he's just sort of... draped... all over his chair, legs sprawled out, arm dangling over the chair-back. "I bring plenty of people back here for tea. I'm not sure if you noticed, but I'm English. It's a bit of a thing with us, tea."

Oh, I noticed. I would listen to you read a phone book. "Just tea?"

Craig's chuckle is warm and deep, rich as buttery toffee. "Forward. I like it." Arching an eyebrow, he gestures to the mugs in front of them. "But we haven't finished our tea, we've barely begun."

"We don't have to." *I want a distraction, and you will more than do.*

"I want to." Still smiling, Craig takes the teabags out of Alex's mug, setting them on a little plastic dish next to the sugar bowl. His own mug gets the same treatment before he slips a spoon across the table. "Milk in the pitcher, sugar in the bowl. Help yourself to as much as you like."

Alex only sits and watches him doctor his own tea with a thin stream of milk, a generous spoonful of sugar. The spoon clinks in the mug as Craig stirs, swirling the milk in a pale spiral before it disappears into the tea and turns the deep amber liquid a warm, light caramel shade. He lifts the mug to his lips and takes two deep swallows. His brown eyes are bright and twinkling and fixed on Alex, who is frozen in his chair with the realization that if he made a move *right now*, Craig's mouth—oh, that very delicious looking mouth—would taste like warm tea with milk.

He's never wanted to taste tea with milk so much before, not ever.

"For what it's worth," Craig says, startling Alex out of his thoughts again, "no, I don't often do this, but I do actually intend on going to bed with you. Should the offer still stand."

It's a good thing Alex hasn't started on his own drink. "Sorry?"

"I think you heard me." The mug clunks back down to the table and Craig is grinning, grinning, altogether delicious and evil. "Drink up."

"If we're going to—" Alex is mostly sober, but only *mostly*. The events of the evening, the lingering alcohol in his system, his utter confusion, they're all combining to make it very difficult for him to understand what's going on. Sex is usually a distinctly more efficient and direct transaction for him.

"We are." Craig grabs Alex's untouched tea. He puts milk and sugar into it, just as he'd done with his own, and pushes it back across to Alex. "Not what I usually do on a Thursday, but I mean, I'd like to if you would. And I didn't necessarily mean right this second, but oh, definitely."

Alex revises his opinion, since he now can't say at *all* that Craig isn't being direct; there's that, at least. Yet despite this small injection of familiarity, the situation is no less puzzling. "I like."

There's that toffee laughter again. "And I like. A lot. Here's my thing, though—I can't shake this idea that you went to that bar to self-medicate after that bad dinner you had. Which, I understand, I do."

Alex, intrigued, considers possible questions and discards them in favor of silence and waiting for further explanation. He tastes his tea.

Perfect.

This is what Craig's mouth will taste like. Once the thought is circling in his brain, he can't stop thinking it.

"I got interested in really talking to you at the Garter because I thought you were good-looking and out of place and I do love a good mystery." Craig keeps drinking the tea that Alex now knows is delicious and soothing and, hey, maybe the English are onto something with the tea thing. "But I don't want to become just another shot from the bottle, Alex."

"I don't date," Alex blurts.

"Am I asking? I'm right there with you, I'm not looking for anything like that." It should be a relief, but Alex sits with no small amount of discombobulation and puzzling disappointment as Craig carries on. "I just prefer that my one-night stands, on the rare occasions that I have them, be a bit more civilized than your average sweaty naked romp. So, tea." There is, however, nothing civilized about the wicked gleam in Craig's eyes, and the distraction does an excellent job of wiping away Alex's inexplicable disappointment. "Tea, and a mostly sober partner who's into it for me, not just as some kind of remedy to a bad date. I want to enjoy our time together. I want you to enjoy it, too."

With this last, Craig's voice drops lower and goes husky; his eyes darken to a deeper brown, almost black, that Alex could fall into and drown in happily. In this instant, Craig is not a charming English baker who keeps sweets in his pockets and plies men with hot tea. He is sex and generosity and playful desire and really—well, Alex has had just about enough of the tea in his mug.

I will enjoy it, I will, oh God, I promise I will, I just—

Some of the sugar Craig put in his tea must not have dissolved completely, because when he surprises Alex with a kiss, the grit of sugar crystals on his lips makes it literally the sweetest kiss Alex has ever experienced. Soft, warm, promising, exactly the antithesis of how his evening had been going when he walked into The Order of the Garter and ordered six tequila slammers from the Goth girl behind the bar.

Flicking out the tip of his tongue, Alex gathers the last of the melting crystals, licking them from the soft pillow of Craig's bottom lip and swallowing. The sweetness glides over his tongue and down his throat as he teases Craig's mouth open and goes in to taste.

Ah, yes. There's the tea, just exactly as delicious as he thought it might be.

"I still want to know what brought you to my neighborhood," Craig mumbles between kisses, pulling back far enough for Alex to see the mischief in his eyes. "I'm not letting that go."

"Tell you in the morning?" If he can still remember by then. Craig's civilized seduction sure seems to have a way of scrambling the neurons. Not that Alex minds.

One last gorgeous toffee chuckle. "Let me make you pancakes first."

It's a deal.

A BACK THAT ARCHES, CURVING UP OFF THE MATTRESS WHILE shoulders press down into the pillow.

Hands that cup, curl, curve to fit the shape of the skull, fingers that thread through the soft twists of dreadlocks to clutch and tug.

A mouth that opens to let out a gasp, a groan, a shuddering whisper of a sigh.

Legs that stir restlessly, calves that tighten and relax, feet that flex and toes that curl into the sheets—Alex is everything and nothing more than the sum of his parts, every shaking, quaking, strung-tight and desperate reaching inch of himself under Craig's hands and mouth.

The soft, slow, sweet kiss that started all this swiftly gave way to something with an altogether darker flavor, still sweet, but more like the rich sweetness of real maple syrup, heavy and deep, one kiss flowing lazily into the next until Alex found himself laid out on the futon, shirtless, arms stretched over his head and pinned at the wrists by Craig's strong hands. Craig, by then also shirtless—how *had* that happened without Alex noticing?—his mouth tipped into a half smile, eyes that deep and deepening brown-black, all puckish and completely irresistible.

If Craig had asked anything in that moment, no matter how outrageous or dangerous, Alex might have agreed without thought or reservation.

The hands that had pinned his wrists to the pillows are now pressed firmly against Alex's pelvis with the heels of each and their long thumbs following the curve of the hipbones, warm palms wrapping around the lean lines of the hips, fingers dipping and denting the skin in an authoritative grasp.

The generous mouth from which Alex had kissed and sucked crystals of sugar and traces of tea tastes his skin, flat of the tongue pressed to the tight strain of Alex's erection, licking slowly up in the smallest of increments; puffs of breath cool the dampness and make him shiver, make his sac tighten with the sublime ache of being teased.

He's used to sex being something perfunctory and desperate, the pleasant means to the end result of release, quick and efficient—he's never experienced anything akin to the near... not worship, not reverence, but not far off, maybe?

He's being *appreciated*.

And he's not sure he deserves it, exactly, has no idea how he will repay the sheer kindness being shown to him by this person on whom, a mere two and a half hours ago, he'd never laid eyes. This man, with his listening ear and cookies, his tea and sympathy, his curiosity and long, slow, languorous exploration of Alex's body.

His fingers flex and pull at Craig's hair, and he chokes back what might be a sob, if he were the kind of person who let go enough. With the sting of grateful tears behind his eyes, he closes his eyelids so tight when he comes that sparkles of false light scintillate in the blackness.

Chapter Three

"*I* WAS FEELIN' LONELY BEFORE…" CRAIG TRANSFERS A fluffy, golden brown pancake from the hot pan to an already crowded plate, sings quietly along with the blues CD he's supposed to review and casts a glance over his shoulder to make sure he's not waking Alex. "*Didn't know then what lonely is… no…*"

Sprawled out over the futon, Alex looks young, very young, more eighteen than twenty-five, all slightly open mouth and tossed-about limbs. He's lying on his stomach with one arm stretched over the pillow he'd drowsily grabbed when Craig eased himself out of bed to make breakfast. Spread out like a cat in a sunbeam, he's taking up quite a lot of the bed.

In the drizzle of sunlight through the linen blinds, the smooth skin of Alex's back lifts and lowers with his even breaths. Craig knows that back quite well now, likes that back and its firm muscles. He can't see the constellations of freckles that dapple it from here, but he likes that he knows they're there.

He likes the loose swag of his maroon jersey sheets around Alex's hips and behind as well, but not as much as he'd like to *remove* those sheets from those trim hips right now.

Hmm. No. That would be rude. He should at least feed the man breakfast first.

Turning back to the stovetop, Craig pours the last of the pancake batter into the pan to make two smallish cakes—they'll go on top of the stack anyway—and lets them heat as he flips the kettle on.

Maybe this time we'll actually finish the tea. A star-shaped flare of mirth tightens the back of his mouth as a smile quirks his lips. He wouldn't mind if they didn't, *honestly.* Last night had been better than he'd anticipated, and he'd anticipated that it would be very good indeed when he made the decision to kiss Alex.

There'd been that moment when he thought about sending the fellow off after a second cup of tea, that moment of doubt when *I don't date* had fluttered across the table and smacked Craig in the chest. It had been a salty moment of insult, sour in his mouth, a clotted knot in his stomach. He had only just restrained himself from zipping *I doubt you're boyfriend material* right back into Alex's face, but Craig had held back when he registered the thin line of pained desperation running through the words and remembered the bad dinner date that had brought Alex into his evening in the first place.

In that instant he had absolutely wanted to both fuck Alex until he forgot his hurt, at least for a bit, and accept the challenge inherent in *I don't date.*

Which would definitely be a considerable break in routine.

It's been a long time since his last boyfriend. And if he *had* been looking for a boyfriend, Alex, on paper, would have been the most avoidable choice in the world: uptight, slightly snobby ad creative with a rebellious streak a mile wide and an apparent aversion to anything more substantial than a fuck and run.

They have nothing in common, so far as Craig's been able to suss out.

And yet.

Yet.

For the first time in a long time, Craig doesn't want this to stop at one night.

Damn it.

With a sigh, Craig flips the last two pancakes onto the plate, slips pats of butter between and on top of them and tends to the tea, pouring the boiling water over the bags of sweet, spicy chai and inhaling the aromas of cardamom and cinnamon as a dollop of warm decadent pleasure spreads through his stomach.

The table is already set and ready in the morning light. It's time for breakfast.

And for answers. Maybe.

"Come along, sleepyhead," Craig says, nudging Alex's hip with a bare foot. "I won't kick you out of bed for eating crackers in it, but pancakes are absolutely out of the question. Much too sticky."

"*I WAS FEELIN' LONELY BEFORE…*" THE SINGING IS LOW, QUIET, but in an apartment as small as Craig's, when it's the only sound apart from the muted scrape of plastic on Teflon, it's still enough to rouse Alex from sleep. He stays still, though, and keeps his eyes closed and his breathing even, not wanting to halt the music, not wanting to get out of the warm bed with its so-soft sheets.. "*Didn't know then what lonely is… no…*"

It's a nice, mellow voice that trails off into a nice, mellow hum.

I don't want you to be lonely.

Alex shies away from that thought and takes stock of himself. He has a slight headache, but nothing as bad as it would have been had he been left to his own devices. He is naked save for a strategically draped, soft jersey sheet covering his ass. His body is still pleasantly sore in spots from the night's events, from being pulled and stretched and pinched and nipped and held down.

And he's going to remember everything long after the aches fade, he's pretty sure, which is interesting because Alex has not had sex worth committing to memory for quite some time.

Interesting—and probably as dangerous as Craig's very good-looking face, and his accent and his tea and cookies.

Wait.

Are those pancakes he smells? Craig was *serious* about that? Holy *shit*.

They have now known each other for... Alex cracks his eye open the narrowest of slits and finds the bright red digits of the alarm clock wedged next to the laptop on the side table. Ah. There. Twelve hours, give or take. Two of those hours he had spent talking, *three* getting leisurely fucked within an inch of his life without having to lift a finger and the last seven sleeping—*sleeping over!* With a one-night stand! Good fucking Christ!—with his arm draped over Craig's stomach.

Not being a cuddler, *ever*, Alex can't begin to form words for *that*.

It's been the best twelve hours he's spent in memory both recent and distant, and now he's getting *pancakes* and he kind of never wants to leave and oh yeah, danger, Will Robinson. Holy, holy, holy, the very holiest of shits.

Craig's still humming as he works, scraping at the pan, switching his kettle thing back on—*Did I just get a Pavlovian erection at the thought of tea? What has this guy* done *to me in just a few hours?*—and Alex chances a glance through slitted eyes. He admires the sun-blurred image of Craig in nothing more than the soft, loose, pale blue jeans that ride low on his hips so that Alex can just see the lean muscle of his lower back, the dips and valleys Alex traced when he grabbed blindly for Craig's ass to pull him closer, deeper, farther inside...

Alex presses his mouth tight shut to keep a groan from slipping out, squeezes his eyes shut again and wonders where his evening went so very wrong/right/frightening/amazing.

It's definitely *one* of those four. Maybe two.

Is he supposed to figure *anything* out with a hot, half-naked Englishman making him breakfast? Is it possible?

And shouldn't he be worried that he seems to be having some sort of argument with himself?

Yes. A little.

But, *pancakes*.

Water streams into heavy porcelain mugs and then he hears the clunk of the kettle set down on the counter and the shuffle of bare feet across sun-warmed floorboards.

"Come along, sleepyhead." Craig's foot nudges him in the ribs. "I won't kick you out of bed for eating crackers in it, but pancakes are absolutely out of the question. Much too sticky."

Hot, half-naked, breakfast-cooking and *funny* Englishman, Alex revises, and this time he does not hold back the groan as he rolls over because, oh, wow, is he ever in *so much trouble*.

Chapter Four

"**Y**OU TALK IN YOUR SLEEP; DID YOU KNOW THAT?" CRAIG cuts through his stack of pancakes and has to hide his grin at Alex's dumbfounded look. "Well. It's more of a grumble. Pass the maple syrup, will you?"

He's not a monster. He'd let Alex get through half of his plate and even waited for him to swallow his most recent bite before casually dropping the question bomb. Incredibly polite of him, really. Craig has been dying to ask about this for *hours*. He's shown incredible restraint, although maybe he should have encouraged the poor fellow to at least put on underwear before the interrogation began. It's just that he's so *appealing* when he's all rumpled hair and wrapped up in just the sheet from Craig's bed. He looks like a slightly scruffy street urchin, not at all like a young, upwardly mobile professional. Craig loves the dichotomy, these two different people in one tightly-wound body.

Alex stares at him with head tilted and eyebrows up, as he pushes the bottle of syrup over the scuffed tabletop. "Do I."

He's going the nonchalant route. It's so much fun Craig almost can't stand it. "Surely you know you do. I mean, Jeff must have brought it up some time."

The name he's not supposed to know is a calculated bomb to drop, but after all, the agreement *had* been that they'd discuss what had brought Alex to the Garter. Now, Alex freezes, hand still outstretched, face very, very still. Any trace of amusement has abruptly left him, and his quick tension is the very opposite of nonchalance. "Jeff."

"You basically growled his name in your sleep."

All right, this isn't all fun and games, of course it isn't; not with Craig's nearly pathological urge to take care of people: his ex, Nathan, new and frightened on his first day at Seattle Pacific eight years ago; Katie at the bar, all those jobs and still too broke to indulge in little luxuries like gourmet croissants; Sarita, with the formerly beloved sister who turned on her when she came out as gay. Craig can't help it, he has to try his hardest to mend hurts and bring unhappy people some small spot of sunshine.

Hearing the snarled name of some other man just hours after he'd had sex with Alex, with a sleeping Alex draped over his torso, yes, it stung—there is no getting around that. He is human. But it also sent a sharp needle of sympathetic pain right through his heart and made him want to make Alex feel better, just as the palpable misery that had surrounded Alex at the bar had prompted Craig to bring him home. Had Alex felt the kiss Craig gently pressed to his forehead as he slept? Did he know Craig was awake for ages, lying there, and brushing Alex's hair away from his face and worrying as he waited to fall into sleep?

Likely not. And that's all right. Craig's pretty sure it would have made Alex bolt and run, clothing or not.

He wants to bolt and run himself, to be honest. This is all a little intense for one night; it's shaking too much of his life already. Still, he can't help himself. He was in deep the minute

Alex lifted his head at the bar and fixed him with those eyes, damn it all. It wasn't entirely about making a lonely soul ache a little less for a little while. He sees that with an awful clarity right now.

Across the table, Alex swallows another carefully chewed bite of his breakfast; he seems a touch less enthusiastic about the pancakes and is quite obviously mulling over a response. At last he takes a long drink of tea and shakes his head. "I'm sorry."

Nothing to do but shake it off and keep going. "Don't be. It was clearly a bad dream, and I'd rather you have one of those about the idiot you started your night with than about me." It's not as difficult as he would have thought to force a bright smile, to be jokey and a little silly. "I mean, I assume that *is* who The Mysterious Jeff happens to be?"

"It is." Alex's gaze is downcast; his face is shuttered like a window in a storm. His fingers toy with a loose wrinkle of sheet at his hip. "Was."

"Boyfriend?"

"*No.*" The answer is much more vehement than seems necessary, and Craig drops his fork. Jerking his head up, Alex looks repentant, but still closed off. "I'm sorry. That was a little harsh. But... no. Jeff was never my boyfriend. Just... a boy who was a friend. So to speak."

Sure. "I've had a few of those." Craig picks his fork up and digs right back into his breakfast, resolving to keep things light. Jokey, even. "To my knowledge, however, I don't grumble their names in my sleep immediately after being—"

The joke misfires, and badly. "I said I was sorry." Lips, forehead and jaw pinch and settle into a frown on Alex's whitened face before smoothing out. "And I'm sorry again. God, I'm a dick."

"Not really. I shouldn't have tried to make a joke like that about what is obviously a sensitive subject." This time, Craig's smile comes more easily as he responds with warmth to the contrition and confusion. *Oh, this one is really so very dangerous.* "Though you *can* be a dick, and I sort of like it about you, I have to admit."

This pulls a chuckle from Alex, and he glances away for a moment. When he comes back to Craig, his eyes are a little less clouded, the gray is a little brighter. "Look, I just... I don't really want to talk about Jeff, right now. I will, because I told you I would and I don't break promises. Just..." His shoulders lift with his deep breath. "I had a nice time, Craig. Last night. I... want to keep that going for a little longer into today." He looks surprised that the words have come out of his mouth.

Fair enough. Craig's not opposed to that idea at all —how convenient. He ignores the fact that both of them swore the one-night stand pact not twelve hours ago.

Letting the topic of Jeff go is easy, especially when Craig can start putting a few more pieces of the Alex puzzle into place from what he's gleaned and he's fairly certain that he can parlay learning the rest into a second encounter. The thought is both exhilarating and frightening as all hell.

Yes. This one is dangerous. This one manages to be open, yet enigmatic: a cocky man, a hurt boy, by turns snarky and vulnerable and filthy and terribly, terribly interesting, more than anyone's been in a long time. Alex is a threat to the casual ramble of Craig's life, because Craig doesn't just want to cheer him up, Craig *wants* him, in a way that is distinctly not casual.

So much trouble. Craig gets up to make Alex another mug of tea. "All right."

"All right?"

"All right." Craig flips the kettle on and spins around to lean against the counter and beam the easiest smile of the morning at the bundle of trouble sitting at his kitchen table. "You could... tell me over dinner tonight after we're both done with work."

Alex's instant tension is sad; it's so predictable already. "Not a date."

Well, all right, at least that much hasn't changed. It doesn't sting the way it did last night, though. "No, not a date, dinner." Craig widens his eyes, opens his mouth to emit a low *ooooo* and wiggles his fingers. "Scary, scary dinner."

Eyebrow up. "Are you making fun of me?"

Tipping his head, Craig makes a show of pretending to think about it. "Mmm... yes. Absolutely."

Silence stretches between them like live power lines, crackling and snapping, until at last Alex laughs and gets to his feet, abandoning the sheet as he saunters over to Craig and snags his fingers in the belt loops of Craig's jeans. "You know, it's a damn good thing you're hot and you make good pancakes."

It's Craig's turn to raise an eyebrow. "You *do* have to go to work, don't you?"

Alex tugs, and their hips are slotted together, warm and snug. This is an obvious distraction from the topic—Craig's not at all surprised that Alex is very good at that, very practiced—but it's suddenly quite difficult to care. "My creative partner flew out to meet with one of our clients today, so I'm going to be working from home, waiting for him to call. So." He looks up from under his lashes. It makes Craig's heart stutter to a stop. "I've got about five, maybe ten minutes. Want to see what I can do with them?"

Craig sucks in a shuddery breath as Alex's palm flattens over Craig's abdomen and his fingers slip under the waistband of

Craig's jeans. Alex's mouth curves into a smile as Craig flails and gropes behind himself to switch off the kettle so they can continue sans potential distractions.

So much trouble.

᠊᠊᠊

AS OBJECTS MOVE THROUGH SPACE, SOME SLIP AND RUSH
right past each other, while others get pulled in to orbit around
larger objects.

And then there's Alex.

Under normal circumstances, he and Craig might have been
slip-and-rushers, two ships passing in the night, a pair of dust
motes in the great big universe of Seattle, the largest small
town in the world next to the phenomenon of New York City.
They might have met—they don't know it yet, but they have
people in common, so it isn't outside the realm of possibility—
but probably it would have been just a tick on the clock, two
pairs of eyes meeting in a club or on a bus or just on the street,
a *simpatico* nod, and then the current of the living city pulling
them apart with neither of them thinking much of it.

In Seattle, as in any large city, there are hundreds of casual
one-second encounters every minute. Thousands. Slip, rush.
Slip, rush.

But that's not what happened here.

Rejection was the slingshot that sent Alex hurtling out into
space, free-falling in hurt and confusion and anger until he
tumbled right into Craig's orbit. He wasn't expecting to be
caught any more than Craig was expecting to catch a falling
star, and yet here they are.

It's been several weeks. More than one month. Less than
four. Who's counting? It's the longest one-night stand in
recorded history, kept determinedly casual with a rigor that
would make Casanova envious. They are not dating. They're
not.

Except, of course, they totally are.

Are not.

They get one day and one night a week, Thursday nights and Saturday afternoons. Sometimes Thursday's a sleepover, most nights not. If it is, though, pancakes in the morning—which may or may not be finished before their traditional pre-work quickie.

Location? The apartment that's closer when they finish dinner.

Dinner absolutely doesn't mean a date; it's just a civilized prelude to fucking each other's brains out.

Sure, if that's what you want to call it.

Saturday afternoons are spent at the bakery, a clutch of hours in which Craig shows Alex how to make sprites, cinnamon roll cookies, miniature fruit tarts, cream cheese brownies and, on one eyebrow-singeing occasion, crème brûlée.

Alex is not allowed to handle the butane torch anymore.

Light, laughter, tea, talking, sex, stability—

Watch it, don't get too close to that thought.

Counting the days between one meeting and the next, not minding too much when an extra few hours sneak in sometimes, it's fine; this is totally casual.

Keep telling yourself that.

It's best friends with the greatest benefits in the world.

Keep. Telling. Yourself. That.

He hasn't seen anyone else besides his work colleagues in all this time.

He doesn't want to.

It's totally casual, though, really.

Casual friends leave spare toothbrushes at each other's apartments, right?

You're so entirely fucked.

꧁꧂

Chapter Five

I's a Saturday when things start to get *weird*.

When Alex walks into the door of Sucre Coeur every Saturday, he's used to seeing Craig. Craig, with his dreads concealed under a fluffy paper hat thing—he must be the only person in the world who makes that look adorable and also hot in the extreme—in the bakery kitchen, waving and smiling cheerfully from his position elbow-deep in dough. He gets the baking situation under control and then comes around the counter, playfully jostling elbows with Natasha or Will or Sarita at the cash register before he greets Alex with a kiss and a chocolate croissant.

It's nice. Something to look forward to at the end of a long week at the agency. And this week has been longer than most, Alex having made his first pitch presentation on which he was the primary creative, and having it received less than enthusiastically. In fact, there is a good chance he's failed entirely.

This week, he could really use that croissant. And the kiss. Mostly the kiss.

Sadly, there is no croissant on this April Saturday and *absolutely* no kiss, because Craig is not in the kitchen and neither Natasha nor Will are at the cash register when Alex butts his way in through the Sucre Coeur door with coffee and all the hope in the world. Hope which is quickly dashed and replaced with utter confusion, because for some insane reason, it's his cousin Samantha of all people—his own cousin, what the hell—wearing the fluffy paper hat and a purple Sucre Coeur apron over her completely bakery-work-inappropriate black and white polka dot dress. She is standing behind the counter with a box of muffins in one hand and a supremely panicked look on her face as she surveys the growing crowd of surly baked goods aficionados before her.

Samantha... does not work here. Not even a little.

Alex hasn't seen Samantha in a while. But the last time he had, Samantha was a thoroughly happy second grade teacher living in Snohomish with her boyfriend Nathan. Samantha has never been any kind of cash register jockey anywhere, which would probably explain the look of pleading, abject horror on her face, not to mention the *help me* she quietly mouths to Alex when their eyes meet.

Nothing, however, explains how Samantha got behind the cash register in the first place. Does she know Will? Or Natasha? Or... no way... Craig? Can the world be *that* fucking small?

It can't, can it? "Peach? What are you doing here?"

"Sasha!" The Russian diminutive of his name, which only Samantha and his mother use, sounds strange in a place where everyone knows him as Alex. This collision of his worlds makes him twitch, even as his cousin looks more frantic by the moment. "Sasha, help! The manager left me alone!"

Samantha is clearly desperate—not a state he usually sees her in, and it's funny. The good news for his beloved cousin is that all his months of hanging out here with Craig, plus a handful of holiday and summer stints working at Aéropostale in college, mean that Alex can easily rescue her from the inexplicable and entirely silly situation in which she seems to have found herself. Within minutes he's rolled up his sleeves and put a very relieved Sammi strictly on dessert retrieval duty, pulling the cookies, cupcakes and blondies out of the display cases and boxing them up for the hungry crowd, while Alex rings up purchases and tries not to figure out what the hell is going on and what his life has become.

In twenty minutes they have the store cleared out and Samantha is slumping behind the counter, clutching a cup of coffee like a lifeline. "'It's the slow time of day,' Craig says," she snaps in a fairly decent and distinctly hilarious approximation of Craig's accent. "'No one ever comes in between two and four,' he says. 'You won't have to actually ring anyone up,' he tells me. Oh, my *God.*" She stretches out one leg and jiggles her foot to indicate the shiny black patent leather heels that match the equally shiny belt of her dress. She flaps her free hand at the fluffy white petticoat under her skirt. "Do I even look like I came here dressed to sell cookies? No."

Craig says. That begins to answer that question, at least—Samantha's definitely not here for Will or Natasha. It does, however, raise even more questions—questions he's not sure it's wise to ask his very nosy and tenacious cousin. "You look pretty, Peach," Alex ventures, forcing the most innocent smile he can muster. "It's nice to see you." *Inexplicable, but nice.* "It's been—" He stops, guilt flooding his chest with heat.

Months. It's been months. And the last time had been a post-Christmas dinner with Samantha, her boyfriend Nathan, and oh, damn it, Jeff. Not exactly a happy memory. "I'm happy to see you," Alex mumbles into a bite of the vegan cranberry scone he'd filched from the day-old basket Craig keeps in the walk-in cooler for the employees. Pushing away all thoughts of the disaster of Jeff, Alex slumps on the counter next to Samantha. A streak of powdered sugar stands out starkly against the green of his T-shirt. It is suddenly the most fascinating thing in his world.

"I know. I'm sorry, Sasha. I've been meaning to call you, it's just..." Samantha tugs off her silly paper hat and runs her fingers through her mop of brown curls, checking bobby pins and adjusting cherry-shaped barrettes. But then her fingers go still as she shoots a sudden, sharp glance at Alex that makes his stomach sink. "No. Wait. Back up—I think I should be asking the way more important question of what the hell *you're* doing here. Do you know Craig?"

"Do *you*?" Alex counters. Fuck, Seattle really *is* a small town, isn't it? But even so, what are the odds of *this*? "And if so, how?"

"No," comes the quick correction, accompanied by a patented Chernikov smirk—their genetic legacy. He remembers now with some guilt all the times *he's* deployed it. "I asked first; you have to answer me."

It's not the first time he's found himself in a standoff with Samantha, but it is one of the few times Alex thinks he can win. He lifts his hands and fixes her with a stare. "Technically, I asked the first question as soon as I walked through the door." His eyebrow quirks almost before he thinks of doing it. "Also, I'm taller and I know everywhere you're ticklish."

Samantha's jaw drops. "You fight dirty."

"It's one of the few advantages of being your first cousin," Alex reminds her, and it's hard for him to hold back his laughter at her furious expression. "Knowledge."

The silence and Samantha's glare stretch between them until she finally throws her hands in the air and gives in. "Fine. Craig was a couple of years ahead of Nathan at Seattle Pacific. They were both in the creative writing program, so they ran in a lot of the same circles, and they've been friends for years now. Nathan being my boyfriend, I am at least somewhat acquainted with most of his friends, and vice versa. Put your hands down and back away."

He leaves his hands up in tickle-ready stance, unconvinced. "And...?" There's more, there has to be, because it's not Nathan here, after all.

"And Craig makes these really great frosted lemon sugar cookies that Nathan loves." Her shrug is more casual than the rapid-fire pace of her speech. "But since Sucre Coeur is down here and we're still up in Snohomish, we just don't get them that often, and *hands down*, Sasha."

Alex cocks his head and drops his hands. She would appear to be telling the truth, not that she has answered a damn thing. "So you just happened to be in the neighborhood today?"

"No. I made a special trip. *We* made a special trip. Nathan's at some kind of writing symposium for the day, and it's near here, and I figured I'd come into town with him. That's where Craig is, by the way." Finally getting to the point, Samantha passes her coffee cup to Alex and swipes the other half of the scone, then takes a huge bite out of it. "Jesus, this is amazing, you totally would never know any of their vegan stuff is vegan."

"There are still Bing cherry muffins in the basket; get your own," Alex grumbles, but he's not too annoyed; he's preoccupied by the news Samantha has just dropped on him. Craig talks about his writing so infrequently, it's easy to forget he's more than just a tea-drinking baking enthusiast and phenomenal part-time lover. For him to have dropped everything and run out in the middle of the workday means the symposium is a big deal. "So that explains that, but how come you didn't call me to say you were coming in, Peach?"

"I had planned to, but Craig recruited me as soon as I walked in the door, so I never had a chance," Samantha mumbles around a bite of pastry. "I guess someone named Natasha couldn't come in today like she was supposed to, because there's some kind of emergency custody drama with her kid's father. Some guy named Will's incommunicado with his girlfriend *and* boyfriend out hiking in Snoqualmie Falls. The owner—Theodora?—is in Singapore. No one else can come in, Craig's panicking—he totally forgot he scheduled this and he really wanted to go—so next thing I know, I'm wrapped in this huge apron and getting *reamed* by some hipster chick for not having the amaretto cupcakes with Nutella frosting today and *what* are *you* doing here?"

With this lightning-fast change of gears, Samantha gets right up in Alex's face. Reflex takes over and sends him backing into the corner formed by the counter and the plate glass storefront window—fast, too fast, and a little panicked. He clocks his head on the glass. "Ow! I came to see Craig!"

Lots of people say really stupid shit when they hit their heads. That's his story and he's sticking to it.

Samantha just stares, scrutinizing Alex for several long, uncomfortable moments. Her mouth is hinged ever so slightly open in what looks like disbelief. Her eyes are wider than usual, searching, astounded. "You what?"

Oh, shit. There is probably no getting out of this, so Alex doesn't even try. He can't help the sigh he drags all the way up from his feet, though. "I came. To see. Craig."

"But I don't understand." Slowly, Samantha shakes her head. But for all she claims not to understand, comprehension dawns like a thousand suns on her face and her mouth widens into a grin. "Like, *see* him see him?"

"Are we twelve?" Alex scoots past Samantha and rounds the display case to give himself a little room to walk and breathe. "Yes, see him. Well, no—get that look off your face!" That look— all big, shining gray eyes and mischief in every inch of her, as if Samantha is about ten seconds away from throwing a tickertape parade—is not usually directed at Alex. It's *really* unnerving, and he really wants to deflect it. "We're just friends."

"Uh-uh, no way, Sasha. You know how to work the register. I heard you greet people by name. You knew their orders." It looks as if sheer delight is about to make Samantha explode in a cloud of glitter and small fluffy animals. "You come here a *lot*."

"No, I—" But it's about as simple to stop Samantha in full-on excitement mode as it is to stop an oncoming train. All Alex can do is give up and let all be revealed.

"Yeah. You spend a *lot* of time here. And I know you and I know Craig, so I know the two of you don't have enough in common to make that happen without something more going on than 'friends' so, you know," Samantha spins around in a flurry of apron and powdered sugar with a huge grin on her face. "I'm thinking you've got a lot of explaining to do."

Great. Maybe someone can explain it to Alex first so he's all clear himself?

"CRAIG!"

The familiar voice rings out across the room, and there's just enough time for Craig to brace himself before his ex-boyfriend, a sunny Puck in an Avengers T-shirt and surf shorts, flings himself across the space between them as if shot from a cannon.

"Hey hey!" Nathan's hug is his usual high-velocity bone-crusher; his boundless cheer fills the large, sunny room to the ceiling. "You made it. I was worried there for a second."

So had Craig been. He's still mentally kicking his own arse for forgetting about this symposium. The meeting center isn't far from Sucre Coeur, but he'd nearly broken his neck biking here thanks to some severely ignorant drivers. The debacle of finding a place to lock up his bicycle doesn't bear thinking about. In the end, he'd cut it so close that he all but had to sprint through the building to make it before they closed the sign-in station, and it had taken him most of the first lecture, on short story composition, to catch his breath.

Not his favorite Saturday in a while, that's for sure. He's still trying to shake it off and level out. "Hey to you too, Nate."

Nate rushes on, pulling back to beam a smile up at Craig. "I would have said hi earlier, I saw you come in, but the script-writing session was about to start so I had to book it." He roughs up the spiky black brush of his hair with his hand; confusion twists the sunshine of his smile. "You don't normally cut it so close! I mean, damn if I'm not glad to see you, but you were even later than usual, which is saying something, right?"

Craig hasn't seen his ex in longer than he likes to think about, but he loves how Nate just jumps into conversation as if no time has passed. In all the years they've been friends, briefly lovers and now friends again, this has been his favorite thing about Nate. No guilt trips or recriminations for the time passed apart, just carrying on as if it's a privilege to know anyone, no matter how sporadic the acquaintance. Which means Craig is free to ignore the slur on his questionable punctuality and the tacit invitation to explain himself. "It's great to see you, man," he says, and means it with all his heart. "Seriously great."

"How about these lectures, huh?" Excitement radiates from Nate, and he bounces in place with the energy of it. "I learned so much in that script class, seriously. Remember that sci-fi script I screwed around with at Sea Pac? Totally thinking of digging it out and seeing if I can mine some gems from it using some of the tips this guy had. I figure you hit short stories first?"

And then there's the exhausting side of Nate's ability to carry a conversation. Craig already has to catch his breath again just listening to him. "Yeah, yeah." His stomach growls before he can expound on the class, which had been absorbing and informative to an amazing degree, once he'd been able to pay full attention. "Nate, pause. Have they got snack machines here? My stomach is going to gnaw through my spine. I didn't pack a lunch, since I forgot this entire thing was happening."

Nate goes still and stares up at Craig with the expression of a man who is sure his friend has lost his mind. "You forgot? About this? Seriously?" He reaches to touch Craig's forehead. "You feeling okay?"

Craig swats the reaching hand away. "I'm fine. *Hungry*, but fine."

"You know, if you're not actually feeling all right, Mama will send me to your place with some chicken *adobo*." Nate tries again to touch Craig's forehead, but pulls back when the next swat makes contact. "Oh, come on. You know it's legit for me to ask if you're feeling all right when you forget about something we've been looking forward to for months. And when you're later than usual. These are things that tell me all is not well in Craig Oliver land." Stepping back, Nate crosses his arms. "I've got a tomato and avocado panini in my bag I'm willing to split, but only if you spill the beans about what's up with you."

Craig's stomach growls loudly enough to catch the attention of several people in their immediate vicinity. "It's a bad idea to attempt to starve me into compliance," he grumbles over their giggles. "You know how I get when my blood sugar drops."

Hostile is how he gets, but with the surety that only long years of friendship can provide, Nathan stands his ground, all five foot, seven inches of him, suddenly as immovable and unperturbed as a marble statue. He doesn't have to speak. All he does is stand in front of Craig and stare.

And stare.

Another growl, noisy to the point of embarrassment, escapes Craig's stomach. As much as he would dearly love to keep his business to himself, hunger—and the deeply creepy implacability of Nate's level gaze—wins out. "I met somebody," he mutters, ducking his head so his chin muffles his voice.

Nathan raises a hand to his ear, miming hearing loss. "Eh?"

May the God he does not actually believe in grant him some kind of strength. "I met somebody."

"I can't *hear* you," comes the sing-song reply.

Craig is not at all embarrassed about Alex. No. He likes Alex, likes him a lot; likes him probably a hell of a lot more than is wise. But he doesn't feel ready to bring whatever they are out of the little space they've created and into the real world. The real world likes to make people define things, and Craig is even less ready to go anywhere near that.

Nathan is not inclined to demand labels or definitions, given that he himself is a bisexual freewheeler possessed of the least possible soul to tether to the ground Craig has ever encountered. But he and his girlfriend Samantha are part of the real world all the same, a gateway out of the comfortable, sexy, peaceful cocoon Craig and Alex have constructed around themselves, and Craig really, really likes that cocoon. It's such a great cocoon.

Nathan is still staring, this time with bonus raised eyebrow.

Craig sighs. *Farewell, cocoon.* "I met somebody," he says for the third time, this time pitching the statement loud and clear.

Pure satisfaction wreaths Nate's smug expression. "And Sammi owes me five bucks. Aw yeah."

"What?" For a second, Craig thinks hunger is impeding his comprehension; but no, when he thinks about it again, he still doesn't get it.

Nathan and his honest streak are all too happy to clarify. "Sammi and I had a bet going when we hadn't heard from you since New Year's," he explains, dropping his bulging backpack to the floor and kneeling to dig through it. He produces a wrapped sandwich and hands it up. "She said she figured you were doing the workaholic thing. But I've got the advantage she doesn't."

Craig unwraps the sandwich, takes half and hands the rest of it back, sighing in happiness as he takes his first bite of food in far too many hours. "What's that?"

"Talking with your mouth full is rude." Nathan stands up. "Sammi hasn't dated you. I have. I know how long you can go before you need to just get yourself laid."

The second bite of sandwich narrowly misses being spat out. "Excuse the fuck out of you?"

"You're denying it?" The look on Nate's face is a smirking dare as loud as any spoken word.

As crude as Nate's statement is, it's not entirely without accuracy. But yes, Craig is going to try to deny it anyway. "I'm objecting to the implication that I'm a sex addict."

"Didn't say that, not that there'd be any problem if you were. No shame, my man. No shame." Nate loops his backpack over his shoulders and shrugs it into place. "I'm just saying, you like your space and quiet time and all, but you know, you also like having sex every once in a while. Many humans do. No big thing." He crams his half of the sandwich into his mouth, making a teasing point of chewing and swallowing before speaking again. "And when you find yourself somebody and you like what's happening, you go off the grid for a while. I remember. Also fine, you deserve to enjoy yourself. Simple as that, man. I know you. I drew the logical conclusion, and hey now, I was right. Right?"

Infuriatingly enough, yes, yes he was. If this is what comes of remaining friends with your exes, Craig is suddenly unsure he wants anything to do with it. "Yes."

"And you won me five dollars from my girl, so thanks for that." Nate winks. "Hey, speaking of Sammi, did you get to see her before you left the shop? She was heading that way to say hi."

"Oh, yeah, she came in. Actually, she reminded me about this when—bloody fuck!" When he stops in the middle of the lobby to smack his head, the sound echoes, earning them both another round of giggles.

The bakery! Shit! *It's Saturday.* Alex is about to—no, already *has* arrived at the bakery for their Saturday lesson, according to the clock on Craig's phone. *Shit!* He'd forgotten to send a text or call or *anything,* and Alex is going to make the trip to Sucre Coeur just to end up facing Samantha behind the counter. *Shit again!* This is not how Craig wanted to start introducing Alex to his friends.

Not that he actually has sorted out how/if/when he wants to introduce Alex to his friends. The cocoon and all. He already misses the cocoon.

"Um. Craig?" Nate's hand lands on his arm and gives it a good shake. "Hey, man. You okay?"

Well, he's going to have to be, isn't he? What's done is done. At least Samantha will be... well, she might not frighten Alex *too* much. Nathan's girlfriend is one of the kindest, funniest people Craig has ever met, but she can also be, like most of the women of Craig's acquaintance, extraordinary in the degree of her assertiveness.

Yeah, um, he might need to rescue Alex.

"I think I need to go back to the shop," he says, wincing at the thought of wasting the money he paid to pre-register for the symposium. Still, he might be able to say he got his money's worth just in the short story lecture, right? He already knew he could write; who needed connections in the industry? Better he should get back to Sucre Coeur, rescue Alex from Samantha and try to smooth over any mess.

Nate's hand slaps against Craig's chest to stop him in his tracks. Craig blinks. He hadn't realized he'd started moving. "Eh?"

"Stop. Breathe. Tell me what's up?" Nathan's face is a study in earnest concern. "Is it Sammi?"

Is it Sammi? "In a manner of speaking, yeah, could be."

Nate has the nearly supernatural ability to turn himself into an immovable force, never mind the fact that Craig tops him by about four inches and a good fifty pounds of muscle. He leans hard on Craig, hard enough that if Craig makes a sincere effort to get away, they'll both crash to the ground. "What *about* Sammi?"

No Saturday has gone so spectacularly the opposite of Craig's way in a long damn time. "I left her at the bakery, and the guy I'm seeing is probably there *right now* getting the third degree from her, and I would like to go rescue him, thanks." He pushes against the little brick wall that is Nate; as expected, no luck.

Nate grins and holds his position. "Ah, so Sammi's with your boyfriend."

"Not my boyfriend," Craig warns.

"No? But if he's at the bakery and you were expecting him, it's more than just you getting it on the regular." With his spiky hair and arched eyebrows, Nate looks like a curious, happy bird as he tilts his head up at Craig. "So, more than a boy toy and less than a boyfriend. Interesting. I need to know more."

"Did you sign up for the magazine writer's lecture?" Craig tries with no little desperation. Never has he felt quite so much like a piece in a teetering Jenga tower. "You should probably get going on that."

"Oh no, I think we both should." Nate steps aside, only to snag Craig's arm before he can take off. "Yeah. I think we need to go to that. Now. Together."

"Nathan Miguel Figueroa—" Craig begins, but a raised finger and eyebrow from Nate cut him off.

"No matter how hard you try, Craig, you're just not Filipino. You are never gonna invoke the same terror with my full name that Mama does, sorry." His broad smile indicates he's anything but. "So. You're gonna come with me to this lecture, because you don't want to waste the money you spent on this whole thing, I'm sure. And I think we're gonna give Sammi some time to get to know your new guy, and maybe you'll write me some notes and fill me in too; how about that?"

Yeah. How about that? Times like this drive home to Craig just how perfect for each other Nate and Samantha are, how cohesive and unified a team they can be. They are a thing of beauty, a strategic force to be reckoned with.

It's great, when it's not being used against him.

 *Chapter Six*

THE BASKET OF DAY-OLD PASTRIES SITS ON THE FLOOR between them, a few pecan sandies and peanut butter chocolate chip cookies all that remain by the time Alex finishes telling Samantha how he and Craig met.

"'That's where the tea is?'" Samantha asks. It must be hurting her cheeks now to have been smiling so broadly for over an hour. "That's what he said, and it actually *worked* on you?"

"You don't have to sound so surprised," Alex grumbles, stuffing a sandie into his mouth and chasing it down with the last of the three coffees he'd brought with him. The bakery has been pretty dead, with only a few customers coming in to clear out the last cupcakes and bundt slices. Without Craig or any of the other staff, the display cases can't be restocked, so they've just flipped the door sign to *Closed* and crashed on the floor to hide from any annoyed, cookie-seeking passersby. "You make me sound like a jerk."

Samantha rolls her eyes skyward and somehow manages to make it an expression of affection. "You *are* a jerk, though. And..." She trails off, forehead furrowing into a dark frown. "I don't know. It was cute, Sasha. Charming. *Craig* is cute and charming. You don't *do* cute and charming. You never have."

"Craig's hot, not merely cute," Alex points out, a little stung by the accurate but unnecessarily harsh assessment of his prickly character. "I definitely do hot and you know it. And so what if I like the fact that he's charming? I can try new things."

"Yeah. Because when we were kids you didn't throw a fit every time Aunt Marina suggested you might want to try a cereal other than Cinnamon Toast Crunch," comes the snappy rejoinder, a reminder that the knowledge advantage of cousin-hood works both ways. "Come on, Sasha. Every guy you've hooked up with since you started having wet dreams has been the same—snotty, preppy and straight out of a J. Crew catalog. In fact, didn't Jeff model for—"

"I think I see your point," Alex says through gritted teeth. They inevitably grind at the mention of Jeff's name. The last of the cookie in his hand crumbles to dust on the bakery floor, giving him the perfect excuse to push up to his feet and stalk off to get the broom. "You're saying I'm not just a jerk, I'm usually a *shallow* jerk."

"With a side of sleazy, if I'm being honest." Samantha squinches her face in a way that's probably meant to take some of the poison out of the insult, which he knows, logically, she doesn't really mean, but it doesn't work.

"First you call me a jerk, then I'm sleazy. That's great. Thanks, Peach." With short, angry strokes, Alex sweeps up the mess he made. But it's a small mess, and he's really angry, and they have no idea when Craig will be back to close, so he begins to sweep the entire shop. Might as well save Craig as much trouble as he can while trying not to punch his cousin in the nose. "With family like you, who needs enemies, right, Samantha? Remind me to give you a call right away if I'm ever feeling suicidal."

His fists are clenched tight around the broomstick; his knuckles are already starting to ache from the grip, and he knows his face is flushed because he feels as if he's coming down with the flu. As critical as he is of himself—and he is—it hurts more to hear everything he's ever thought of himself coming out of Samantha's mouth. If his own cousin, the relative he's closest to out of his whole family on both sides, thinks he's basically an undateable waste of space, then what must Craig think, deep down, that maybe he's not saying because he's just so *nice* and the sex is good, so why rock the boat?

After years of refinement, Alex has spiraling into self-loathing down to a sadly efficient science, and he doesn't realize he's lost in his thoughts until Samantha tries to tug the broom out of his hands. "I'm sorry," comes the simple apology, with a deep breath and a sigh. When Alex looks up and blinks, Samantha does look contrite; she bites her lip, casts her eyes down. But then, she always looks contrite when she realizes she's crossed a line. With another tug, the broom is out of Alex's hands, and Samantha is yanking him into a hug. "You're right. I... I am being so gross," Samantha admits, her voice muffled from speaking into Alex's chest. "I was surprised and concerned about Craig, and that got away from me. You're really not a bad guy, and I know it and I apologize."

Doesn't make me a good guy. "Yeah, but you have a point," Alex mumbles, shrugging her off and moving to retrieve the broom and resume his work. "Craig and I are very different people, and maybe I'm not necessarily the good kind of people for him."

Samantha's eyes bore into his back for a long time. "I think he could be the good kind of people for you, though." Her heels tap away, the sink in the back runs, and then there's the squeak of wet cloth on metal as Samantha quickly wipes down the countertops before moving on to the empty display cases. "I mean, if you keep letting him be." Silence. "Do you want to let him be?"

"I'm still seeing him, am I not?" He knows he has a reputation for love 'em and leave 'em, but goddamn, he's not heartless—and it's not as if he's always the one doing the leaving.

Just ask Jeff.

"But is that why you're still seeing him?" Samantha persists, pulling the empty trays out of the cases. "I know I'm being nosy. I'm just trying to figure it out. Without, you know, being a complete horror show again." The trays rattle as Samantha stacks them in her arms, preparing to carry them to the dishwasher. "I just think it would be nice to see you happy, Sasha. With someone who's actually nice. So. Without being a jerk, based strictly on your methods to date, casting no aspersions on your character or Craig's, I'm stating for the record that more than a few... ah, *encounters* is usually not your thing, and visiting your hook-up at his place of business is definitely out of the ordinary. Do I need to put soap in this thing?"

Alex has to pitch his voice louder to make sure Samantha hears him in the back room. "Craig should have filled it this morning. Just shove the rack in and shut it to make it come on. And I'm aware of my *thing*, as you put it."

"And I would like to know why the change-up," comes the answering call as the industrial dishwasher fires up and fills Sucre Coeur with steamy, lemony soap smell and the sound of gallons of running water. Samantha emerges from the kitchen again, drying her hands and inspecting her cherry-red nails for chips. "Craig can take care of himself, so I'm not exactly worried, but I would really prefer it if you weren't dicking him around just for the sake of getting laid. And I still don't know why the tea pickup line worked on you."

"I just... I like him, all right?" It hurts to admit it out loud, as if his teeth are being pulled. Alex cringes from the space in the air where the words seem to float, as if they could touch him, could burn him, He knows Craig isn't Jeff, there's *nothing* of Jeff in this... thing... Alex has with Craig at all, except for the lingering and pervasive sense of panic and anger that still floods him whenever he thinks of his... ex. Former. Erstwhile. Whatever Jeff was before he became a bad dream.

There's nothing of Jeff in Craig. The words are a mantra he repeats to himself when he feels the panic on the rise, as he does now. "I like Craig. I have no intention of hurting him," he repeats firmly, as much to convince himself as Samantha.

But he still sees worry in Samantha's clear gray eyes and the lines of her heart-shaped face, and when she opens her mouth, Alex can almost hear her saying, *Yeah, you never do.*

Before she can say a word, though, their cell phones ring.

For all that Craig is getting out of this lecture, he might as well have left, money be hanged.

It's not the fault of the speaker—she's fascinating, the editor of an aerospace magazine, of all specialties, and while what Craig knows about that topic could fit into a thimble with room to spare, she knows writing well, knows how to make the most dubious subject interesting. Were he able to focus, he'd be learning a lot that could help him pitch more articles to local mags.

Instead, his leg has been jiggling for the last hour while he worries about Alex, about how he's surely having the screws put to him by a well-meaning Samantha. By the time Craig extracts him from the situation, Alex will be the prickliest of prickly hedgehogs. He is not at all sure how to remedy that.

No. That's not true. He knows exactly how to remedy that, he's just not sure he actually has the stamina for the amount of remedying that will be required. At least he can say he is absolutely willing to do his best.

In the pocket of his jeans, his phone zaps a text message notification at the same time Nate's gentle elbow prods his ribs. When he slides a glance Nate-ward, Nate just smiles and points at the phone in his own hand, nods his head and raises his eyebrows.

Why are they still here? Craig heaves a sigh and digs into his pocket to get his phone and thumb it on to look at Nate's message.

Calm down and listen to the nice lady.

Nate's flinch at the double-barreled irritation in Craig's glare is satisfying, for a moment at least. Craig bends to his phone and taps back a message of his own.

Get fucked.

That, too, is satisfying.

His phone buzzes again. *Okay. Calm down and tell me about your guy?*

He's going to end up with carpal tunnel in his thumbs or something, he's typing so furiously. *He's trapped at my bakery with your very nosy girlfriend.*

Buzz. *She's not gonna murder him, Craig. Come on. Tell me the real stuff about him.*

Fine. *We met in a bar. He was having a bad night; I thought he was cute. I like spending time with him. I want that to be a thing that keeps happening, so Sammi better not scare him off.*

Nate's eyebrow quirks. *Is he of a delicate nature?*

The fact that Craig has not yet crushed his phone in annoyance seems a minor miracle. He doesn't answer; instead, he crosses his arms over his chest and focuses intently on the lecturer.

His phone buzzes again. He ignores it. It buzzes a second time.

This time, Nate's elbow to his ribs is a lot less gentle, and it's a good thing the lecture is starting to break up because Craig can't hold back the pained grunt that would have disrupted the goings-on entirely. He ignores the strange looks they're getting from the people who were sitting near them. "Goddamn it, Nate."

Holding his hands up, Nate backs off. "Okay. I'm sorry. That was a bad joke. I shouldn't have said that. That's what the last two messages said."

"And maybe you could not hit me in the ribs." Craig touches the sore spot through his T-shirt and frowns. "That had better not bruise. Jesus, some apology."

Nate ducks his head. "Sorry. Really, Craig. I'm sorry." He gets to his feet and holds his hand out. "Come on, please?"

Tempting as it is to draw things out and see how far Nate will go with his apology—getting him to really beg is always entertaining—Craig sighs, shakes his head and accepts the hand as both a handshake and a hand up out of his seat. "Yeah, okay. Fine. Apology accepted." He picks up his satchel, slings it across his chest and picks his way through the chairs as fast as he can without tripping or bruising himself. "I should get out of here."

"Hey! Wait!" Nate grabs his own bag and picks through the chairs with considerably less care, if his muffled curses are anything to go by. "Fuck! Come on, Craig. Are you that worried about Sammi? Seriously, she's an elementary school teacher, not a murderer."

Craig stops without turning around, fingers tight around the strap of his bag. "No, yeah, I mean, I just..." He doesn't know what to say, or how to explain that he doesn't really know Alex, even now, or that what he does know makes him protective and selfish and anxious to see what's behind the high walls. He doesn't know how to explain that, as much as he does like Samantha, he's afraid that her gregarious, inquisitive nature might undo the miniscule progress he's made so far.

He doesn't know how to explain any of this to Nate, because he still doesn't understand much of it himself; he only knows that he likes Alex, and wants him and doesn't quite fathom how a random uptight white guy has gotten so far beneath his skin.

"You really like this guy," Nate says, interrupting Craig's attempt to, for the thousandth time in months, work things out for himself. "I mean, you like him."

Craig can't help the eye-roll. "No bloody kidding. Yeah, 'course I do."

"No. I mean—*damn*, you *like* him, Craig." He steps around to face Craig again, and the wonder in his voice is echoed in his eyes. "He's got you good, you can't even say why. How'd that happen?"

"Fuck if I know." Craig falls into a chair. "That's all I can tell you, Nate."

Pressing his mouth into a tight line, Nathan observes him in silence, tilts his head and tucks his thumbs under the straps of his backpack. His thoughts are just about loud enough to hear, but Craig has no real idea what's going on inside his head until he announces, "Okay, so I totally have to meet this guy."

Worst. Idea. Ever. "Uh, no, no you don't."

"No, I think I do. It's only fair; Sammi's getting to meet him." Nate pulls out his phone. "I think we're gonna need to go out dancing, my friend. Do you want to call your guy or do I just need to have Sammi extend the invitation?"

SAMMI GRABS HER PHONE AND ANSWERS IT FIRST, BUT THE look on her face says clear as anything that she's not finished with Alex, not by a long shot. "Hey, baby!"

Ah. Must be Nathan. Alex pulls his phone out and looks at it. *Craig.* His face goes feverish with a rush of blood under his skin. Samantha's giggle tells him she spots it—how could she not, they both have the same paper-white complexion—but he ignores her and turns away to answer before the call goes to voicemail. "Hello?"

"Babe. Hey." Craig's voice is steady and warm, a low thrum of good humor that weakens Alex in the knees. "Listen, I'm sorry about not being there this morning... well, for not being there and for not texting you to tell you. I hope Samantha explained why I left?"

"Ah, yeah." Casting a glance back over his shoulder, Alex watches Samantha speaking with considerable animation to Nathan, nodding with an emphatic enthusiasm that for some reason fills him with dread. "Samantha and I know each other, actually. Um. We have for a long time."

"Are you fucking kid—never mind." Craig's laugh sounds as helpless as Alex has felt most of the morning. "How small is this city?"

Alex looks at his cousin again. "Very small. Very, very small."

"Amazing." This time when Craig chuckles, he sounds more like his usual self. "Well, I'm here with Nathan—you know Nathan, too, then, I'm sure—and we're all done here. He suggested we all go out tonight, does that sound all right?"

No, not really, it doesn't. Because it sounds like a double date, and Alex is having enough trouble working out the blurry lines of his feelings and tolerance and understanding. It's too much, too fast, too weird.

Samantha, of course, is no help. She's standing with the phone tucked between her shoulder and her ear, both thumbs up and a hopeful, encouraging smile on her face. *Say yes*, she mouths, no doubt wanting to see for herself how Alex and Craig get on so she can go on trying to "figure it out." Or laugh at it. Or both. Alex sighs and returns his focus to the conversation. "What did you have in mind?"

"Clubbing in your neighborhood? We can go back to yours after. If you want."

He wants to say no, make his excuses, say that he's tired, do *anything* but go on a possible double date-like thing, but then his mind supplies a fleeting image of the two of them under the lights of a club with the pulse of a bass line running under their feet and up into their close-pressed bodies, with sweat and heavy breathing and the promise of *later* hot in his ear.

He's never entirely sure whether he hates his brain more when it's dragging him into the murky depths of self-loathing or when it tempts him into circumstances his first instinct is to avoid.

He wonders if it'll get warm enough, and if Craig might get tipsy enough, to strip down to his undershirt as he sometimes does when they go dancing and tucks whatever T-shirt he's worn through his belt. Alex imagines Craig's strong arms, shaped by exercise and excessive dough-kneading, dappled with the different colors of the strobes, sweat running alongside that one vein on his dark forearm that Alex likes to trace with his finger—

The Nathan and Samantha factor of the evening is now entirely out of his consciousness, replaced with naked skin and slow kisses, gentle teasing tickles and gloriously throaty laughter.

Alex can put up with a lot for the promise of that, though he doesn't want to examine why at the moment. "I'm in," he answers, mostly with his dick; though yes, a less hormonal part of him simply sings in delight about getting to see Craig today after all. "We're nearly done cleaning up here."

"Oh, you didn't have to." Alex can all but see Craig's warm, appreciative smile, which calls up a corresponding... er... warm and almost *fuzzy* feeling in himself because he made that smile happen. That thought, too, is shoved away for later—or never—as Craig continues. "Samantha's going to go meet Nate at some Vietnamese restaurant for dinner. I'll meet you at the bakery so I can finish closing up, and then you and I can go have a shower and get ready at my place? You left some stuff last time we went dancing; it's clean, I washed it."

I think he's the good kind of people for you, comes the echo of Samantha in his mind and a resurgence of warmth in the pit of his stomach.

Yep. He's screwed.

Chapter Seven

"Stop pacing," Nathan advises, standing on his tiptoes to better scan the throng of people on the sidewalk. "You'll just get all rumpled and sweaty. I mean, I think you're cute all rumpled and sweaty, but unless you want to go home right now and change..."

Samantha sniffs, surreptitiously brushing a slightly sweaty palm over the full skirt of her dress. "I do not sweat. I gleam." Nate has a point, though. With effort, she manages to bring herself down from a steady pacing stride to a moderately excited bouncing in place. "And hush. I'm just really excited about this night out with Craig's new guy."

Really, *really* excited. For hours now, she's been picturing the look that will dawn on Nate's face and she knows the real thing is going to be *amazing*.

Nate's smile is fondly tolerant. "I know you are, sweet cheeks."

Oh, but he has no idea, Samantha knows. He *can't*. "You don't *really* understand, Nathan." It's hard not to pace. Maybe she should suggest heading inside the club to get a drink so she can calm her nerves. "This is important. I've wanted to see Craig find someone for years, and so have you—"

"Sammi, I *know*. Better than you, actually." Nate's tolerance becomes amusement. "He is *my* ex, remember? Not yours?"

She waves it off. "He's a really good person; he deserves to have what you and I have." She's not bragging or being smug, Samantha tells herself. Not much, anyway. What she and Nate have *is* good, amazing even, warm and loving; and if not perfect, well, it's all the better for not being so. It's perfect for *them*, and Craig deserves to find that same sense of compatibility, of coming home, of fun and sex and fights and making up. He's been so nice to her since she and Nate got together, and it seems like a crime for such a perfect specimen of manhood go to waste in the trenches of near-celibacy. Craig has needed to find someone for a long time: someone who will put up with Craig's baking or writing at odd hours, his goofy sense of humor and his predilection for excessive tea consumption. No—not just put up with, but *enjoy* these things. And who will in turn be funny, intelligent and excellent in bed, of course.

She's a little surprised that her favorite cousin is in the front-running to be that kind of ideal match—well, she doesn't know about the bed thing and doesn't want to—but when she thinks about it, Alex deserves happiness just as much as Craig does, so in that weird way, they could be a good match. Maybe?

"I have a good feeling about this one," Samantha announces despite her conflicting feelings. She begins to pace again and ignores both Nate's indulgent grin and the irritated glares of the passersby she's forcing out of her way. "He's clearly got good taste, and he's at least articulate and passably good-looking by Craig's standards."

Nate snorts out a chuckle. "You make Craig sound shallow for liking the guy. You know he's not."

"He has eyes, doesn't he?" It's difficult to slow her pace, but Samantha tries, forcing her heels to click at a rate of one per second on the sidewalk. She can't manage it for long, though.

The best thing, really, is that Nate doesn't know; Craig hasn't even told him the guy's name. Or what he looks like. Samantha managed to keep Nate in the dark all through dinner. *I should earn a medal.* He doesn't believe that she didn't get the guy's name, or even notice what he looks like, but he still doesn't know. Samantha's lips tilt into a smile. Well, she's never been a good liar, but she's always been excellent at keeping secrets, especially secrets that are huge surprises when revealed. She loves surprises—loves them best when they're happening to other people.

Nate stretches up on his tiptoes again. "I wouldn't worry, Sammi. I'm sure this guy is really good for Craig. Or Craig's good for him. Or both! Both would work. I'm sure it's both."

She ignores Nate and checks her phone for the time. "They're late." To hell with keeping her pace slow. Anticipation is going to eat Samantha alive. Her heels clatter along the pavement, the racket she creates akin to a stampeding herd of vintage-store-shod gazelles.

"By five minutes." His voice is irritatingly calm. "They... " He lets out a chuckle. "They're probably having sex."

This does stop Samantha in her tracks. "Craig would never be late for anything just because of sex. Even if it was the best sex in the world. He's not like that."

Nate's eyebrows shoot up toward his spiky black hairline. "Seriously? Mister Late himself? Yes, he would, and you know I would know. It doesn't happen often, but I can guarantee without question that some tardy spots in his history are a direct result of sexy times. He can be distracted."

"Too much info," Samantha replies with haste. Now is not the time to allow herself to be diverted by her fantasies of Nathan and Craig together. She spins on her heel and recommences wearing a hole in the sidewalk she's claimed in the name of her excitement. "In fact I'll bet you ten dollars, Nathan Figueroa, that there was a bus delay. That's all." Samantha smiles sweetly. She has more than cleared her debt from this morning's bet by paying for their dinner, but there's nothing wrong with trying to get her initial investment back. Doubled.

One eyebrow cocked up, Nate grins. "Well, Samantha Chernikova," he says, mimicking her tone. "You sure you want to chance that? You already lost once today. I told you, you just don't know him the way I know him."

She spins on her heel and points her finger at him for emphasis. "I know people. I'm good at people. Bet's on."

Still grinning, so brightly he could light the night sky, radiating an air of confidence that would worry Samantha if she weren't so very sure of herself and her people-knowledge, Nate sticks his hands in his pockets and rocks back on his heels. "Then you won't mind if I see your ten dollars... and raise you two weeks of you doing anything I want you to do."

Samantha lifts her chin. "Bring it."

"That includes you cleaning the apartment in that corset and the knee-high boots you bought for Halloween that year," Nate warns. "I really like you in that outfit."

"It wasn't a Halloween costume. I wear that on weekends quite regularly, thank you," Samantha retorts, smirking at her beloved boyfriend. "And frankly, I look forward to chaining you to the bed and not letting you come for at *least* two hours." She sashays back over to Nate slowly, languorously, skirts swishing and heels clicking as she watches his face go a little pale and sees him swallow as if his mouth's gone dry. "And you have to feed me peeled grapes any time I ask. In those vinyl booty shorts I bought you, the hot pink ones. Oh! And—"

She had more in mind. She really did. Samantha keeps a running list of slightly kinky, sexy and silly things to make Nate do when they have these bets. It is quite the comprehensive list, and she committed it to her normally reliable memory a long time ago.

It's just that she's completely lost her train of thought because Craig is strolling up to them right now, with Alex, and damn it. They have definitely, judging by the grins on their faces and the completely disastrous state of Alex's hair and rumpled, blue-striped button-down, been fucking. She's lost the bet; but on the other hand, what a stupendously hot couple they make, even if half of said couple is her own cousin. And in the end, the look on Nate's face is very much worth losing ten dollars and a housework bet anyway. Samantha has won the night in every possible way. Her fingers entwine with Nate's and give a reassuring squeeze. "Surprise?"

"Yeah, gotta say, didn't see this coming," Nate says, nodding his head in an apparent stupor.

She squeezes again. "I didn't tell you who it was because I wanted to see the look on your face."

"Nicely done." He shakes off his surprise and waves them down. "Okay, great surprise, and you just won me ten bucks and two weeks of Sammi cleaning house in lingerie and leather boots," Nate informs them cheerfully. "Your first drinks are totally on me."

"Too much information," Alex says, with his face drained of color and his voice half-strangled.

"Yeah, little bit, sorry," Craig agrees, slinging an arm around Nate in an affectionate half-hug. "Sammi, you're gorgeous, you know it, but I don't need to know about your sex life with my ex-boyfriend."

Alex jumps as if he's been electrified, and his mouth falls open as he turns to Craig. "Your ex-boyfriend!" He turns again, pointing at Samantha. "You said they were friends! You didn't tell me Nate was Craig's ex!" He spins back to Craig. "You didn't tell me Nate was your ex!"

This really couldn't be going any better on the entertainment front. Samantha almost wishes she had popcorn. "I didn't tell you because I wanted to see the look on your face," she tells Alex, dimpling her most innocent smile in his direction. The narrow glare he directs at her makes her roll her eyes. "Oh, come on, Sasha. It's funny."

Craig's eyes slip to the side in a sharp glance. "Sasha?"

"It's his nickname in our family," Samantha volunteers when it becomes clear Alex isn't going to say a damn thing. "He calls me Peach. Can't remember why, but… yeah. We have nicknames."

Craig looks between the two of them, and then he looks hard at each of them and finally throws his hands in the air. "Same eyes, I should have seen it. Don't fucking tell me. You're brother and sister? Twins, since you're the same age, right?"

"We don't even have the same last name, silly. Close, though," Samantha says. Alex continues to stew and glare at her. Yes, she knows she's in trouble if Alex ever gets her alone for two seconds, but everything, *everything* continues to be absolutely worth all the mischief she's shelling out. "It's parental. My dad, his mom, they're brother and sister. And I'm cuter."

Nathan's chuckle startles them all. "This is hilarious. Man, Craig, you weren't kidding when you said you didn't really know your guy."

"Oh, because you were going to volunteer the cousin information?" Craig asks, raising a single eyebrow in interest. "I mean, you had the opportunity—"

"Actually, I didn't," Nate points out with a huge grin. "Because *you* didn't feel like telling me anything about the guy. And then *Sammi* sure wasn't being forthcoming, so how was I supposed to tell anyone anything?"

"Sammi is a menace," Alex snaps, clearly not amused and not letting up on his glare. "Her whole thing for wacky hijinks is funny until it's aimed at you. Fuck, but I have a headache now."

"The point is, I'm basically an innocent in all of this." Nate nods, takes Alex's arm and steers him to a nearby bench. "Come on, have a seat, take a couple of deep breaths. You buttoned your shirt crooked, by the way."

Alex's glare switches focus from Samantha—well, there's a relief—to Nate and then Craig as he fixes his shirt. "Explain."

"It's quite simple, babe," Craig begins, and Samantha cannot help but giggle at the endearment; it seems so *strange* to know it refers to Alex, of all people. Her cousin, her Sasha, the last person in the world to tolerate pet names and endearments from anyone apart from Samantha and his mother. Yet when Samantha looks, it's to see Alex's glare melt into a smile that can only be described as goofy—well, as goofy as Alex ever gets, which isn't much, but still—as Craig continues. "Nate and I dated for a while at uni. And a little after I graduated. It was fun, but honestly, he's much better suited to Sammi than to me. They are a lot alike, you might have noticed."

"Nate is less of a menace." Alex looks up at Samantha and shakes his head. "I will never understand why they allow you to work with young minds, to have an active role in molding the future of this country and the free world."

"That's because you're a jerk, Sasha," she fires back and pouts. "Meanie."

He ignores her in favor of looking back up at Craig. "Small town."

"World's largest village." He pulls Alex and then Nathan to their feet. "Well, fuck. I don't know about anyone else, but I need a drink."

"I'VE BEEN IMAGINING YOU IN THOSE BOOTS FOR THE LAST two hours," Nate confesses in Samantha's ear, putting her fresh drink in front of her. "I can't think of anything else."

It's not exactly subtle—the music in the club is loud and thumping, and everyone's shouting to be heard over it. To Samantha's relief, Nate's breathless declaration is only loud enough for her and the handful of people in her immediate vicinity to hear. She offers them a tight smile and a nod as they whistle at her.

Sipping her martini, she sniffs. "I don't think our bet counts when you cheated to win. You had foreknowledge. That is completely unfair." And so, she has no intention whatsoever of fulfilling the bet. *It's not welshing if the other person cheated,* she tells herself with no small sense of uplifting virtue.

For a second, she wonders if Nate's cheating can be leveraged into a lacy panties fashion show. He does look good in a pair of red lace cheekies. *Ooh.* The thought is filed away for later.

Nate coughs in incredulity as he drops into the seat next to her. "Um, I hate to break it to you, but I told you outright I had foreknowledge. It's not cheating if you decided to ignore the warnings, baby. Besides, do I need to point out *your* foreknowledge? I don't think I'm the real cheater here." Leaning over, he kisses her on the cheek. "I'm cutting you off; you've hit your revisionist history point of drunkenness."

"I'm not drunk," Samantha protests, almost believing the lie herself. "I'm distracted."

"By wh—oh." He peers over the railing of the second floor mezzanine, zeroing in on the spot where Alex and Craig are still glued together on the dance floor, hands in each other's back pockets. "Wow."

Samantha looks over the railing and shakes her head. "In fact, please get me another dirty martini, and make it a double," she says, downing the one Nate has just brought her so fast her head starts to swim. Maybe phō hadn't been the wisest, most alcohol-absorbent dinner she could have chosen. Or maybe it was, because now her cousin and her friend are straight up making out in the middle of the dance floor, furiously thumping The Naked and Famous remix be damned. She picks up her martini glass and shakes it in Nate's general direction. "Drinky, drinky, my love."

He plucks the glass from her hand, sets it aside and scoots close enough to pull her into his arms. "Nope, definitely cut off. What's up, baby?"

"Nothing." She slumps into his embrace, and—yes. She is sulking. She is definitely sulking. Samantha waves her hand toward the dance floor. "Them."

All right, maybe she is a little drunk. It's taken the last two hours of dancing and drinking to get nicely liquefied and able to pause and think without her inconvenient fantasies getting in the way. The bartenders at this club don't skimp on the alcohol, which is one reason why it's so popular. That isn't usually Samantha's favorite reason to come to Laser, but tonight it certainly helps. Nate's frown is audible in his voice as he tries to follow her train of thought. "Them? Craig and Alex? What about it?"

Samantha focuses her watery gaze on the dance floor and locates the happy couple with what she considers to be a fairly impressive immediacy, given that she is five good, strong dirty martinis in the bag. "I dunno about it."

Not her most articulate moment, but it gets across the point she's been wobbling toward for two hours. Nate starts, and for a moment he squeezes her a little too tightly. "You liked it fine two hours ago. You liked it fine an hour ago, actually." His grip relaxes, and he jiggles her gently. "Alcohol always makes you suspicious."

"No, I mean, it's..." Okay, sipping that last martini would, in retrospect, have been wise. Samantha squints and tries to pick words out of her muddle of a brain. "It's legit, Nate. That's why the drinky." She squirms in his embrace and stretches her fingers in the general direction of her confiscated empty glass. "Please can I have another?"

He sighs. "Sammi..."

No joy, then. She relaxes against him. "I love my cousin. I love him very much."

Nate's cheek shifts to touch hers. "Uh huh."

Samantha watches the dance floor while she gathers her thoughts. It's mesmerizing, to see Craig and Alex dance. They've been in their own little world this entire time, completely absorbed in each other and paying no attention to anyone else, not even when Samantha and Nate joined them. And since her escape to the mezzanine, Samantha has watched two guys, at two times, start grinding on Alex's ass while eyeing Craig up and down, only to wander off with confusion written all over their faces when neither Craig nor Alex acknowledged their existence with so much as the flicker of an eye.

They are into each other to the exclusion of everyone else, and *that* is why her earlier, cautious delight has whirlpooled right down into the depths of doubt.

"Sasha's like my brother," she says, eyes still locked on Craig and Alex. "Always has been. I love him. I know him."

Alex's button-down is open to his waist; the sheen of sweat on his skin reflects a rainbow from the laser show overhead. Craig ditched his burgundy Henley an hour ago and is down to his low-slung jeans and a white undershirt. His fingers are hooked through the belt loops of Alex's jeans, holding them together so tightly there might as well be nothing between them at all. *My God, why don't they just fuck on the dance floor?* Samantha marvels as Alex's hands slip further into Craig's back pockets, the flex of his fingers around Craig's ass cheeks clearly visible behind the denim. *Just strip down and go at it, I don't think anyone would mind…*

Fifty people around them in various stages of undress, many of them doing things much more explicit and possibly illegal in public, but it's Craig and Alex everyone watches out of the corners of their eyes. Even Sammi is fascinated, despite herself.

Enough. She shakes herself alert and picks up where she left off, waving down at the floor. "They are so into each other, I don't think they even remember they're here. And that… that is not Sasha. At all. It has never been Sasha. Sasha does not connect like this."

And it *is* a connection. It's easy to see that whatever is between Craig and Alex is more than just sex— Samantha can almost reach out and touch the magnetism between them. This is what baffles her, despite her earlier approval, even when she was sober, chasing itself around and around in her mind until she *needed* the alcohol to calm down. The fact that they take pleasure in each other is not a surprise. They're pleasure seekers of the highest order. No, the sexual attraction isn't the confusing part at all.

Her head aches when she tries to work out what, exactly, *is*.

Nate's hand rubs her arm. "Sammi." There's laughter in his voice, and she sees concern in his eyes when she turns to face him. "Come on."

No problem. "This shouldn't be happening," she blurts. "There must be a reason it never occurred to us to introduce them before, right? Because deep down we never thought it was a good idea, did we?" She winces at the hysteria in her voice, but whatever. She's tipsy and she knows her cousin and Craig is her friend, so maybe she's entitled to a little hysteria.

Nathan sucks in a deep breath; his face is a little twisted in thought, and Samantha recognizes him trying to work out the best way to say something he knows she isn't likely to throw a party about. Lips pursed, he finally takes her arm, then pushes through the sweaty, pulsing crowd of clubgoers to get to the far wall, where curtained alcoves conceal trysting lovers. Nate peers into each of the alcoves, ignoring Samantha's protests, until one turns up empty. He shoves her inside and down onto a padded bench and yanks the heavy velvet curtains closed to muffle the club noise. "Okay, not a word until I finish. Okay?"

"Nate," she starts to protest, but a hand over her mouth in the dark shuts her up.

"Sammi. Please." Nate takes another deep breath. "First things first. Craig is a big boy."

Not the most promising of starts. She peels Nate's fingers from her lips. "Craig is—" But that's all she gets out before the hand returns to silence her.

"Craig is a big boy," Nathan repeats. "A big boy who really, really likes your cousin. A lot."

Samantha ducks out from under Nate's hand and lets out a humorless approximation of a laugh. "This isn't supposed to be funny," she replies.

"I agree." The alcove isn't big enough to allow Nate to pace, but the energy Samantha can feel coming from him means he wishes he could. Nate always thinks better when he can pace. "I'm not joking, Sammi. Craig really likes Alex, in a way I have not seen Craig like anyone in the entire time I have known him."

"And that doesn't *worry* you?" She throws her hands wide, grasping for the sense Nate isn't making. "That he's getting in deep with my cousin, the serial dater? Alex, whose recent taste in men has been, in case you have forgotten, Jeff the Jerk. Remember him? Fucking Fucker Jeff? *Your* nickname for him, I remind you."

The handful of double dates they'd had with Alex and Jeff had been almost, but not quite, as entertaining as a series of visits to the dentist. "Who could forget? Such a charming dickhead."

"A charming dickhead completely and totally in... ind... dicative of Alex's taste in men: pretty, snobby, heartless, bullet-proof assholes without two brain cells to rub together." When did her tongue get so unwieldy? "That's literally the only kind of guy Alex has ever dated. Like, that's his type. And Alex himself? Alex flirts with guys, he sleeps with guys, he walks away from guys." She flops back against the velvet-covered wall of the alcove. "And you're still not worried?"

Nate taps at his chin. "Wait, but didn't Jeff have an anthropology degree? He had some brain cells, at least, even if he didn't exert himself much using them."

"Nate! A little focus!" She snaps her fingers in his face. "Craig is not like those guys! Not even a little! How can this not end in tears and blood?"

"Sammi." Kneeling in front of her, Nate takes both her hands in his and rests them in her lap. "They're adults, they make their own choices, and they're not stupid men, baby. I mean, Craig does not make decisions like this lightly. He hasn't seriously dated anyone in a long, long time. If he's doing it now—or at least playing at it, I guess—he's weighed the pros and cons and said fuck it, you know?"

She does know. She does, and Nate would definitely, absolutely know, as her wallet and reckless bet record today can easily attest. That doesn't exactly ease her worries, though.

Nate threads his fingers through hers. "As for Alex... he's a big boy, too, baby. And I think Craig will be good for him. Better than Jeff, anyway, not that it's a stretch."

I think he could be the good kind of people for you, her voice echoes from just a few hours ago, and a blush of guilt burns Samantha's cheeks like fire. She'd actually believed that when she said it. She believes it now.

And she still believes another thing she thought earlier— that Alex *deserves* it, on some deep level. She's always wondered what he might be like if he let go enough to really let someone in.

"'M drunk, I'm being gross again," she says, thinking of the awful things she said to Alex before she got her head on straight, and she buries her face in both of her hands.

Fingers close around her wrists. "Maybe a little bit," says Nate, never one to sugarcoat. "And you are kind of overreacting. But it's sweet of you to be concerned."

"I..." she begins.

The curtain of the alcove swishes open, and the sight before Samantha's eyes shocks her speechless, completely derailing her train of thought. "God, it took for-fucking-ever to find you guys," Alex announces, Craig draped shirtless over his back, both of them grinning as if they just got away with robbing a bank. "We pissed off two twinks, a bear and his cub and a drag queen fixing her falsies searching for you. I wish I had a Gay Bar Bingo Card right now."

"We're ready to go," Craig adds, running his fingers up Alex's throat. "You don't have to if you don't want to."

Samantha stares at the two of them. "We've only been here like, two and a half hours."

"And we're ready to leave," Alex begins, only to cut himself off with a shudder when Craig lowers his head to the curve of Alex's neck and begins to mouth slow, wet kisses along its length. "Fuck."

"That's the idea," Samantha vaguely hears Craig mumble against Alex's skin. *Oh God.*

Alex sags and only keeps himself from hitting the floor by tightly gripping the curtains. "If you want me to be able to get us out to a cab, you need to stop," he warns, his eyes half-shut with pleasure.

With a warm, filthy chuckle, Craig slides his other hand down Alex's chest. "Think of it as a challenge, babe."

"Gotta go, bye Peach, bye Nate," Alex groans, and they're gone, leaving Samantha and Nathan staring out of the alcove after them.

Samantha recovers when her open-mouthed shock completely dries out her tongue. She blinks and shakes her head. "That just happened," she croaks.

"That *is* happening," Nathan corrects. He rises and pulls Samantha up. "It's happening, Sammi. It's obviously a voluntary and mutual thing. Whatever it is."

"What if it..." She *wants* to be happy for them, she *does*, but worry still fills her throat like cotton and she can't get the rest of her sentence out.

But Nate understands her, as he always has. "Let's just be happy for them in the now." Pulling Samantha close, he runs his hands up and down her arms, soothing, comforting, an oasis of calm in the pulsating madness of the club and the evening. "Is it really so hard to believe that for some very strange reason we don't know yet, this could actually work out?"

Samantha's head is really, really starting to throb—no, wait, that's the dubstep. It doesn't help. "A little," she mumbles, pressing a hand to her head. All the alcohol is making her head spin now that she's standing.

Nate pulls aside the curtain, gently escorting her back out into the main part of the club. "You're cute when you're worried and drunk. Let's get you home. You need a nice glass of water and a foot massage. Hmm?"

Maybe she is thinking about this too hard. Maybe the alcohol is making her all kinds of suspicious. Opposites attract, right?

They exit the club just in time to see Craig and Alex successfully flag down a cab and tumble into it, still linked at hand and hip and lip and anywhere else they can touch. They are so, so connected, and so, so into each other, that Samantha thinks maybe she can afford to feel a little, tiny scrap of hope.

Looking up at the night sky through the fog of light reflected from the city, she can just about spot a single star. And she only needs one, one star for one wish.

They should just be happy... I'll just wish for them to be happy.

Chapter Eight

"W HERE TO?" ASKS THE PRETTY CABBIE WITH THE SPIKY dark hair. A smile curves the red bow of her lips as she takes in the two men who have all but fallen into the back of her taxi. Craig knows what they must look like, all sweat and debauchery and freely roaming hands. He resolves to tip her very well, though the appreciation in her eyes makes him wonder if the real bonus, in her mind, isn't money at all.

"My place," Alex growls. Not a point Craig is going to fight. He wants Alex *now*, Alex certainly seems to want *him* if the aggressive way he's sliding his hand up along Craig's bare ribs is any indication, and Alex's apartment is a much shorter cab ride away. Craig nods his agreement and does his level best to make Alex's job of giving his address very, *very* difficult.

The cab driver winks, touching a kiss to her black-nailed fingertip and pressing it to the scuffed Plexiglas barrier that separates driver from fare. "Don't get anything on the seats," she cautions before pulling into Seattle traffic with a lurch that sends Alex sprawling over Craig's very receptive and delighted body.

Ten minutes is plenty of time to bring Alex to the brink and pull back, over and over again, holding him tight and close while Craig rolls his hips up, undulating against the rock-hard erection that has to be painful by now, he's been teasing Alex for so long. *How long are you going to hold out on being polite, babe?* he'd whispered on the dance floor, while his hand slipped down inside Alex's jeans and his gentle but nimble fingers stroked through the briefs at Alex's cock.

Craig loves Samantha and Nathan and enjoys spending time with them, but a nightclub isn't really conducive to long conversations and the cheerful exchange of gossip. It is much more conducive to tormenting one's lover, especially if said lover had been left high and dry from a sadly shortened session of shower fun earlier in the evening.

Poor Alex. Craig has every intention of making up for it.

"Hope I get you again the next time you guys need a ride," the cabbie calls after them as they scramble out of her taxi and into the courtyard of Alex's brown brick apartment building. They trip up the garden steps as they try their level best to get inside and upstairs without allowing more than a hair's breadth of space between their bodies. They don't succeed, but oh, what fun it is to try. Craig is particularly pleased with the ridiculous way they scramble up the darkened staircase; he tugs Alex back every few steps so his arse is nestled against Craig's cock while Craig reaches back down into his jeans. Craig is mesmerized by the sleepy droop of Alex's eyelids when he looks over his shoulder, how their languor clashes hard with the strain of Alex's body against his and the hands curled into clawing fists at the seams of Craig's jeans as Alex tries to pull them even closer together.

He wishes they had an elevator to play around in, but that would require Alex to live in a building taller than two stories. Ah, well.

They spill out of the stairwell at last and—"That's not my pocket," Alex babbles when Craig pins him against his door and slides a hand down the front of his jeans yet again. "My keys, they're in, they're... fucking hell... "

"I know where your keys are." It's not easy, but Craig manages to keep his voice calm despite his racing pulse. He wants to be inside, laid out, naked and desperate, right now. But it's more fun to keep teasing Alex, to watch him come to pieces, and it's all that keeps Craig from just breaking down the door.

His palm rests along the length of Alex's cock, fingers cupped just under the taut, heavy hang of Alex's balls. Slowly, ever so slowly and carefully, he presses the heel of his hand against the heat and firmness, pulling up just a little, flexing his fingers, keeping friction gentle yet relentless. "Come on, babe," he whispers against Alex's temple, brushes a kiss across the flushed and fevered skin, then comes away with the faint taste of sweat and salt on his lips. "It's better when I make you wait, yeah?"

Fingers scrabble across the pale oak of the door as Alex seeks any purchase to keep himself upright; desperate little mewling groans spill from his lips while he pushes his pelvis forward, up, seeking and needy. "Please..."

"Aw, you said the magic word. All right." Craig pulls his hand back and flips Alex so that his chest is pressed against the door and Craig is right up against his back, hands rummaging in pockets for the wayward keys and keeping up the playful groping through the fabric.

Craig barely remembers to kick the door shut behind him before tackling his lover to the fluffy flokati living room rug and trying to pull off both their pairs of shoes at once, and to hell with the bedroom. His need is outstripping his control; his libido is responding with gusto to every pant and groan and plea that Alex lets slip. Though his demeanor in public is that of a strangely appealing, cocky jerk, in the bedroom Alex allows himself to give in to need. He lets Craig pull him apart. And if there is one thing Craig finds absolutely irresistible it is that submission, that willingness to lose himself that only happens when they're alone.

It is a gift. Craig is aware of this. It is not one he understands, nor is he ready to ask why he is the lucky recipient, but he is aware and holds it close, pours everything he has into meeting that need.

Alex's shirt is gathered at his elbows, exposing long expanses of skin to Craig's lips and tongue as he straddles one tightly clenched thigh and whips his own shirts out from where they've been looped through his belt. One swift motion sends them flying across the dim room and frees Craig to pay full attention to the straining body beneath him.

"Wait—" Alex wriggles free of blue-striped cotton and scrabbles at the end table, flopping and slapping around amongst the detritus there until he finds a remote control. "Thin walls—remember—"

A click of a button and Justin Timberlake's voice spins out of the speakers of Alex's stereo system, mellow and sweet over the slow throb of synth and bass. Craig muffles a guffaw against Alex's chest. "Oh, my God, why don't you just give in to the full cliché and play some Barry White?"

"Shut up and fuck me now," comes the impatient, jagged-edged reply, accompanied by an insistent pelvic grind, and Alex pulls the knitted cap from Craig's head and flings it away to join their shirts. "Judge later."

Craig shoves Alex back down into the soft white cloud of the rug and lies flat all along every inch of that lean, sprawling body, letting his fingers roam and tickle and twist into smooth skin and pebbled nipple. Every harsh groan that climbs up out of Alex's throat Craig swallows like warm spiced rum, just as delicious and three times as intoxicating.

Just a little longer, Craig bargains with himself; the side desperate to strip Alex naked is putting up a fierce argument against his sheer love of the tease. *Just a—*

But the tease has gone on too long. A strangled gasp catches and hangs in Alex's throat for a millisecond before his lower body arches upward hard against Craig; shivers and shakes rocket along his every taut line as he comes. His fingernails scrape Craig's back, making sharp welts of pain on his skin, and Alex's eyes are screwed more and more tightly shut as gasps rattle from his mouth.

Tension hangs in the air, dissipating as Alex slumps to the floor in a pliant pile. His eyes open slowly, one at a time, and a sigh heaves its way out from his chest. "Well, shit."

Craig can't help but chuckle. "Sorry?"

"Like hell you are." Alex's fingers slip along Craig's back and slide down his side; one hand falls to the rug. The other moves with lightning quickness to wrap behind Craig's neck and pull him down into a kiss; Alex's tongue, deep and hot and dirty, licks into Craig's mouth,. "Damn it, Craig," he mumbles, sucking Craig's lower lip between his. "Didn't even get my fucking jeans off."

"Oh, I can help with that." Craig nods, pulling back to trace the tip of his tongue up along Alex's throat. Satisfaction fills him to see goose bumps stipple Alex's skin, to feel a shiver spread under its surface. "I trust you did not think I was done here. You came. I didn't."

Alex seems to be having trouble speaking as Craig rocks his hips downward, rolls back, rocks down again. His eyes flutter shut as his mouth works, soundless and desperate, until at last—"Fuck," he manages, the single word sounding as if it's fought a battle to get free. "Craig—"

"Yes, that's sort of where I was going with that." He slides his hands around and down Alex's back, wriggling past the jeans, past the waistband of the briefs, until his hands cover the tight warmth of Alex's ass, cupping and kneading and pulling their bodies even closer together. Already, anxious need tightens Alex's body again; little groans thrum through his chest. "If you're up for it."

Alex doesn't answer, not with words. Eyes narrowed in a dark glare, he wedges his hand between the two of them, with fingers fumbling for the buttons on Craig's jeans, slipping in behind the fly and down into the boxers, wrapping Craig's cock in the soft warmth of his palm. "Oh, I'm up for it, but if you're going to keep on being a cockteasing asshole, you can take your dick and go the fuck home."

Oh, really? Craig lets his own fingers wander, allows his middle finger to dip and slide ever so slightly along the valley of Alex's arse. "I can do that," he says, dropping his head so every warm whisper feathers along Alex's neck and earlobe. His finger slips a little further, tracing the softer, more sensitive skin deeper in the crevice. "I can go home... alone. Get into bed all by myself. Wrap my hand around my cock and get myself off..." Deeper his finger slips, slow, careful, until the tip brushes against the soft gathering of skin he's looking for. He lets it rest there, moving so slightly against it that he might almost not be moving at all. His teeth nip at Alex's neck. "I'd be thinking about you, here, alone... seems like a waste."

"Ahh..." Alex doesn't seem to know which way to move, up against Craig's cock, which he still holds in loosening fingers, or down against the teasing, drifting fingertip between his cheeks. He is reduced to wordless sounds of pleasure and writhing movement, exactly the way Craig likes him best.

Craig slips his hands out of Alex's jeans with some regret, regret that dissipates when he pushes himself up to look down at the gorgeous man beneath him. He traces across the prominent collarbones, down well-formed pectoral muscles, then follows the trail of dark hair from Alex's chest to where it just disappears into his half-unbuttoned jeans. Alex watches him, eyes storm-dark and heavy-lidded, with a smile tilting his kissed-pink, slightly swollen mouth.

Too much to resist. Craig slides his hand back up, palm down and fingers outspread. His thumb brushes feather-light over Alex's left nipple, already tightened into a pebble. Under his palm, the thin skin over Alex's ribcage ripples into goose bumps. "This is better than if I go home, isn't it?" he asks in a low voice as he applies a gentle twist that makes Alex squirm and groan under his hands: a hypnotic sight. "Rather see you like this than try to imagine it... "

Alex's back arches, and the swell of his reviving erection is easily felt where Craig straddles his hips. "Stay," Alex says, the words as insubstantial as a breeze.

Easily done.

"Thank you," Craig mumbles. He dips his head to occupy Alex with a kiss as he slowly undoes every remaining closure on Alex's button-fly jeans.

Focus. It's futile, restraint is a myth at this point. Now is the time to slow down, savor each moment and touch and motion, but the tease of the night has been as long for him as it has for Alex and he's still hard; his cock pushes against his jeans, about to cross the line from pleasurable ache to just ache. With care, but not too much, he yanks both briefs and jeans down Alex's legs in as near to one motion as he can manage and shoves them aside. "I can't really wait anymore," he confesses, voice low and rough. "I'm sorry."

"Thank fuck," is the only response he receives as Alex returns the jeans favor and they're both utterly, gloriously naked and wrapped as close together as they can get. Justin Timberlake fades into Ellie Goulding, into Florence and the Machine, slow, soft music that twines and throbs and moves through Craig's veins, thick and sweet as honey.

Craig turns Alex over as the bass drops, letting his erection slip into the crevice between Alex's cheeks and lie there, cradled and warm and straining for more. "Are you..." he begins, knowing he doesn't have to finish the sentence and hoping that the answer is yes.

"Yes," Alex breathes, flooding Craig's entire body with sweet relief. "Now, ple—now, Craig. Come on. Fuck me."

Two hours and then some of teasing and perpetual cockstands: it's no wonder Alex is almost needy enough to beg again. Craig feels a fleeting urge to see if he can push it all the way, get another broken, desperate *please* that's so very sweet, but no, he meant it, he can't wait anymore either.

Condom retrieved from his pocket, lube from the end table, and it's right at the end of Craig's ability to maintain control when he finally, carefully eases into Alex one snug millimeter at a time. A moan escapes, and Craig lets his eyelids droop as he savors the slow push.

He can see through his eyelashes that Alex has laid his head on the floor, one cheek pillowed into the carpet, eyes tight shut, mouth open in a long, nearly silent exhalation. Under Craig's fingertips, Alex strains, fights not to push back and all the way down onto Craig's cock, and the muscles held tight in restraint shiver in Craig's grip.

They're both holding back with so much effort they're shaking, and all Craig wants to do is lose himself in the bliss, the overwhelming sensation of being enveloped in sex.

He lets his hips rock forward and push his cock inside the last inch, and revels in it for just a moment, just a little, just enough to enjoy knowing he's as close as he can be to another human being and how much he likes that it's Alex. He drapes himself along Alex's back, skin to skin, hand sliding down to cover Alex's. "I won't last," he whispers, hips already impatient to move.

"Don't try." One gray eye opens and rolls back to fix on Craig. "There's always time to do it again... not like we ever stop at one..."

Fuck, but dirty sexpot Alex is one of Craig's favorite Alexes.

"Alex," Craig groans, a desperate mantra carried on a thread of breath, the last and only word he can make his brain form. Straightening, he rests his palm at the base of Alex's spine for one moment, one moment of warmth and trembling pale skin under his hand before he pulls his hips back and begins to move.

He's learned to hold Alex's hips hard, almost bruise-leaving hard, when Alex is wound this high and tight. The muscles under his hands shudder with the restraint of not being able to push back against Craig's cock. All Craig allows Alex to do is take each thrust. His fingers twine into the fibers of the rug and hold on, white-knuckled and desperate, and little moans tumble out of a mouth curved into a blissful smile.

It makes Craig smile too, before he lets his head fall back with his own pleasure and bites his lower lip. He closes his eyes to heighten the feel of Alex under his hands and around his cock, focuses on the sounds of their breathing and the music in the background. The moment is sex, fucking and skin and bitten-off dirty words, a flood of sensation. Craig had started with long, languid thrusts, but soon there's no rhythm as he pushes into Alex and pulls away.

He falls forward and reaches down to find Alex so hard, so warm to the touch, the tip of his cock already slick and wet. His thumb slides over the slippery warmth as he begins to stroke, struggling to keep time with his own stuttering thrusts. He wants to speak, to spill enticements into Alex's ear, to whisper and moan and encourage and beg him to come, but it's all Craig can do now just to remember to breathe.

Alex is heavy in his hand, hot and full and straining. So eager, so ready—

In a few strokes, Alex comes for the second time, eyes springing wide open as his fingers spread out taut and tense over the rug before curling back into fists so tight Craig will have to kiss away the red crescents Alex's fingernails will leave in his palms. His mouth is stretched wide; a broken creak of a moan is all that comes out.

He's tight, almost too tight around Craig now, and the feel and sight of Alex coming yanks Craig over the edge with him. His body is full, as if he's taken in the energy of both of them for himself, collected it until it warms his skin and tightens his muscles, floods every inch of vein and artery with electricity for one second before it flares away and sends him gasping and sprawling out over Alex in a tangle of warm, loose limbs and short breaths.

For a moment, Craig is blind and deaf to everything, knowing only Alex's breath expanding his ribcage under Craig's chest. Momentary panic gives way to contentment as he lets the familiar-as-his-own-skin sensation guide him back to reality.

When he drifts back to earth, the playlist on Alex's stereo has mellowed out even further, and Craig lets it carry him down into sweet relaxation, Emeli Sande's voice smooth and melancholy as a whiskey sour, leading his thoughts down trails he only wanders at times like this. *You could fall in love in a moment like this.*

You could be in love in a moment like this.

His eyes open at the startling thought, and only super-human effort controls him so this is his only reaction. *That's not supposed to happen.*

It's not, was never supposed to happen.

Has it happened?

Craig holds himself still, barely breathing as he gropes for understanding. *He's got you good, and you can't even say why*, Nate had told him a handful of hours ago, and it should have been a laughing matter, but he hadn't laughed, even a little bit. Because no, he couldn't say why—a million years wouldn't be enough time to articulate it—but it's true, too true, truer than Nate could have guessed. Definitely, it was truer than Craig had known, or at least, more than he'd admitted to Nate.

He... loves Alex. Or he's getting there in a hurry.

There's so much to love—Alex's overtly sexual nature, his shy, pleasured disbelief at little kindnesses, the feel of his skin under Craig's palms, the freckles on his back, the way he falls into such concentration on work tasks that he has to be physically pulled back into the world. There's the little frown-crease between his brows, his eyes, his very nice backside, his strong hands, his guarded heart. There's the way the energy of movement crackles from Alex even when he's sitting still, the way his mood is so clearly inscribed in every expression; even the dark pool of anger that Craig can't touch, even that is fascinating and in its own very strange way, loveable.

In this moment, open and pliant in body and mind, Craig can't push any of this away, neither its existence nor how he feels about it. He also can't say a damn thing about it, because Alex—skittish, anxious, cautious and wary Alex, who still won't talk about Jeff, still mutters darkness in his sleep— would take off running in a heartbeat, and that is the very last thing Craig wants.

His feelings sit heavy on his tongue like a lead weight. They taste as if he's holding a battery in his mouth.

He doesn't want to pull back, to disengage completely, so he lies on Alex's back, cock softening, breath slowing, his cheek pressed to Alex's skin. He lets one hand trail down Alex's arm, over bicep and elbow and forearm until he can curve the palm of his hand around the back of Alex's and let their fingers intertwine as they catch their breath together.

It's love, for him, or something really close to it, because there's no one else in the world he can share this kind of silence with, no one with whom he would even want to think about trying it.

Old routines have shifted and broken and reformed into this new life, this life of surprising contentment. He's never felt them change; his life has just flowed into this new normal.

He should be worried. He should be discomfited, uneasy, concerned.

But Craig matches his breathing to Alex's and feels nothing but right, at least in this moment.

There will be time enough to worry about his sanity later.

〰〰〰

ALEX AWAKENS THAT MORNING NEXT TO CRAIG. NOTHING unusual for a Sunday.

But today the light is different—the way it plays through the sheer curtains in Alex's bedroom and over Craig's skin. Shadows of passing birds make temporary tattoos on Craig's back; the skin itself is lit from within—warm brown, velvety smooth. Alex's breath catches in his throat as he observes this perfect moment, imagines it captured forever and framed on his wall.

For the first time in too long, the thought of a camera in his hands doesn't burn.

He lets the moment pass, waits until they kiss goodbye and part for the day before he runs to his bedroom closet. The large plastic containers are still stacked in the back, each one stuffed full of carefully boxed and wrapped equipment—lenses and cameras, his priceless collection. Even the antique and toy cameras he'd kept for fun and decoration are all here.

Months ago, he'd packed away everything to do with photography and worked hard to forget that his first and best love had ever existed.

The familiar weight of his Canon doesn't quite feel so much like an extension of his body as it used to, but it's good, a comfort; it makes excitement cascade down his arms and into his fingers. He turns it on, checking the settings and blowing a stray speck of dust from the picture viewer. In precise order, he goes through the box and checks his flashes, inspects his lenses.

The next thing he knows, he's down on the sidewalk outside of his building with yesterday's clothes on; his bag is slung over his shoulder, exhilaration is propelling his feet toward the nearest bus stop.

Alex limits himself to one roll of film, one roll carefully slotted into his camera. One roll. It's a struggle. *Just do two, one more roll, tuck it in the pouch there just in case, it's nothing.* But he doesn't want any waste, not of film or time or anything. So he has only one roll of film and no digital backup. Thirty-six exposures are all he will have to tell him if he can still do this.

The limit forces him to be circumspect in his choice of subjects, to select and frame scenes with extra care. *No waste, no waste, no waste...* Even so, it seems as if no time has passed before he's traveled all over the city and has thirty-six photos on his Canon.

Now he has to see if there's still something there, after too many months of nothing.

And to do that, he has to face mending some bridges...

∿∿∿

Chapter Nine

GETTING OUT TO MAGNOLIA IS STILL SECOND NATURE, even if Alex hasn't made this particular trip in many, many months.

Too many months. His fingers tighten around the strap of his bag as he thinks about it. He's not expecting a great reception; he knows damn well that he doesn't deserve it, that part of him wants to run screaming in the direction he came from. That part, fortunately or not, does not seem to be in charge of his feet, however.

He peers at the window of the shop. It hasn't changed in the months of his absence—though to be fair, it's never changed much in all the years of its existence. The door remains in a state of perpetual dustiness on the outside; the glass storefront will forever be crammed with flyers and photos in varying stages of fade and curl. The display equipment does change a lot; it's always the latest, top-of-the-line stuff, as anything this shop carries would certainly be. But it's all on the same stands and scrupulously dusted glass shelves, separated from his itching fingers by the same bulletproof glass and a decades-old line of forbidding iron bars.

Before his life went upside down and sideways, Alex used to come out here all the time. At least once a week, for years, since he was a twelve-year-old with a pocket full of three years' worth of birthday and Christmas money. This shop, and all it represents, was his one constant, and then... then it wasn't.

Things should never have gotten to that point. He is angry that he let them, that he allowed that absence to occur, but also grateful that he's finally woken up and allowed his feet to carry him back to this doorstep. Terrified, but, yes, grateful.

And when he finally moves and walks through the shop door, the smell of film developer and glossy paper fills his nostrils and brings him all the rest of the way home.

The short, dark-haired man behind the counter is helping his lone customer choose a new camera lens when the bells on the door—the same string of cheap, loud jingle bells as ever, with maybe a few more flakes of gold paint gone—catch his attention, and it's gratifying to Alex when Connor realizes who he's seeing and his eyes go wide and his smile even wider.

Before Alex can take another uncertain step inside, Connor is in front of him and has him wrapped in a huge, warm hug bigger than his stocky little frame. "Holy shit. Alex Scheff, you fucking asshole."

He hugs back as tightly as he can, his eyes squeezing shut. "Connor." If the clean but cluttered crush of Monaghan's Photography had been his second home for half his life, then Connor had more or less been the brother he never had. Being back here is already like regaining the use of a damaged limb, and seeing Connor fills a hole in Alex's heart that he'd been ignoring for way too long.

That he'd turned his back on all of this twists his stomach with guilt. He hasn't so much as sent a text message to Connor in far too long, let alone set foot in the store. Like most of Alex's friends, Connor had fallen by the wayside when the whole... Jeff... thing was going on, and Alex had been too preoccupied and embarrassed to do anything to remedy the situation. Just thinking about it makes Alex's face flood with the dull burn of angry shame.

He's almost ruined so many things.

"You fucker, you gold-plated motherfucker." Connor pulls back to look at him, anger and concern and relief all over his face, and Alex has to blink back a suspicious sting in his eyes at the sight. He's still becoming reacquainted with being someone people give a damn about. "Fuck. I don't know where you've been, but are you okay?"

Deep, steady breaths and Connor's hands on his shoulders help bring him back to center and to his reason for being here. "Yeah. Mostly. Kind of." His relief at not being immediately thrown back out on the street still threatens to overwhelm him. When he brings a hand up to cover one of Connor's, he can't stop it from shaking. "It's good to see you, Connor. So good."

"Yeah, well, you're like seeing a ghost, I gotta say." Connor claps Alex's shoulder and turns back toward the counter, jerking his head for Alex to follow him through the forest of postcard and film racks. "A ghost I am fucking glad to see, though. Asshole. Where the fuck have you been?"

Gripping the woven canvas of his bag strap is wearing a stinging welt into Alex's fingers, but he can't stop. The ache is penance as much as the action is a balm to his nerves. "Not here."

"That, I worked out for myself. Excuse me." The customer at the counter has been waiting patiently for Connor to come back and finish helping her. With a glare glittering in his dark eyes that says more clearly than any words that Alex should stay put, Connor crosses to the counter, leaving Alex to look around the quiet shop and process being here again, to process the way he had turned his back on this shop, on his best friend. And for what? For Jeff. No. *For* nothing, but definitely *because* of Jeff. Alex's anger has not abated as the months have passed. If anything, its fires are stoked higher and higher as he mends bridges burned.

Alex places his hand on the cool glass of the display counter and closes his eyes, taking in a deep, calming breath redolent of paper and chemicals. So far he's been lucky in that none of the damage he's done has been irreparable. Some rifts haven't been comfortable to mend—Samantha has yet to stop dropping pointed remarks about him missing family occasions up to and including their grandparents' golden anniversary, and she's well within her rights to do it, *what* a dick move on his part—but slowly, he is rebuilding. Slowly, he's getting a real life again.

And so much of it is due to Craig, even today, although Craig doesn't know about this or his part in it. Not yet.

Today, Alex's intention is to reclaim the largest part of himself that he'd torn out and set aside while Jeff shredded him to pieces. Alex is still pretty shredded, but enough of him has been stitched back together through affection and cookies and kindness that he might be able to do this. He *wants* do this.

Connor finishes ringing up his customer and follows the girl to the door, locks it behind her and flips the sign to *Closed*. When he turns around, his arms are crossed over his chest and the look on his face can only be described as forbidding. "Gonna assume you came out here for a reason."

"Um. I did. Yeah." Alex tugs up the strap of the camera bag slung across his chest and grins at his old friend. "I know I've got some nerve, but I've got a roll of undeveloped film and no idea if I can still shoot or not. Can I borrow your darkroom?"

HOURS LATER, SQUINTING IN THE DIM ILLUMINATION OF Connor's darkroom, Alex pulls the last print out of the fixer bath and holds his breath. Except for a brief period while his negatives dried and Connor forced him to go get something to eat, he's been working alone all afternoon, anxious to get his solitary roll of film from negative to print.

Never religious, Alex is nonetheless sending prayers for an at least decent result to whomever will listen.

"How's it looking?" Connor slips through the blackout door and sets a bottle of Fat Tire on the shelf near the drying line. "Any luck?"

Alex pegs the print up on the line with the others and takes a step back, closing his eyes. "I'm afraid to look."

"Talk about words I never thought I'd hear. Fine. Let me look." Alex hears Connor step over to the line of drying prints and stop in front of the first print.

The silence is brutal. And very, very long. Alex closes his eyes even more tightly, stuffs his fists into his pocket and tries not to claw the palms of his hands to pieces as Connor paces down the line and takes occasional sips from his beer bottle.

At last, Connor reaches the end of the line and a low whistle escapes him. "Damn."

Shit. "That bad?" It takes significant effort for Alex to pry his eyes open and face the music. "Fuck."

"No, asshole. They're fine. Your sanity and judgment are questionable, but these shots are fine." Connor is shaking his head and reviewing the line of prints. "Goddamn. I never want to hear you question your ability again."

Alex can't move. "What?"

"I mean, the subjects are pretty pedestrian, but at the same time they're classic Seattle. And in that context, your shit is still top-of-the-line, buddy." When Connor turns around, he's smiling. Alex finally pulls his hands out of his pockets and relaxes. "I'd sell these postcards, is what I'm saying. I don't think you've lost a thing. Of course, now you're gonna have to test yourself. No more of these brownstones and bridges. The Space Needle is absolutely the fuck off limits. You already knew you could do all this, these are like riding a bicycle for you."

"You mean it?" He knows his eyes are as wide as salad plates. "Seriously, Connor."

"I don't bullshit, you know that. Not a good business practice in my line of work." Connor turns back to face the prints and sips his beer, shaking his head in what looks almost like admiration. "Naw, these are good, you gotta know that."

"Well. I haven't really looked at them yet." He forces his feet to move toward the shelf where his own beer waits, still not looking at the prints—not yet. He will, just, not immediately. In fact, changing the subject seems like a good idea while he pulls himself together. "So, hey, how've you been? How's Rayna?"

For a split second Connor looks surprised, and then... then he looks angry. When his eyes slide over to meet Alex's, they're narrow and dark and very, very alarming. Though Connor is shorter than Alex, he's got the stocky frame of the ex-boxer he is and is therefore rather frightening when he gets upset. Connor's empty hand flexes into and out of a fist before he speaks again. "Rayna had the baby we were expecting when you disappeared. You remember that?" Alex probably should have seen this coming. He walked right into it. *Fuuuuuuuuuck. I am an idiot.*

Obviously the discussion of why he'd dropped off the face of the earth couldn't be put off forever, but he could totally do without having slingshot himself into it via the normally innocent medium of small talk. And he has nothing he can say, no excuse to give. Not with Connor's angry eyes pinning him in place, not with regret clogging his throat.

There's a snort before Connor pulls a long swallow from his beer and continues. "Kira's six, almost seven months old now. And you haven't seen her. Not once. Because you didn't answer texts or emails or phone calls... did you even know her name before I just now told you? Did you read the birth announcement?" Hurt is as sharp as a knife blade in Connor's voice and suddenly shows all over his face. "What the fuck, Alex? She was born in December, it's goddamn June now. You were supposed to be her godfather. You're like my brother, asshole."

The thing is, this discussion was easier with Samantha and Nate because they expected him to be an asshole. But Sammi's family, and Nate's been around for years, and Alex has pulled a lot of dumb shit over the course of his life. They're used to forgiving him. To having to forgive him. To not asking too many questions.

Not so Connor. He's never pulled anything like this with Connor. This is the first time Connor's had to deal with any direct results of Alex being a selfish dick. And Connor's like a terrier; he sniffs down his quarry and latches on, digging in his heels and his teeth. He does not easily forgive and he will not let go of something until he understands it.

Alex has been avoiding Monaghan's for quite a few reasons, and this is definitely one of them. Still unable to speak, Alex keeps his eyes on Connor as he takes several bracing swallows of his own beer. It tastes like sawdust.

Belligerence shines in Connor's eyes when he lights back into Alex. "Nobody knew where you were. Nobody heard from you. You know I actually even ran into that fuckin' jerk in a Caribou one day and asked him about you?"

This is a jolt—enough to dislodge Alex's voice. "You mean Jeff? You saw Jeff?"

"And even talked to him." Connor's mouth twists.. "Not that he'd heard from you either. Unlike me, though, he didn't seem too concerned about it, so I'm not sorry that I guess he's gone." Folding his arms, Connor leans on the table. "You gonna tell me what the hell happened? And do not tell me *that* douche is why you stopped doing photography, because I already don't like him. If I move on to hating him, it could be a physical problem." It would be, too, Alex knows. When Connor cracks his knuckles and grins like a wolf, it's unnerving as hell. "For him."

Breathe in. Breathe out. Craig dropped the Jeff questions a long time ago; Alex can only assume this is because he's decided that Alex will stop being evasive about it when he's ready. Connor is not Craig. He won't be put off.

But that doesn't mean Alex is going to give direct answers. All these months later, his weakness is still a gaping hole in the pit of his stomach. It's too much. "No, don't... I mean, there's no need... a lot of things went wrong."

"Tell me something a little less obvious." Connor snorts and doesn't let his gaze waver an inch.

"I got in over my head. It wasn't worth it. I'm glad it's over." This last is, finally, not a lie, as it had been the first couple of months he'd lost himself in Craig. He wishes the mention of Jeff's name weren't still like a clutch of glass shards roiling in his stomach, but he is glad it's over. "I was in it way too long... it took me a while to get my shit back together. It still isn't, really. I'm sorry, Connor. That's all I can tell you right now."

He can't, he just can't yet talk about letting himself fall so hard he gave up everything he loved. He still can't face the shuddering weakness of wrapping himself entirely in his relationship with Jeff, of his years-long obsession with making it work. He certainly can't talk about the series of emotional knife wounds that led him to shove his collection of cameras and everything that reminded him of photography deep into the back of his closet.

Jeff had poisoned it all so badly.

Connor purses his lips and stares at Alex, stares piercingly over his beer bottle and waits. But no, Alex can be stubborn too. Alex can keep some things for his own. He'd meant what he said.

Finally, Connor sighs and shakes his head. He doesn't look pleased, but he does look resigned. "Fine. Okay. I'll let it go... for now."

"Thank you." Not that this means Alex is finished walking the tightrope. He braces himself for Connor's next line of attack.

It's neither long in coming nor subtle. "So who's the guy that got you to pick up your camera again?"

Oh. Ha ha. Ha. *No.* If Alex can't tell Connor about why he *stopped* taking photos, he certainly can't tell Connor why he's *started* again. He can't talk about this morning, about the sunlight through the curtains passing over drowsy Craig's dark array of dreads, tousled from sleep and the debaucheries of the night before. He can't tell Connor about the way the dark blue sheets cut across and contrasted with Craig's hips, their diagonal tangle revealing only the barest hint of the curve of Craig's backside. And he's not even talking to himself about how the burning desire to capture the moment on film caught in his chest and throat until he couldn't breathe.

Connor clears his throat and drags Alex's attention back to the present. "Hello?"

"Yeah, I..." Alex picks at a clothespin while he thinks, picks and picks until a splinter slides under his nail and he winces and sets it aside in favor of his drink. "Ow."

"Don't try and get out of this one," Connor warns. "I know you. I know there's a guy. You're too happy." He pauses. "At least this time it's a good happy, not the weird desperate happy."

"Fuck you," Alex blurts, having narrowly avoided choking on the beer he's just swallowed.

"No, fuck you," Connor retorts. "Look, you can't get away with not telling me *anything*. You disappeared, man. We've known each other for a long fucking time, and you disappeared. Because of that motherfucking shitstain. And okay, fine, I'll let you get away with not telling me the whole story on that for now, but I am not going to let you disappear again, so hey." He finishes off his beer and sets the bottle aside, stalking over to poke his finger into Alex's chest. "You better tell me about the new guy, so I can figure out the odds of you pulling a David Blaine again."

"Ow," Alex says again, scowling as he rubs the new sore spot on his chest with his sore hand. "I'm not going to disappear!"

"Yeah? Pardon me if I'm not convinced." Stepping back, Connor fishes in his back pocket for his wallet, then rummages through it until he pulls out a photo that he shoves into Alex's face. A baby girl with creamy beige skin and dimples, a fluffy fuzz of dark hair and her father's brown eyes smiles at the camera, frozen in a moment before she bursts into baby babbles. "I got a baby girl who's never met her godfather, Mister I'm Not Gonna Disappear. Try harder."

Alex swallows dryly as his gaze fixes on the small photograph and his fingers flex. "Connor, I'm sorry. I'm fucking sorry, okay?

I know I made a mistake. I'm admitting that. I am admitting I'm a fuckup."

"You think?"

"Of course I think." *I will not get angry. I have earned this.* "I am a fuckup. Okay? And the thing with Jeff was fucked." Sucking a deep breath down into his lungs, Alex decides to give a little. A very little. "But Jeff is gone, and yeah, there's a new guy. And I promise he's not Jeff. Not even a little bit."

This is not enough to dissolve the skepticism in Connor's eyes. "I'm gonna have to meet him."

That's a big one. A huge concession. Letting someone who isn't Samantha or Nate or one of the Sucre Coeur employees see him with Craig? Really see them together? That might be putting things with Craig on a level Alex isn't equipped to handle. "I'll think about it."

"Months, Alex, *months*—" Connor begins, gritting his teeth.

"I know. I know, Connor." Panic inches its way through Alex's body from the feet up, squeezing him tightly and threatening to cut off his breath again. "I know, I just... please, okay, it took a lot for me to come here and face you today, knowing what a dick I have absolutely and completely been. I can't give you everything at once; I'm almost out of what's keeping me on my feet." It's pouring out now, ahead of the vise grip of fear, tumbling, spilling and frantic. "I swear to God, I'm not going anywhere, and you will find out everything, but Jesus, even this guy I'm seeing, *he* doesn't know everything, and I—"

"Whoa. Whoa." This time Connor's touch is back to brotherhood, with calming and centering hands on Alex's arms, and a worried look replacing the anger. "Okay. I'm sorry. I get it now. Okay? Do what you need to in your own good time. I'm not going to push it anymore. Okay?"

Relief closes Alex's eyes again, as his chest relaxes and allows breathing to resume. "I will tell you, you know. Really. When I can."

"I'm gonna try real hard to believe you," Connor tells him, gentle and worried and so reminiscent of the kindness keeping Alex linked to Craig that Alex nearly collapses and spills everything then and there.

"I don't deserve a friend like you," Alex manages to say, opening his eyes and forcing himself to smile and keep things simple.

"You really don't. But you're stuck with me." All anger and fear is gone from Connor's eyes. He's still worried, and Alex feels that guilt again at causing the worry and not knowing how long he's going to have to work to make it go away—but at least the anger is gone and the pushing is over for now.

Well. The emotional pushing. Alex barely keeps his feet as Connor physically grabs him and shoves him over to face the line of prints. He does not manage to keep the best grip on his beer, and winces as liquid splashes out of the bottle and onto the front of his button-down. "Connor!"

"I gotta finish closing up. Take a look at your work, will you?" He slaps Alex on the back. "A real look. Real close. Because I do not want you to give up on yourself again. I want you to look at this good stuff and then get the fuck out of my shop tonight and come back next week with *better*. Take risks again. Okay?"

This makes Alex laugh, the kind of full-on belly laugh he doesn't let out too often, and oh, God, he can never, ever let his almost-brother slip away again.

Or himself.

When Alex nods, Connor slaps him on the back and lets himself out of the darkroom, leaving Alex alone with the fruits of his first photographic labors in close to a year. His breaths come so deep now that his lungs fill with the smell of developer and stop bath and fixer and he's dizzy.

But then he stops, shakes his head and focuses, taking the step forward that will bring him close enough to really *see* what he's done.

The first and unavoidable impression is that Connor is correct—Alex's subjects are classic Seattle scenes, nothing that can't be seen in any stock photo gallery. A brownstone, plants in pots and slender trees in iron cages, the Space Needle and the EMP Museum, the skyline seen from a ferry. Children contemplating a chalked grid on a street near his apartment. Fishmongers at Pike Place. They're all everyday moments in Seattle that any photographer could have captured, that dozens if not hundreds *had* captured for *Time* and *National Geographic*. This was deliberate, though, these subjects had been selected as though Alex was calibrating his focus all over again. So their pedestrian nature is not surprising.

It's the second look that counts, the closer one, and here are the touches and balances that identify all of these as *his* work; the captured slants of light and ripples of shadow, the child gazing right into the camera with a solemn face. He sees everything that marks these moments as ones only he could have seen and frozen in time, and it's like looking through his own eyes. This was the purpose of his work today: to bring his own vision to life once again.

And he's done it.

He takes a long breath in, all the way down to his toes, and feels as though his dislocated soul has slipped back into place at last.

Chapter Ten

"**H**OW MANY WEEKS?" SARITA ASKS, HER EYES EVEN larger than usual. Craig sighs, both at the question and the fact that her hands have stopped decorating sugar cookies and are now squeezing soft, hot pink icing all over the kitchen island.

"Frosting," he says irritably, with a sharp gesture of his index finger. "And I've already said it once; you heard me."

"That doesn't mean I believe it." Setting aside the frosting bag, Sarita grabs a damp tea towel and cleans up her mess. "Joined at the hip since January, and now you tell me you haven't actually seen him in three weeks? Your first major separation in six months, no wonder you're cranky."

Craig does not get paid enough to listen to this kind of cheek. "I'm cranky, as you put it, because you're being nosy and spilling frosting everywhere, which are two things that do not get this order filled." He stomps over to the oven and pulls out two more trays of sugar cookies. "I would like to *get* this order filled, please. I'm getting retina-burn from the frankly obnoxious color scheme the O'Brien girl picked for her wedding shower, plus I've that blasted wedding planning story deadline with the *Post-Intelligencer*. So can we work?"

That earns him one arched dark eyebrow and a bonus smug half-smile. "So touchy. One might draw the conclusion that you're annoyed about having to write about people getting married, or baking cookies for blushing brides-to-be, when it's been three weeks since you last got laid."

"I do have the power to fire you," Craig points out, dropping the cookie sheets on the clear end of the island with a crash. This sort of badgering, he does not need. It has not just been three weeks, it has been an absolutely interminable three weeks; and no, drowning in the wedding crap of what seems to be the entirety of Seattle does not help at all.

Sarita tosses her wet, pink-stained towel on the floor and yanks off her paper cap. "Great. It's too early on a Sunday morning to deal with the lime green frosting that's coming next anyway."

"No! Wait." Never mind his own problems, some things in this world should never be borne alone, and sugar cookies frosted in an eye-searing clash of neon colors are among them. "Don't go. I won't fire you. I'm sorry I've been a fucking crotchety bastard."

"And?" Her fingers pause on her apron strings.

"And..." *And what?*

"And you'll tell me *why* you've been about as fun to be around as an angry porcupine?" Sarita takes careful backwards steps to the paper hat dispenser on the wall, never taking her eyes off him. "I mean, you're not *just* mad because you haven't been able to get your mad crazy bang on in almost a month."

"How do you know?" he retorts. Some people are too insightful for his own good. "Maybe it is just that. I've been working quite a lot lately. So has he. It could be simple frustration, for all you know."

And some people are also much too eloquent, even in silence. Sarita stares at him as she tucks stray curls up into her fresh cap. It is a stare that says a lot, but mostly it just says, *You must be joking.*

Craig can only sigh.

"All right," he says, picking up a spatula. Her gaze is still burning into his head, but he simply cannot look at her while he talks about this. He begins to scoop cookies off of the sheets and onto cooling racks, concentrating too hard, working too methodically on such a simple task. "Well. It's complicated."

"Love is, from what I understand." This is such a surprising statement from Sarita that Craig accidentally flings two cookies to the black and white tiles of the floor when he looks up at her. "What? Did you think we didn't know?"

"Well, given that I certainly didn't until a couple of months ago, no, I didn't think you did!" His hands shake, and a third cookie joins its crumbled compatriots on the tiles. He shoves the mess aside with his foot. "Shit. Fuck! How the hell did you figure it out?"

Confusion fills Sarita's eyes. "How did you not?"

"Oh, I don't know, maybe because I've never been *in* love before?" It takes some doing, but Craig gets his hands under control, at least, and resumes moving cookies without further mishap. "It's a bit of a new thing for me."

Sarita doesn't look any less puzzled. "Yeah, but you've *seen* love, presumably. Like, your parents are still married to each other, right? So I'd guess there's at least *some* love there. And your ex, you see him and his girlfriend a lot. Don't they love each other?"

"That's different." One tray emptied, he sets it aside and works on the next. "Seeing something from the outside isn't experiencing it."

"All right. That's fair." She picks up her frosting bag and drops big dollops of frosting onto soft cookies, spreading it smooth and sprinkling candy flowers over the hot pink surfaces. "Is that what's complicating things?"

"No, you knowing is just a bit of a shock, is all." Craig gets the second tray cleared and carries both the cookie sheets to the dishwasher. He takes his time loading them into the plastic rack, situating them with care. *How to explain?* "Sarita, have you ever been in love?"

"Nope." It's a quick, easy answer. "Hasn't really come up, not that I'm looking too hard."

I wasn't looking, either. But she already knows that. And, he supposes, that's when everyone says it happens, anyway. And despite the bravado he displayed to Nate during their very first conversation about this whole thing all those months ago, Craig is really scared quite shitless about his feelings and all that they mean. "Would you want to be, do you think?"

Sarita laughs. "Sure, one day, maybe. I mean, I'm not opposed to the idea. Actually, I think it would be pretty nice. I'd like to bring a girl home to dinner for more reasons than to piss off my sister, you know?" She cocks her head. "You want love, don't you? It's always seemed like a natural thing you might fall into, to me. I've always felt like you have a romantic heart beating underneath that cool loner surface you have going."

Interesting. "Have you?"

"Sure." She waves him over and hands him a frosting bag. "That's why I always gave you shit for not dating. Come on. You can talk and frost."

"The romantic heart," he prompts, pulling over a rack of cookies to work on. "You were saying?"

"Well, I just… " Her hand twirls in the air as if to pluck words from the ceiling. "I don't know, Craig. It's just a feeling. I haven't been watching you with any guys but Alex. There's just always been something that made me think your heart was looking for something, even if you weren't."

"All I was looking for when I met Alex was a pint of oatmeal stout," he retorts, reaching for the bowl of candy flowers. "Then when he chatted me up, I just wanted to cheer him up. Make him feel good. Maybe have a nice enough time myself—that would be extra. That's all I was looking out for."

"I know, your sacred routine, blah blah." Sarita stabs a finger in his direction. "But all that's pretty romantic. Most people wouldn't give any thought to making some sad drunk guy happy. They'd just think, 'Hey, drunk guy hitting on me. Easy score.' You never would."

"Of course I wouldn't, that's not nice," he protests. "I'd never take advantage of anyone like that."

"Okay, but you also gave him the cookie you were saving for yourself, didn't you tell me that?" She bats her long eyelashes. "That's cute. That's kind of romantic."

"It was just supposed to be one night, one nice night for the both of us!" Candy flowers go flying, and Craig spares only the briefest of thoughts for how furious Theodora would be to see how he's wrecking her bakery and wasting her inventory. Placing his hands on the smooth steel top of the island, he draws in a deep breath and tries to calm his spinning thoughts. "Which brings me back to my actual problem. The point is, fine, you nosy brat, I might be in love with Alex, and that is a problem because I might be insane for it." He shakes his head. "I'm in love with him, and we've never even said we're dating. He could be seeing someone else for all I know." He doesn't think it likely, but it's a thought that buzzes by to bother him sometimes.

"You're the one who let me get us off track. I'm just saying." Sarita brushes her hands down her apron front, assuming an expression of mock piety for a moment. In the next instant, she's sweetly serious once more, bowing her head to her work. "Let me see if I understand you correctly. You're angry because you thought you were going to have a one-night stand, but now it's the end of July and you might be in love and... that's a bad thing?"

"Not angry, just vaguely annoyed and questioning my sanity," Craig corrects. He rubs his forehead, realizing too late that there's a smudge of hot pink frosting on his palm. Or was. By the feel of it, it's now decorating his forehead and nose. He drops his head as Sarita giggles. "See? I've clearly lost the plot."

She snorts. "I don't know that you ever had it." She tosses him a towel. "But specifically with this, come on, Craig, Alex is great."

"Alex is high-strung." *Never mind that I like that. Evidence: Nate, for one thing.* He shakes off the irritating reminder. "Neurotic. Closed off! Did you know I don't even know his parents' names? That's not normal, Sarita. I can't get him to talk about anything—it took me two months to get him to admit he likes banana peppers on his pizza."

Sarita's mouth twitches, but if she wants to laugh again, she's doing an excellent job of keeping it behind her teeth. "I don't think that's the end of the world. Disgusting, ugh, banana peppers, but... it's not like he's a complete mute or anything. He's just not like you, with everything laid out for everyone to see."

Craig has to admit this is true. It's not fair to say Alex is completely closed off. He's just slow to allow layers of himself to be revealed. Samantha and Nate have indicated that it's always been this way—although they admit that now he is even more reticent, the layers a bit pricklier. "Most people would say he's an onion," Nate had mused one day over coffee. "I've always said he's more like a pineapple. A sea urchin. A hedgehog. No, wait, a cactus—"

"I get it," Craig had growled, apparently so intimidating Nate that he dropped the subject of Alex for the rest of that day.

Maybe it's better to approach this whole thing from a slightly different angle. "I'm not sure I ever saw myself with someone who's so completely my opposite," he says at last.

Sarita lifts that single eloquent eyebrow. "You would have preferred to date yourself?"

"No! No, not that." That's possibly the most genuinely alarming idea he's ever heard. "I suppose I always saw myself with another version of Nate. We were good together, Nate and I, you know, we just sort of... fizzled out there at the end."

She frowns. "So...Nate, but with less fizzle, more fizz?"

"Maybe. Perhaps. Oh, I have no idea, Sarita." Sometimes he wishes he'd taken some public speaking classes in university, something that might actually aid him in the effort to articulate his thoughts aloud. "I just...well, what about you? What would you look for in a girlfriend, if you were looking?"

"I don't know, Craig. I have nothing specific in mind." Sarita sets her frosting bag down and gazes at the ceiling and twists her fingers in the hem of her T-shirt. "I mean, I have ideas. I look at my brother and his husband a lot—they love each other. I'd like to think I could meet someone who looks at me the way Devesh and Sunil look at each other. Someone I like. Someone I enjoy spending time with who isn't scared off by my crazy sister. Ideally I'd meet someone I'm attracted to, someone I can talk to, someone who just does it for me, you know?" Pushing aside her completed tray of cookies, she pulls over a rack of fresh ones and picks up a bag with lime green frosting oozing from its tip. "I think that if you go looking for specific traits and qualities, you're just asking to be frustrated. I want to meet a cute girl that I like, who likes me back. Keep it simple."

"You've met a lot of those," Craig points out, setting his own finished tray aside.

"Mm hmm." She's looking down at her cookies, focusing hard, but he can see her smug little grin all the same. "And Craig, I've never felt the urge to make pancakes for a single one of those girls the next morning."

That is, perhaps, a valid point.

Sarita straightens up. "Craig. You like Alex? Maybe you feel a little more than that, but basically, you like him?"

"'Course I do," he replies, reaching up—with a hand he knows is clean this time—to smooth the frown that's begun to furrow his brow.

"You want to spend time with him? You enjoy it?"

"I do."

"Personal topics aside, you like to talk, and you're attracted to him?"

"Correct on both counts," he answers.

"Then by all my personal basic criteria, it's probably not so crazy to be in love with him, is it?"

She stands there expectantly, arms crossed over her chest, and even her silly paper hat seems somehow stern. It's odd to be schooled by a pint-sized grad student who, by her own admission, has never been in love; but... she could actually be right.

"Relax," Sarita says, grinning. "Maybe just go with it and see what happens."

Well, it's no worse an idea than any other I've heard.

With a sigh, Craig looks down at the trays of cookies. "These look terrible. Beautifully decorated, but absolutely awful. These aren't her wedding colors, are they?"

Sarita comes around the island and tucks her arm through his. "No. I believe we're doing her cake in mauve and forest green. The wedding's in November." She slips her hand into his and gives him a good squeeze. "You're going to see him soon, right?"

"For my birthday, at the end of the week," he confirms. "We're going out to dinner."

"Then spend time with him," she says. "Talk to him. Enjoy it."

He looks down at her. "Simple as that, is it?"

She's the picture of serenity as she says, "If you let it."

Chapter Eleven

"**I** CAN NOW ABSOLUTELY DOUBLE CONFIRM THAT YOU HAVE not lost your touch." Shaking his head in admiration, Connor strings an eight-by-ten of his very pretty baby girl—not that he's biased or anything—up on the drying line and takes a half-step back to get a better look at it. "Actually, I think the break maybe did you some good. This is the best stuff I've seen you produce."

"I'll take that with a grain of salt," Alex retorts, carefully washing another photo. "You're automatically biased, since that's your daughter. And I'm pretty sure it's impossible to take a bad picture of Kira."

"Yeah, she got her mama's looks." He grins at the print, as in love as he'd been the first moment he held his daughter. Kira's skin is perfect, rich and smooth, with deep dimples in each cheek. She got Connor's big brown eyes and Rayna's dark curls, and is as round as a ball of butter. And fortunately for Alex, her photographer of the day, she'd been a dream subject, with her constant smile and direct flirtation with the camera.

She'd made Alex laugh and relax, and Connor thinks it might have been a good day for the guy. Not usually one for children, he'd looked as though he enjoyed holding Kira the few times Rayna let her little girl out of her arms. He'd grinned as she babbled and drooled, even when her little dimpled fingers smacked gently against his face. It had been a sight to behold. Today, Alex looks more human than he did when he first stumbled back into Connor's shop all those weeks ago, which is only to the good.

However, he also looks as if he hasn't slept well in a few days, and that begs for prodding. Connor arranges his face in an expression of perfect innocence before he turns around and leans against the sink. "So, you been gettin' it pretty good lately?"

The rickety table they've jammed into Alex's shower to hold the chemical baths for the prints rattles as Alex spins around, wide-eyed, and sets the chemicals sloshing in their plastic tubs. "What the actual hell?"

Innocence has never been an expression Connor can maintain for long. His grin spreads way out of bounds as he cocks his head while Alex flails. "Eh, I'm just noticing the circles under your eyes and the three large coffees you've had today, Mister Jitters. I'm putting two and two together here. Not sleeping much?" He wiggles his eyebrows, biting back a grin as Alex's face collapses into a frown of annoyance. Alex has always made the *best* grumpy faces.

But in the next instant, he's facing Alex's back as the guy resumes rinsing the print he'd been holding. "Not that it's any of your goddamn nosy business, but no, Connor. I have not been getting it lately. Good, bad or indifferent."

Ooh, interesting. Connor holds out his hand for the print so he can rinse it and hang it up. "No? Then who or what the fuck's been keeping you up at night?"

Silence. Well, except for the excessive splashing of chemicals as Alex angrily bathes another print and hands it to Connor.

Connor rinses and hangs the print. "Al."

Another round of angry—hilariously angry—rinsing. Still not a word.

Connor takes the next print from Alex with one hand and grabs his arm with the other to stop him from picking up another print. "Hey. Alex. Stop. Breathe. Explain."

The glare Alex shoots over his shoulder would wither lesser men. "I don't have to explain shit."

"Well, you didn't *before* because I was kind of joking, but *now* you do." He tugs Alex around to face him, frowning at the tight set of his mouth. "Aw, fuck, you didn't break up with your mystery dude, did you?"

Alex's eyes roll. "No, not that there would be anything to break up, since he's not my boyfriend."

Yeah, and I'm your great-aunt Olga, but that's a story for another time. Connor isn't blind, the *not my boyfriend* thing is the biggest river in Egypt he's ever seen. Label or not, the guy is the most likely cause of Alex's insomnia, for sure. "Have you seen him lately?"

Alex doesn't answer; his lips just press tighter, and his eyes won't meet Connor's.

Two can play this game. But Connor plays it better. "Al."

"I've been busy with work, big campaign for camping gear, you know." It comes out in a sharp snap, with Alex still staring off at some point over Connor's head. He would clearly like it very much if Connor would shut up and they could finish these prints. "He's been busy too. Wedding season. Writing. Lots to do."

There is definitely a puzzle to be solved here—one Alex would prefer remain unsolved, if his general crankiness is anything to go by, and it usually is. Connor taps at his bottom lip with his finger, observing, as Alex—with his usual ridiculous stubbornness—refuses to observe any goddamn thing at all. He's got all the pieces he needs, he's sure of it. If he can just—

The light bulb illuminates. "Oh. You can't sleep without him anymore, can you?"

When Alex's face shutters completely, Connor knows he's hit the mark. "Fuck off, Connor."

"Oh, my God." It's a discovery on the level of, fuck, a lost Vermeer painting, or fucking Atlantis or something. It is an earthquake, a tornado, a tidal wave out of nowhere. Connor has no idea where to even begin with it. "Holy fuck, Alex."

"Jesus. Don't fucking make a big deal out of this, Connor." Alex's white knuckles, clenched around the edge of the wet table, tell a different story. "Look. I got used to it, that's all. It's not a big deal."

"Have you met yourself? Of course it's a big deal." The words spill out before he can reorder them to sound less incredulous, and Alex's jaw tightens. Connor shakes his head and tries to make sense of it, to find better words. "I'm sorry, Al. What I mean is, you know, this isn't a usual thing for you. I think it's kind of..." If he says *cute*, he's going to be thrown out on his ass before he finds out anything more. Diplomacy is not Connor's strong suit, but he tries. "Interesting?"

"Sweet Christ. This is why I don't talk to you about shit." Alex looks back over his shoulder, less angry but no less annoyed, by the look of him. "It's not interesting. I can't sleep. I don't like that I can't sleep, I don't like *why* I can't sleep. It's affecting my work and it annoys the hell out of me." Dropping his head, he takes long, deep breaths and shakes his head. "I don't want to talk about it. Can we finish up with these prints?"

Without waiting for a response, he gets back to work washing photographs in the chemicals, jaw set and mouth tight shut. And that, Connor understands well, is that. For now.

The long months of not seeing Alex, of worrying about him and how deep he'd gotten in with Jeff, make Connor want to do anything but drop the subject; yet if he pushes too far, Alex will shut down completely. Which, since Alex is acting almost like himself again, is the last thing Connor wants. Connor much prefers this Alex—closed off and irritable as he is—to the one he always saw with Jeff: a brittle shell of pretense over an inner layer of trying way too hard.

Connor takes down a couple of the dry prints to make room for the ones Alex is rinsing now. Yeah, it bugs him that Alex won't do a lot of talking about this mystery guy. It bugs him that Alex won't talk about what the fuck went so wrong with Jeff that he locked up his cameras for months and didn't see any of his friends or family.

But. He pauses to look at one particularly lovely shot of his little girl, with her eyes wide and sparkling, holding a soft stuffed ducky toy in her dimpled fingers. It's beautiful work, the result of a careful eye for lighting and a talent for catching the right moment. Whatever happened, Alex's skills were barely dulled, and Connor's been watching him sharpen them for weeks.

Maybe getting to the bottom of The Lost History of Alex doesn't matter. What does matter is that every moment he's behind the lens, Alex is sinking deeper into his own skin, re-memorizing it, loving it; anyone with half a brain can see that. For these snippets of time, he's not an advertising creative or a fuck-up or someone's maybe-kind-of-let's-not-talk-about-it-boyfriend.

Once upon a time he was just Alex, and Connor thinks maybe these days the guy's really starting to remember who that was. So whoever the mystery guy is, at least he's not fucking things up the way Jeff did—that is a good thing. He may even be actively helping Alex, and that's even better.

And Alex isn't going to be able to hide the guy forever. Connor is willing to bide his time.

He tugs down another pair of dry prints and turns to set them aside. Too late, he realizes that Alex is turning to hand him a freshly washed print. The collision knocks Alex back against the table and sets all the chemicals to sloshing. "Hey!"

"Sorry!" Connor reaches around to steady the trays. "Man, your bathroom is too tiny for this. I told you we could use the darkroom at the shop."

Alex bats him out of the way and grabs a dishrag to mop up splotches of liquid. "It's not like you had to come along just because I'm developing prints of your kid. Besides, I told you, I have plans tonight. It's easier to just do this here instead of having to rush back from your neck of the woods after shooting all morning and developing all afternoon." He tosses the rag aside and gets back to work.

"Oh yeah. The boyfriend."

Okay, yes, Connor is willing to bide his time, but seriously, as if anyone would have resisted the opportunity for that little poke.

Alex freezes in the middle of grabbing the next photo. "He's not my boyfriend." He physically flinches from Connor, which sets the trays of chemicals sloshing again.

Anyone more sensible would take the reaction as a warning, but Connor can admit that he has never been known, to anyone, as a sensible person. He fills his response with sarcasm and front-loads it with a good snort. "Okay, sure."

"He's not." Alex bangs the fixer tub a little harder than is strictly necessary to get bubbles off the print, and Connor can't hold back a chuckle. At the sound of it, Alex grits his teeth and hands off the photo with narrowed eyes. "We see each other. I've explained this."

But do you see anyone else? Connor would bet his favorite vintage Hasselblad that he already knows the answer. "You like him."

"You're as bad as Samantha." Alex heaves an exasperated sigh, fluttering the prints on the line. "Yes, I like him. Of course I like him. I don't take people I don't like out for birthday dinner."

"You..." Connor strangles a howl of laughter. He knows Alex knows he's deeply in denial. The way Alex denies his denial is the funniest thing Connor's seen in a long, long time. "You don't take *anyone* out to birthday dinner, Al."

"I took you out for your birthday," Alex protests, crossing his arms over his chest. "You've taken me out for mine."

He's about to find out if he really can die laughing, or die from holding it in. "Someone's defensive. You don't sleep with me, and neither one of those was dinner. Unless we count Guinness as food."

It's too red in the room to be sure if Alex's face is burning, but Connor would lay odds on yes. His arms tighten over his chest. "We're also celebrating his new article in *Eat The State!*, the one about being an expat observing American politics. Better?"

"Nope, but I'm gonna drop the subject because I know you, and this bathroom is too itty-bitty for me to dodge while you try to drown me." After clipping the print back to back with another, Connor glances around for the next one. "Oh, hey. Was that the last shot?"

Alex looks around and shrugs. "Looks like it for now. Even pinning back to back, we only have room on that line for ten prints. I'll do the rest tomorrow." He snaps off his rubber gloves and tosses them down on the toilet tank. "Let's get out of here. It's got to be getting late, and I'm feeling claustrophobic. I want to get a little air before I break down the wet table." He sniffs at his shirt. "Ugh. I stink."

"Yeah, it'd be a shame if you couldn't clean yourself up before your big date," Connor chuckles, stripping off his own gloves and goggles. "Hang on. Let me get past you so I can see those first photos again. I think Rayna's really gonna like them—"

"It's not a date, damn it." The rubber strap of Alex's goggles snags in his hair, and he stops in the last inconvenient sliver of space between the table and the sink to yank at the mess. "Hey, Monaghan, watch it!"

Oops. Connor's effort to squirm between the wet table and Alex sends fixer sloshing up the front of his shirt and even tags Alex with a few splashes. "Aw, damn."

If the look on Alex's face means anything, his feelings are running a little stronger than *damn*. He extracts the goggles from his hair and throws them down. "If you just poured hazardous chemicals down my shower drain, I actually am going to drown you in what's left of them."

"Relax. It was just the fixer, and nothing much got down the drain. It got all over you and me." And he's gotten the worst of it. With a mournful sigh, Connor looks down the front of his completely soaked Clash T-shirt. "Man. I can't replace this."

Alex is wearing an old soccer T-shirt from college. He pulls it off now to inspect where fixer splashed the purple vinyl of his number. "Good thing I've got about ten of these and they're all falling to pieces anyway. Why would you wear a shirt you can't replace to develop photos? You know better."

"Wasn't thinking." True enough. When Alex came over to his place, Connor hadn't planned on following him back here;

not until he'd mentioned his it's-not-a-date. It hadn't occurred to him to change shirts. It's his own damn fault—okay, with a little tossed Alex's way for piquing Connor's curiosity. He tugs his wet shirt away from his chest. "This blows."

In the light of the living room, the extent of the damage becomes clear. Connor's shirt is ruined entirely, Alex's less so. Alex shakes his head at Connor as he tosses his own shirt into a laundry basket. "Get that into a vinegar bath in the kitchen sink," he advises. "Maybe we can at least get the smell out before you go home. I think you're stuck using it as a developing shirt forever, though."

Connor lifts an eyebrow, yanks his shirt off and heads into the kitchen to look for vinegar. "You got something I can borrow to get home in? I can't leave here half naked."

"Serve you right if you did, for being such a bull in a china shop in my darkroom. And for picking on me." Alex pulls on another soccer T-shirt. "Besides, any shirt I loan you is going to be too tight across the chest and it'll hang almost to your knees." He pauses halfway through tugging the shirt down. "And you'll probably just wear it to develop photos in, and then *I'm* out a shirt."

Rude. "Fucking have a heart, asshole," Connor snaps, as he pours vinegar into a sink full of water. "I'll bring it back intact, swear to God. And even if it goes to my feet, it won't be covered in chemicals."

"Fine, I'll find you something." There's a knock at the door as Alex disappears into his bedroom. "Can you get that while I'm looking? I don't think it's time for Cr... for my friend yet. He's always late anyway. It's probably just kids trying to sell magazines or candy or something."

"No problem." Connor tosses the shirt into the sharp-smelling vinegar water and plods across the living room. He hopes it is the candy kids. Rayna likes the caramel bars they sell; it might be good to go home with a bunch of the things.

He knows it's not the candy kids as soon as he opens the door. It's also not the magazine kids. It's not, in fact, any kind of kid at all. It's a six foot-tall black guy with a bakery box in one hand and a startled look on his face that quickly narrows into suspicion as he stares at Connor.

Connor has never been more acutely aware of being shirtless and short in his entire life.

But given the timing—a glance at the clock on the microwave lets Connor know now that it's much, *much* later than he and Alex had guessed—there's only one person he could be, so Connor isn't too worried. *Well, well, well.* He didn't have to bide his time for so very long after all. As Alex bolts out of his bedroom with a panicked look on his face and his phone in his hand, Connor holds the door open wide and shrugs. "I am gonna guess," he says, waving Mystery Guy inside, "that you're not here to sell us subscriptions to *Sports Illustrated*."

BABE, DON'T TELL ME YOU'VE FORGOTTEN OUR DINNER PLANS.

Craig thumbs the message to "sent" and plucks at the string of the bakery box sitting on the hallway floor next to him. It's a marvel, this turn of events—he's usually the tardy one, and Alex is quite scrupulous about punctuality. *And yet here we are,* Craig considers with a rueful grin as the clock on his phone ticks to a half-hour past their meeting time and he's still sitting outside Alex's apartment door. Well, there's a first time for everything. Just... did it have to be tonight? After they've both been so busy, finally a night together and Alex decides *now* is a good time to experiment with tardiness?

Jesus, he misses Alex.

Still. Maybe it's good that he's been too busy to see Alex—as tired as he is running Sucre Coeur and hauling himself all over Seattle for music gigs and museum exhibitions and wedding mini-interviews and political rallies, Craig could do something stupid like confess his feelings.

Which would be problematic, if not outright disastrous.

He checks his phone again. No messages. Time's moving steadily toward eight, and their reservations are at eight-thirty. Where the hell is Alex?

Craig doesn't even want to go out to dinner. The celebration was all Alex's idea. To Craig's mind, a perfect celebration for his birthday and success would be to order in dumplings from the Chinese place around the corner and then go to bed with the man he's just about sure he loves right after they eat. Or before. He's not picky.

The bakery box string makes dull music under his absently plucking fingers. Love. He's still not entirely sure how he feels about it, not even after talking to Sarita. It still feels too much like going over a cliff he'd missed spotting on a map. And it's not as if he has something against love; of course he hasn't, nothing against it at all. He just also has the right to question the sanity of his mind and heart for throwing in their lot with this unlikely and somewhat volatile candidate.

I just thought we'd only ever have the one night…

No message, still. He sighs and sends another one.

Helloooooo?

Despite his frequent sanity checks, Craig has to admit that he likes the slow burn of whatever it is they've got going. He can see how finding out little things about Alex is almost like a treasure hunt. Discovering Alex's punctuality, the banana pepper thing, the fact that he likes lemon slush drinks and wears glasses for working and reading is not unlike uncovering artifacts on an archaeological expedition.

What is with this lateness tonight, though? he wonders.

You're really quite late, you know. Did a bookshelf fall on you?

But this time, as soon as he hits send, he hears Alex's voice through the door, muffled but clearly annoyed. Scooping up the bakery box, Craig scrambles to his feet with a smile on his face and a hand raised to knock at the door—

Then he hears a second male voice.

Craig freezes; his mind races.

Two options: one, it's a friend that Craig hasn't met. Logical enough; Craig hasn't met any of Alex's friends outside of the two he happened to already know. Alex hasn't mentioned having other friends, but of course he must. Maybe this is one of his old friends from school.

Or two, the thought that idly bothers him from time to time: Alex is seeing someone else.

This is not the most comfortable of notions. Craig's stomach curls into a tight knot while he stands in front of the door, listening to a conversation he can't make out.

It would be fair for Alex to see other people; it would. They're both free. They aren't dating, have never declared exclusivity. Craig's unconfessed feelings don't change that fact. He wouldn't *like* it, but it would be fair, and he would figure out how to deal with it.

He'd thought, though, that if it *did* come down to that kind of thing, they'd discuss it first? That would be polite, the civilized thing to do with the rather informal arrangement they have. Craig wouldn't blame Alex for seeing someone else, given how limited their time together has been lately. He just... would have liked to discuss it.

Also, for the record, he still doesn't like the idea of it at all. Fair or not. Especially not on his *birthday.*

But maybe it's just a friend, after all.

He pulls in a deep breath in a vain effort to uncoil the knot in his stomach. Not much sense in standing out here working himself up over something he knows nothing about. It's unnecessary anxiety, and thinking this way is insulting to Alex; it gives him no credit for decency whatsoever. Drawing back his shoulders, Craig forces himself to knock on the door.

"No problem," he hears after a moment. It's the second voice, crystal clear but unfamiliar. When the door swings open to reveal a short, stocky man with dark hair, a barbed wire bicep tattoo and no shirt who is just as unfamiliar, the knot in Craig's stomach melts into a steaming hot lump of jealous hurt.

"I'm gonna guess that you're not here to sell us subscriptions to *Sports Illustrated*," Shirtless Guy says by way of cryptic greeting, pushing the door open wider and beckoning for Craig to come inside. He's acting as if he *lives* here or something, he's so casual. "Hi."

The string of the bakery box bites into Craig's fingers when he clenches his hands into fists. It stings enough to keep him alert and in control of himself. Only just, but it's enough. He lets the hurt tilt his chin into the air and lift an eyebrow, but he says nothing.

Shirtless Guy's smile is much too cheerful and casual for Craig's liking. "Are you early?"

Deep breaths. "As it happens, I was in fact early for once, but I've been out in the hallway waiting for my dinner companion for quite some time now." He does make a small effort to keep the acidity from his remark, but it's very small and so fails entirely. Behind Shirtless Guy, Craig finally sees Alex, standing there with his panicked face as white as snow.

"Not what you think!" Alex yelps as he hurls a wadded-up ball of fabric at the stranger. "Put that on. Now." As his... his *friend*... complies, Alex looks at Craig, his face all-over desperation. "Craig, it's really, *really* not what you think," he nearly whispers, eyes pleading for understanding.

Craig forces a smile. "I'm terribly interested in what it *could* be, babe."

He feels bad when Alex recoils; he knows his tone borders on cold and he's probably got an alarming expression on his face. But only *slightly* bad. Surely Alex understands how awful this situation looks, no matter their arrangement. The walls go right back up as Alex stands very straight.

"It's complicated."

Shirtless Guy has been watching the two of them while he shakes out the fabric Alex had tossed at him, resolving it into a T-shirt that he pulls on—Craig is trying not to think about why the guy gets to wear a T-shirt that fits him so badly, it's obviously Alex's—and understanding begins to dawn on his face. "Complicated? Al, wait up, does he not know—"

"Not helping," Alex snarls, and his voice is angry, his eyes still opaque and fixed on Craig. "Go home, Connor."

"I don't think I should, not if he thinks—"

"Connor!"

The guy rolls his eyes, ignores Alex and steps forward to face Craig. "Hi. Connor Monaghan. I'm married." Instead of thrusting out a hand to shake, he holds it up in front of Craig's face, a heavy gold band on full display. "And *not* to Alex, if you were thinking of going there. I'm straight."

It's welcome information that does nothing to sort out Craig's confusion. The situation has moved much too quickly from *This is terrible* to *What now?* He's quite unable to get a grasp on anything. "Right."

"You're the mystery guy." This Connor guy looks for all the world as if he's *assessing* Craig. *What nerve!* "He never said you were English."

"I... see..." says Craig.

"He's obviously told you less about me than he's told me about you. Incredible." Connor shakes his head, chuckling. "It doesn't look like he's ever mentioned me. Al, I'm hurt."

"You were going?" Alex suggests through clenched teeth.

Connor ignores him. "My wife's English, too," he says. "London." Looking down, he spots the Sucre Coeur box in Craig's hand. "Oh, hey, she loves that bakery. They made her special orders when she was pregnant with our kid."

Sucre Coeur gets a lot of customers, but *English*, *pregnant* and *special orders* rings as clear as the church bell in his hometown. "You're married to... ah, Rayna, wasn't it?" Here's an evening full of shocks, when all he wanted was a nice dinner and a blowjob.

Nodding, Connor looks pleased. "You work there? You remember her? Amazing, she'll love that."

"Hard to forget a heavily pregnant Englishwoman coming into the shop and threatening my life if I didn't make her a real English apple crumble straightaway." Strangely enough, Craig does remember the experience and with quite a lot of fondness. It helps ease his tension. "Yeah, I do remember her. It was my pleasure to make what she wanted. You can tell her I badgered my mum into giving me the Cunningham family recipe. It's been a secret for generations."

Connor's smile gets even bigger. "Excellent. Hey, if she never brought Kira in, I'll tell her to stop by. You oughta see what your desserts helped to bring into the world, right? And she can bring me some of those butterscotch cookies you do, I love those." He winks, heads into the kitchen and pulls a wet, smelly bundle out of the sink. "Speaking of Rayna, I need to get home. Traffic's a bitch heading my way this time of night." He locates a plastic bag, stuffs the bundle into it and ties it off. "My shirt. We had a chemical accident. I'm gonna go home now and let Al explain everything."

"Okay." It's all Craig can say in the wake of yet another reminder that the world is small, and that is more than Alex seems capable of at the moment.

Connor snatches a large sheaf of keys from the end table by the distressed leather couch. "You're an idiot sometimes, Al. Craig, we weren't formally introduced, but it was nice to meet you. See you guys later."

And he's gone in a wave of jingling keys and chemical stink, leaving Craig and Alex to stand staring at each other. The silence is very nearly deafening, and Craig tenses all over again.

He breaks the silence. "So. You played football in college." Uncovering this tiny factoid treasure about Alex should be delightful, but he keeps thinking of Connor in the shirt and his lips purse tightly. He's so irritated, his mouth tastes as if he's licked a lemon.

"Soccer." Alex nods, with his hands in his pockets and his shoulders nearly up to his ears.

"Well, I'm English, so it's football." Craig puffs out his cheeks. "We're late."

"I know." Walls still up, eyes still unreadable, Alex rubs his face. "I'm sorry. We ran way later than we thought."

Despite Connor's clarification, a wad of jealousy sits luke-warm and sour in Craig's stomach when he hears the word "*we.*" Connor and Alex might not be lovers, he can accept that, but they clearly are close. Connor knows Alex. Knows him well enough to get away with calling him an idiot, well enough to use a nickname, well enough to ignore his angry instructions, well enough to answer the door as if he's been here a dozen, a hundred times before.

Who *is* he? And what were they doing that involves chemicals? And why won't Alex let Craig in, the way he's clearly let this Connor person in?

Craig takes a deep breath and tells his circling thoughts to *stop*. "I hope you'll explain what's going on. I thought you'd been working all these weeks."

Alex's mouth opens, closes, opens again and then purses in a grimace. "I have been. I…"

"Because I will take you at your word and Connor's that nothing was going on, not that you and I can't see other people, of course," Craig goes on, watching Alex's face for any clue at all and, for the first time since they started seeing each other, allows himself to feel actively annoyed that he *has* to do this. Alex has every right to keep to himself, but it doesn't make it any less frustrating to be the one shut out after all they've shared. "I just wish you'd let me *in* sometimes. You're so difficult."

This last comes out in a rush, spiked with the frustration and unhappiness of the last several minutes. Craig hadn't meant to say it, but neither does he regret letting his frustration get the better of him for at least one small moment.

He's not superhuman. He *is* in love, or something really damn close to it. There is only so much he can do. Or take.

The outburst makes Alex jump, startled enough to drop his mask and look, for all the world, like a kid surprised by a dog barking at him. "Oh."

But the mask is back on in the next instant, and though Craig wants to scream he manages not to. In times like these, Sarita's philosophy of simplicity just does not work. "I'm not trying to pry."

"I'm not trying to be *difficult*," Alex snaps back. He shakes his head as if he's shaking off water and a sigh lifts his shoulders. "I just... I... fuck it. Here." He takes Craig's hand. "Come see, okay?"

"See what?" Craig is being tugged towards the bathroom, which, even given the benefit of the doubt, seems a distinctly odd place to do anything with another person that *isn't* sexual in nature. He sets the bakery box down on the end table and follows.

Alex gropes inside for the switch and flips it, but the light doesn't come on with its usual brilliance; the light from the fixture is a dull red. "This."

At first Craig can see only outlines of unusual things—the shower cubicle, and what looks like a table wedged into it. Gloves and goggles heaped on the toilet tank. The pedestal sink with a line of... something... stretched over it. The entire room reeks of chemicals, despite the whirring extractor fan—

Alex stands near the door with all the nervousness of a bird prepared to take flight. Tension, visible even in the near dark, is wired through the length of his body. His face is blank, a studied mask, a clue for Craig as to the wariness with which he is being observed.

"Take a look," Alex says, voice an expanse of forced calm, as he gestures with the hand that isn't clutched, white-knuckled, around the doorknob. It seems as though he'll say more, but then he swallows the words and tips his head up... and waits.

The gesture indicates the line strung over the sink. Craig takes a step forward to better see what hangs from it.

His breath catches in his chest.

Photographs.

A baby girl, round and dimpled and fluffy-haired, with skin as luminous as pearls, smiles out at him from the eight-by-ten rectangles, looking so alive Craig almost wants to pluck her free from the confines of the glossy paper and tickle her. In the first photo that catches his eye, her huge dark eyes peer flirtatiously from behind a stuffed duck. Her dimpled hands squeeze the cuddly toy to her face.

He can almost hear her squeals.

Another photo shows her flat on her tummy, head up and alert as she reaches for a baby rattle. Her determination radiates from the still image, giving it depth and dimension. In yet another she's held in the arms of the woman Craig recognizes as Rayna, the apple crumble lady, who shares the baby's smooth, luminous skin and long, long eyelashes. Rayna's tight dark curls spiral down around her face, and she smiles as the little girl reaches up in clear delight to grab at them. Craig nearly expects to hear happy shrieks and tender admonishments, to see curls tugged gently out of chubby fists, for the distance between their noses to close in an Eskimo kiss.

"These are amazing." He's only just aware that he breathes the words, so captivated is he by the sheer beauty and life in the images. As hard as it is to tear his eyes away, Craig looks over at Alex, who is still poised for flight. "My God. Who... Connor?"

Alex's hand slips off the doorknob and he tucks his balled-up fists into his jeans pockets. "No. Me."

"You?" It's the last thing Craig expects, yet what a delightful surprise.

"Me." Alex won't meet his eye. "The baby is Connor's daughter, that's why he was here developing the photos with me. I mean, he does photography too, but I did these. Me." He shuffles over to the line, pulls a photo from the back row and hands it over. It's Connor, with the baby and Rayna. "It's a hobby."

"It's quite brilliant for a hobby." The photos are breathtaking, light and lovely and so real it aches deep in Craig's chest. And Alex is talking about himself; that's something Craig can't begin to examine. "These are incredible. Really. How is this only a hobby?"

"It just is." Apparently the revelations are over. But if Craig squints, he can see that the mask has slipped again, just a little, and Alex is smiling, sweet and bashful. "You do like them?"

"Of course I do!" He loves them, in fact. He would not be at all surprised to see them in an exhibition. "They're incredible, Alex. Really beautiful work." He brushes a finger over one of Rayna's long spiral curls. "I can't believe my apple crumble customer is married to your friend. Honestly, what a terribly small world this is, after all. First Samantha and Nate, now this." If he were the sort to believe in fate, this would be an unmistakable sign.

"Yeah…" Poor Alex. How infinitely small the world can be!

Craig traces the baby's—Kira, he remembers Connor saying—photographed cheek. "But come now, really." Time to stop teasing his poor lover. Alex clearly doesn't find all this as amusing as Craig does. "This is lovely work, Alex. She's a beautiful baby and you've done her justice. I mean, these are seriously amazing. How long have you been doing this?" He's almost afraid to ask it, afraid Alex will close off again…

But no. The inquiry into something Alex knows seems to wake him, to guide him onto steadier ground. He allows himself another small smile before answering. "Since I was six or seven. Started with some of the super old cameras in my grandfather's attic and just sort of went from there. Connor's dad used to own the shop where I bought my first camera; that's how I met him." Alex's shrug is a little too casual, his studied nonchalance a poor facade over the quiet happiness

Craig can see sparking to life. "I did yearbook and school paper photography in high school, and took some classes as an undergrad."

"You never said. Still waters." With a grin he knows is huge and silly, Craig tugs one of Alex's hands free. It's just too lovely to see Alex happy with something he's done. "Has this been going on the whole time we've been seeing each other?"

He feels, rather than sees, the moment Alex's entire body goes rigid. The brightness fades from his face. "No. Just... it was... I put it away for a while. Before you."

Ah. It doesn't take a genius to realize that *that* had to do with the mysterious Jeff, whom Craig could cheerfully dip in shellac and hang as an art installation, should they ever meet. *Asshole In Resin*, he'll call it. If he's feeling particularly irked, he'll do it all up Damien Hirst style, dissected and displayed in parts. "That's a pity."

"Connor is from... before, obviously." Alex tells him, the words halting and slow. "Before... anyway, so he knew..."

"I understand." Craig squeezes the hand he holds and smiles, hoping it's reassuring. As much as curiosity eats him alive regarding whatever happened to Alex before they met, he won't push. It seems difficult enough for Alex to even hint that *something* happened.

He wishes he could make it better, though.

Alex takes a deep breath. "And all of this is from... before, too," he continues. He waves his free hand to encompass the line of prints. "I thought I was done with it, but I woke up one morning a few weeks back... I decided to try it again. I'm sorry I didn't tell you. I was still getting comfortable with it again."

"I understand," Craig says again, and means it. There is a light of joy in Alex, even under the tension and worry; Craig is happy that it exists, however complicated it made things for a minute there.

He would like to do something so that things aren't so complicated in the future, though. Craig looks down at the photo in his hand and rubs a thumb over its plain white border. *Uncomplicating things is rather complicated in its own way, isn't it?*

A careful tread will be required. Cautious negotiations. A delicate hand. They should probably talk.

But not tonight. Tonight ought to be about celebrations, not negotiations: a time to rejoice in talent and unexpected revelations and the feelings he can demonstrate but never, ever divulge. He gives Alex's hand an extra squeeze and starts for the bathroom door, forcing Alex to back up with him. "We really are terribly late for dinner," he remarks, allowing his smile to beam well out of control.

Alex gasps as his back collides with the door and Craig presses up against him. "I... uh... I think we've actually missed our reservations."

"Probably made some hungry tourist couple *very* happy, if you think about it." Their faces are almost too close together to see each other clearly; the gap is so minuscule as to be easily closed with a kiss, if Craig wishes.

He does. "Brought dessert," he murmurs, close enough to Alex's lips to feel every hiccuping breath. "If we order in, we don't have to leave your flat until tomorrow night."

"But..." It seems difficult for Alex to form coherent sentences. Good. "It's your birthday..."

"And as the birthday boy, I should get to choose what I want to do, shouldn't I?" Craig's free hand slips under Alex's shirt and skims the warm skin. "Don't you think?"

"I..." It's too dark to really tell, but Alex's eyes might be glazing over.

"And if I want to celebrate my birthday and celebrate your incredible talent by staying in with you, that would be good, wouldn't it?" A little line of skin along Alex's ribs, when stroked with a feather-light touch, reduces him to jelly. Craig, of course, knows exactly where it is. "That would be a nice sort of celebration, don't you think?"

Alex groans and capitulates. "What kind of dessert?"

"S'mores brownie pie. You liked it last time I made it."

Another groan, this time ending in the tiniest of whimpers. "With the little marshmallows?"

"With the little marshmallows, and I used the torch to make them all crisp and brown on top." Craig sets aside the photo in his hand to better enable the very slow unbuttoning of his shirt. "We can pop it into the oven for a minute or two and make it nice and warm."

"Not fair," Alex gasps as Craig, now successfully shirtless, reaches over to helpfully extract Alex from *his* shirt. "I can't concentrate when you're getting naked and talking food porn."

"That's the idea." Skin to skin now, oh yes, Craig likes that. "Do you approve?"

"Yes, oh God, yes, absolutely." Alex's mindless babbling might have something to do with the fact that Craig's just slipped a hand down the front of Alex's jeans. "Whatever you want."

"Good. Right." Back out comes the hand, and Craig opens the bathroom door. "I'll order dinner and warm the pie and you'll shower?"

The light from the living room slants in to illuminate Alex's abruptly forlorn face. "But, we, you..."

"I love your photography," Craig assures him, slipping past him with a kiss. "And I think you're amazing, and I absolutely want to celebrate. I just also think you *reek* of chemicals, babe."

He leaves Alex pouting in the bathroom doorway while he hunts down his phone so he can order dinner. Jealousy, wonder, sensuality, reluctance, eagerness—there's not a feeling Craig's experienced tonight that he doesn't love, if only because their collective intensity rushes through him like electricity and leaves him feeling alive in a way no contact with another human ever, ever has. Complicated and unlikely as he and Alex are, this is the best relationship... or whatever it is... that Craig's ever had.

Except for the fact that he can't really *tell* Alex that.

Yet.

Chapter Twelve

Sarita has an apologetic look when she turns to Craig, shop phone to her ear. "It's Mrs. Cartwright," she tells him with even more apology in her voice. *Oh dear. Bad news.*

"I'll handle it," he says, forcing a brighter smile onto his face before setting aside the basket he's just filled with breakfast pastries. "Hello, Mrs. Cartwright! Happy day-before-family-reunion day! What timing, we've got the last batch of cupcakes out of the oven and cooling, all five dozen will be frosted and ready by the end of the day—"A flurry of apologetic babble fills his ear and, as he deciphers it, makes his heart sink. "Three dozen *more*? Oh, good lord."

The apology shifts into coaxing, pleading appeals as Craig considers the bakery schedule for the day and makes some shifts. It's Saturday, a day they're not usually closed, but they needed a full day without customers to decorate the Cartwright order for five dozen cheerful rainbow-decorated cupcakes, deliver an elaborate wedding cake to the event center on Mercer Island and bake an order of vegan lemon poppy seed muffins for a small regional Unitarian Universalist conference.

And, Alex and Connor are coming in today for a photo shoot, so maneuvering in the kitchen is going to be tight. Craig pinches the bridge of his nose against the nascent headache.

"No problem, Mrs. C," he tells the increasingly frantic voice on the other line. "I'm from a big family myself, I absolutely understand last minute additions to parties! We'll get that extra three dozen in, no problem. Two chocolate, one vanilla?" The voice now gushes noisy gratitude. "You're very welcome. We'll see you at six tonight, then? Bring Madison, I'll have a special treat for her—yes, a nut-free caramel brownie, and I've got one for you too, 'course I have. All right? See you then." He clicks off the phone; only now can he let out the explosive sigh he's been holding back. He takes out his exasperation on an innocent blueberry muffin by tearing a huge bite out of it. "Fuckbugger."

Will looks up from applying the initial layer of sky blue frosting on some of the Cartwright cupcakes. "Three dozen *more?*"

"I'm afraid so. Bugger, fuck, shit." Craig sighs and hands the cordless phone to Sarita. "I think we can just manage it."

Sarita clicks the phone onto its charger and looks at him nervously. "Don't forget I'm out of here at four, Craig. I have to be. Mama will kill me if I miss Grandfather's birthday dinner. She'll kill me if I'm even a minute late getting to Tacoma, come to that. And you know what the I-5 is like."

"Not a problem." He sounds more reassuring than he feels. "You'll be able to leave when you need to, and you're off at five on the dot, Will. Today will just take a bit of rearranging is all. Starting now." Taking a deep breath to fortify himself, Craig heads for the refrigerator, where the six tiers of a raspberry cream-stuffed wedding cake—alternating layers of chocolate and lemon cake festooned with dozens of Will's perfect red buttercream roses over a layer of more buttercream in a pearly antique ivory—are waiting to be delivered and assembled. "You two will have to take this over to the island immediately."

Will nearly drops his frosting spatula. "Craig, it's barely after seven in the morning, no one—"

"Poppy Lawrence is doing the catering for the LaPorte wedding," he interrupts, making his smile even more reassuring. "We all know Poppy is always three hours early for setup so she can finish cowing the event center staff into leaping sky high when she says jump. She will be there and she adores you, Will. It should be no problem to get her to give us fridge space early, and she'll want to do the cake placement herself anyway. Just get there, charm Poppy, assemble the cake and get out."

"We don't have enough frosting made for another three dozen cupcakes," Sarita points out and frowns, and if Craig's smile gets any more reassuring, it's going to slide right off.

"Are my fingers broken? I'll get the new batch made and bagged while you're delivering the cake, and I'll start piping the rainbows onto the cupcakes you've already frosted. When you get back, you'll both take over frosting while I get started frosting the new cupcakes. It's all going to be fine, you two." Hey, he almost believes it. "The photographers will be here at eight, but don't rush yourselves, they'll need time to set up."

It almost sounds sane. As if they could actually manage it. Maybe they can. Craig wonders how handy Alex and Connor are with frosting bags.

No, no. Best not.

His employees still seem uncertain. Craig gathers them into a nice, reassuring squeezy hug. "Don't worry about it! We'll manage it and even get the muffins done for the Unitarians, that's a small enough order. No problem. I'll stay late if I need to since Vanessa and Natasha are opening for me tomorrow." He squeezes his employees one more time. "We can do this.

You two are the best, fastest decorators that Theodora's ever hired. I have faith in you!"

Sarita raises one skeptical eyebrow, but still manages to muster a smile. "Can we stop for coffee on the way back?"

"Make them very, very large coffees from the Java Stop for all five of us, and it's a deal." A great deal more cheery with his work staff on board for today's insanity, Craig opens the safe and pulls out a couple of twenties. "I have a feeling we're going to need the caffeine."

"No argument here," Will says and offers his own tremulous smile. "Come on, Sarita, I'll get the big tiers into the van." And they're off in a flurry of frosting and highly-resonating nerves, with the LaPorte cake carefully loaded into the Sucre Coeur van and the boxes strapped down, and Sarita the alert custodian of the top tier in the front seat.

Once they're gone, Craig looks around at his kitchen. Since they've been here for two hours, it's a disaster, with Cartwright cupcakes everywhere in various stages of decoration—and no room for him to make more frosting. "Right, then," he announces to the empty bakery, popping in his iPod earbuds. With music in his ears, it doesn't take him long to clear a space and line up bowls, frosting bags and food coloring.

Industrial mixers make buttercream a snap, even at quantities large enough to frost and pipe cloud-tipped rainbows onto three dozen cupcakes, plus a little extra just in case the Cartwrights produce even *more* relatives before the day is out. Craig mumble-sings along to his Proclaimers playlist, bobbing his head to its bouncing guitars as he tints and compares, checking to be sure that there is little to no variation in his colors.

Some bakeries might not be so exacting, but there is a reason that the team at Sucre Coeur has been climbing to the top of event planners' recommendation lists for the last year. This attention to detail is what got them the Cartwrights and the LaPortes—and what prompted Theodora to email Craig: *Darling boy, we need a website and brochures. Make it happen, will you? No pinstripes or cartoon cupcakes is all I ask. Something nice. I trust you. Sarita plays around with web design, doesn't she? So just find a photographer.*

Hence Connor and Alex's imminent arrival. Theodora didn't give him the biggest budget in the world, but it is enough to pay a dubious but willing-to-try Sarita a bonus to design the website around the digital photography Alex has agreed to do for a small fee.

"Why me?" Alex had asked . "I'm just a—"

"Great photographer with a real eye for people and for what might make a good picture?" Craig had responded, smacking Alex's lips with a kiss. "And I was hoping, since I'm sleeping with said photographer, that he'll work for the unfortunately tiny fee Theodora has offered..."

Craig hadn't mentioned how interested he is in seeing Alex at work, at work doing something he really loves. The advertising agency is just a job; Craig has no interest in seeing Alex there. No, Alex likes that well enough, but he *loves* photography, that much has become clear in the weeks since it was revealed. And he's seen Craig at work dozens of times. It was well past time that the tables were turned.

"I feel like a gigolo," Alex had complained, but jokingly. He'd taken the job with an eagerness that surprised Craig in its intensity. And he'd even gotten Connor to agree to assist him—for cookies. "For *cookies*. What do you put in those things, Craig? Crack?"

"Butterscotch schnapps."

"Ah."

Craig smiles at the memory and drips one last miniscule drop of coloring into the bowl. A quick stir and he holds it up to the light. Finally. Perfectly sky blue buttercream. He moves on to the rest of the colors, ending with a rainbow of bowls and no small amount of satisfaction as he grabs the frosting bags.

Scooping the frosting into the bags and twisting them off is easy work; Craig has gotten it down over the years. Singing along to "500 Miles" is even easier. He falls into a rhythm and a trance, slapping frosting in time with the music, not noticing when his head bobs along, or when a bad imitation of his mother's Glaswegian accent surfaces, or when he starts trying to sing both the Reid brothers' parts.

The next filled frosting bag doesn't make it into the Rubbermaid container with the others. Not with the penultimate chorus coming up in eight beats.

Wielding a fierce frosting bag guitar, Craig abandons all pretense of work and takes full advantage of the empty bakery, bouncing around the kitchen and cranking the volume of his iPod up to deafening levels as he sings about all the miles he'd walk. Today is going to be fine. More than fine. They're going to get all their cupcakes baked and frosted, Alex and Connor will do amazing work for the website and, if Craig's very lucky, he'll get to take Alex home afterwards because once again, time has gotten away from them. That is far from Craig's favorite thing, and it is time to fix it.

But right now, everything is fine and the frosting bag is a microphone as he spins in place, opening his mouth, ready to belt out—

Oh.

On the far side of the bakery counter, Alex stands wide-eyed while a grinning Connor holds up a key ring, wiggling it. The keys catch the sun and cast glints of light around the bakery. "So... you gave us a key."

Craig lowers his frosting bag microphone. "That I did."

Alex is biting his lip and Connor's grin just grows. "Got an encore for us?"

There is only one thing to do.

With his biggest smile, Craig trades bag for breakfast basket and makes an offer. "Scones?"

"HOLD YOUR HANDS STILL." IT'S THE FIFTH TIME IN AN HOUR that Alex has asked this of Craig, who obediently pauses in piping fluffy white frosting clouds while Alex leans in with his camera and adjusts the focus. "Hold... hold... and..." The camera clicks and buzzes. "There. Okay."

All right. This is less fun than Craig thought it would be. Connor and Alex have been here for *hours* taking pictures, and it's completely thrown off his hastily rearranged schedule. Sarita is pulling the last sheet of cupcakes out of the cooler with one eye on the clock, since it's nearly three and she really does live in mortal fear of her mother's displeasure.

He has two dozen more cupcakes to go plus the muffins to bake, and he could use his best decorator, but he promised. "Get out of here, Sarita. Go get ahead of traffic."

"No, it's early yet. We've still got this last big pan... and the Unitarians—" But she's whipping off her paper hat and apron even as she protests.

"We'll manage." As he did this morning, Craig makes this sound much more reassuring than it is. Out of the corner of his eye, he can see Alex peering from behind his camera. "Go on, love. If Mrs. Cartwright comes in and we're not done, she'll just have to wait, won't she?"

Sarita looks so relieved, he knows he made the right call letting her go early. "Thank you, Craig." Without waiting for a reply, she's out the door and running for her car.

Craig pipes another white cloud at the other end of the rainbow. "Don't even think of volunteering to stay past five, Will." He grins as he sets his finished cupcake on a nearby tray to join its completed compatriots, ready for boxing.

"I could. James and Ginny won't mind—"

"It's your anniversary, absolutely not. Out at five. I'll do the muffins. We'll be fine. Keep rainbowing." *If I never see another frosting rainbow again, I'll throw a party. I expect I'll dream about them tonight. Ugh.* "Alex, babe, how much longer?"

"I think I've got all the shots I need, maybe." Alex clicks the storage card out of his camera and slips it into the MacBook he has set up on the bakery's lone, rickety café table. "I'll go through them and see if there's anything else I might need."

"I'm afraid I'll have to ask you to get any others on another day." *There's just no time for any more "Okay, hold still."* "Sorry. I didn't know..."

"I should have warned you I'm kind of a taskmaster," Alex admits with a rueful smile as he sits down at the laptop. "I don't really do candid."

"So we've seen." Craig winks at Connor, who stifles laughter as he gets some final shots of Will drawing rainbows onto blank blue cupcake tops. "Is that the difference between you and Connor, here?"

"Well, that and the fact that I don't own a profitable camera and film shop, so I can't afford to work for alcoholic cookies." He taps away at his computer for a moment before wandering into the kitchen again, camera-free. He leans over Craig's shoulder and rests his chin in the crook of Craig's neck. "I didn't mean to take up so much of your time. I'm sorry."

"Please don't worry about it. We've got nearly everything done, and besides, I liked watching you work." Behind the camera is the only time—other than when they're in bed together—that Craig has seen Alex completely lose the wariness in his eyes, to stop scrutinizing and assessing the world around him for potential pitfalls.

And he really does know and love his work. As intrusive as the constant "hold that" has been, Alex has a real eye for a moment, even in a context as mundane as mixing batter or sliding a tray of cupcakes into the oven. He works with precision, if not always swiftness, and there's no doubt that this is his element.

Craig wants to know more. But for now he contents himself with leaning back into Alex's embrace while he gets on with his own work and Connor snaps a few extra shots.

Freed from the interruption of posing, Craig and Will manage to get all the cupcakes decorated, if not boxed, by the time Will's partners come to retrieve him for dinner. And while the happy trio offers to stay, Craig all but has to shove them out the door. "You are not... boxing... cupcakes... on your anniversary! Out!"

He finds he can, however, ask Alex and Connor for boxing help, and Rayna too when she comes to meet her husband. Craig is pleased to be allowed to play with a giggly Kira, and he tickles her until she squeals and bats at his hands. He's even more pleased to hand her over to Alex, who looks panicked that he might drop the cuddly bundle until she pokes him in the nose with a dimpled finger and makes him laugh.

Best not to examine how *that* makes Craig feel.

The Monaghans leave to grab dinner at their favorite Thai place after Mrs. Cartwright comes in with her daughter to pick up her eight dozen cupcakes. "Ah, alone at last," Craig sighs, locking the door behind the happy family.

"Yeah. You, me and an order for three dozen vegan muffins," Alex chuckles, peering at his laptop screen and clicking through the day's photos. "You did promise dinner when we're done here, right?"

"I made my legendary spaghetti sauce last night. We'll pick up a loaf of French bread on the way back to my place and then all we have to do is boil some noodles while everything warms up. Quick as a flash." He pulls down the ingredients for the muffins—they're one of the shop's best sellers, so he's got the recipe memorized. They should easily be out of here by seven-thirty.

The sound of a noisy stretch and a yawn creaks from the general vicinity of the MacBook. "Sounds great. We've been so busy at the agency this week, I could definitely use an easy night."

Craig winces. "Then I am sorry to have made you wake up early and work on a day off." Fluffy yellow lemon zest falls into a glass bowl under the onslaught of his microplane grater.

"It's fine. I wanted to do it." The reply is slightly absent as Alex clicks and drags. "Photography and spending time with y—here." He coughs. When he continues, he sounds more alert. "I like Saturdays here already, so getting to do this was a bonus. Really. And we went with digital instead of film, so I get to stay here and work instead of having to run off to develop the negatives and prints."

Flour, sugar, salt, baking powder. Craig tries not to let his smile wander out of control. It is easier to concentrate on his dry ingredients than it is to respond in any way that wouldn't be... gooey. It's just that every little relaxation of Alex's guard makes Craig want to throw a parade in the streets of Seattle.

Let it handle itself. Don't push.

He holds his hand over the bowl and sprinkles in the poppy seeds. But the click and flash of a camera comes out of nowhere, making him drop the rest of the seeds into the middle of the dry ingredients. "I thought you didn't do candid."

"I don't—on a job." Alex lowers the camera to reveal an endearing, bashful smile. "This one's for me."

Craig never blushes, ever, but this... his face warms as if with fever and he can't look up from his mixing bowl. *You make it so difficult to remember that it might be a bad idea to love you.* "I see."

"I wish I'd had a camera ready this morning when we walked in." Peripheral vision only just shows him Alex, grinning. "You put on quite the performance."

"Tsk. Damning me with faint praise." Poking fun helps the fever in his face cool down and melt away. In another moment he's able to face Alex with a genuine smile as he blends wet ingredients into the dry. "I put a lot of myself into being that ridiculous, I'll have you know."

"I didn't think it was ridiculous. I thought it was fun." Alex sets the camera aside and perches his glasses on his nose while he works. "God, I haven't heard that song in years, though."

Craig scoops the batter into muffin tins. "Whereas I heard it nearly every week of my life from the time I was little to when I moved to the States."

"Really? Why that song?"

"Why that band, would be the better question." Tin one is set aside. He's making pretty good time with these. "I told you once that my mother is from Scotland, didn't I?"

Alex glances up. "Yeah. When we met, I think."

Craig finishes filling tin two. "That's it. My mother is from Scotland, and the Proclaimers have been her favorite band since she was a teenager. She actually met my dad at one of their concerts, an early one, before they were famous."

"He's from Scotland, too? You said he was from the British Virgin Islands, didn't you?" Aw. Geography would appear to give poor Alex a headache. He's rubbing his temples and frowning; Craig wants to soothe the headache away, but he's got to get these muffins in the oven. "So how are you English, again?"

He'll have to settle for explaining while he fills the last tin. "Dad actually is English-born—his family went over from Tortola before he was born. But he went to university in Glasgow because he liked their maths program. And he got dragged to a concert for a band he'd only vaguely heard of and while he was queuing for beer..." *Four... five... six...* "He met this very short and terribly mouthy local punk schoolgirl who was trying to get a beer of her own with fake identification. Which was going about as well as you would expect something like that to go."

"It would have gone *very* well if she'd had one of my fake IDs," Alex says, chuckling behind his computer screen. Craig's eyebrows shoot up. *Oh goodness, isn't that interesting?*

"You don't say." He congratulates himself on his restraint.

"I am a man of many hidden talents, past and present," comes the reply, delivered with a very self-satisfied smirk. "Go on."

That's going to be chased down later, Craig resolves. "Well, you can guess that things didn't go well for my mother with the beer man, but my father liked her spunk and her spiked purple and red hair and, he tells us all, much to our dismay, her very short skirt."

Nine... ten... eleven... and twelve. Craig scoops up the tins and carries them to the oven. "I won't say it was love at first sight, but it was certainly affection at first illicit beer. A little help?"

Alex scrambles to open the oven door and help slide the tins in. "And they've been together ever since?"

"Mm hmm. One graduate degree and a kid later, they moved back to the tiny little English town that my dad calls home, got married and had three more children." Muffins safely in the oven, Craig moves to clean up the kitchen. "And the Proclaimers are still my mother's favorite band, so I've heard their music all my life. Don't your parents have a favorite band?"

"I think my dad likes the Eagles. Maybe." The oven door shuts with a thump. "Which are you?"

"Hmm?" There's a particularly sticky spot on the mixing island where Kira had flung a fistful of red icing. "Which am I what, now?"

Circling the island, Alex shoves his glasses up on his head and picks up the bowls Craig's just finished using. "I counted four kids. Which are you?"

Craig pauses in the middle of scraping at the red icing splat. It occurs to him that this is a conversation that encompasses more than the events of their day or week or month. It's not confined to work or the city or their immediate friends or what to order for dinner. This conversation is—he hadn't even noticed it happening as naturally as the sun setting—personal. It's a minute cracking open of a tightly shut window.

Only last month—last *week*—it would have been unthinkable. He has to resume scrubbing to hide the fact that his hands want to twitch. He can only hope the deep breath he takes to steady himself went unnoticed. "We're talking about my family?"

"Well, it's just..." Alex raises the dishwasher door, considers, shrugs. "You've never talked about them before."

"Not something that really comes up with us, though, is it?" Craig asks, striving for lightness. The question is bold; he feels as if he's crossing a border checkpoint into an unknown land. There could be anything on the other side. *Not all cupboards lead to Narnia.* "Families and all that." He pauses to breathe. "We can talk about something else. If you like."

At last, understanding seems to dawn on the other side of the kitchen. Alex takes a step back from the dishwasher, lips pursed in an "O" as he exhales and lets his gaze wander far away. In his hands, the glass bowls clatter against each other and bring him right back. "No, I... I want to know. It's... fair."

"Fair?"

"You know about my photography," Alex points out, putting the mixing bowls in the dishwasher. "That's a... a thing, for me. It's important. So... yeah. Your family is important; I could know about that. If you... if you want."

The words emerge as if dragged by a sloth, and it's a rather businesslike way to get to know each other, but Craig will take it. Immediately, before Alex rethinks whatever made him decide to open up, Craig tosses his sponge aside and makes his own dive into the sea of tension, ignoring the churning of his stomach. "All right, but fair's fair. One for one. Tell me something about your family. Like... what about you? Any siblings?"

For a moment, Craig thinks Alex won't play along, thinks Alex will bolt from the shop, leaving him with the scent of lemon muffins and a vast gulf of regret for taking the chance.

But at last—"Samantha's as close as I ever got, unless you count a Pomeranian named Trixie."

Relief. Craig puts on a face of mock solemnity and grabs a wooden spoon, holding it out as if he's interviewing Alex. "And are you close to your canine sister, Mr. Scheff?"

"Not really, she's the baby of the family so she's everyone's favorite." Alex jokes back, pretending to have to compose himself to go on. "I'm afraid they never could get my shedding problem under control, and I just could not learn to stay off of the furniture."

Both of them crack up, and it snaps the tension like a rubber band. It's a game now, nothing frightening. Craig's nerves fizzle, buzz... go silent. He can breathe again. "No, but really, no siblings at all, ever?"

"Uh-uh." Alex waves a chiding finger and resumes filling the dishwasher. "One for one. That's the deal. Your turn. Which kid are you?"

"The middle child, sort of. Although to be fair, I was the baby until I was about fourteen." Craig gets back to scrubbing down the mixing island, still watching Alex for any sign of trouble. "My mother writes romance novels for a living, you see. Sort of popular ones."

Alex's eyebrow quirks up, along with one side of his mouth. "So, what, was it enthusiastic research?"

"Mm. Not quite." He chuckles, thinking back. "No, one year she sold her first set of film rights, the ones for her bestselling book. A bottle of champagne, a night of celebration and nine months later... Surprise! Baby twin sisters. It was a bit of a shock."

"I'd fucking guess. No wonder you're good with Kira; that's a hell of an age gap. And your mother writes, that explains you..." The dishwasher is full except for the three muffin tins in the oven, so Alex retrieves the shop broom and sets to sweeping. "I always kind of wished I had a real sibling. I mean, there's Peach—Sammi—like I said, but... Connor's like the brother she can't be, and I always wanted that. An embarrassing, loud, sometimes jerk of an older brother, but a brother."

"I hate to break it to you, but that's all older brothers. Trust me, I grew up with one." Craig is almost afraid to keep asking questions; he wonders if the wrong one will slam the window shut again. But *can* the window shut again? Maybe they've come too far to go back... "All right, you know how my parents met. What about yours?"

Alex shrugs. "Nothing fun, like yours. They met in law school. They're kind of like the Clintons, except not political. They're both in law—Dad's a partner in a firm, Mom's a law professor at UDub. They're both smart, both workaholics, both content with one kid and a fluffy dog." He finishes up and allows a smile as he sets the broom aside. "They are from different places, though. The Scheffs are from D.C., and the Chernikovs moved here from St. Petersburg back when it was still Leningrad. So they have that in common with your parents."

"Sounds like they're still together, so they have that, too." They smile at each other across the kitchen. The island between them is clean. The floor is swept. The muffins are nearly done. *What happens once we're outside the shop, though?*

Craig circles the island, slipping his hand along the stainless steel surface until he's standing in front of Alex. "Just so you know, I like this. That is, I like knowing more about you." He tugs at Alex's belt loops and smiles into the pale, worried face that he loves too much. "It makes you a real boy."

"I never wasn't, I just..." Swallowing hard, Alex pulls his glasses from his head and hooks them into the collar of his T-shirt for safekeeping before cupping his hands around Craig's forearms. "All right. Look, it... it's not easy for me. I think you know... but I like it, too. Just, you know. About you."

That's more, so much more than he ever hoped for or expected, ever. "Is it terrible if I confess to wanting to know more?" He feels greedy, nosy, but with the window beginning to open, it's as though the world is his to own. "Is that all right? I mean... we can stop. Go back to how things were, never talk about ourselves again." His mind and heart are in full-scale rebellion at the very idea, but he has to make the offer.

The look on Alex's face is anything but resolute, but he manages to keep his gaze steady on Craig's face. "Something tells me you don't really want to do that."

"That would be true," Craig admits, heart in throat. "Alex, I—"

What a moment for the oven timer to buzz! At least it makes them both laugh. Craig tucks his face into Alex's neck. "Would it be quite all right if we continued this at my flat?"

"Well," Alex says, a little breathless still with chuckling, "Yeah. I could really use a cup of tea right now, and I have it on good authority that that's where I'll find it."

Chapter Thirteen

ALEX LETS HIMSELF FALL INTO MEMORY.

Years ago—he's not sure exactly how many, but he thinks it must be fifteen or more, because in his memories he's maybe eight or nine years old—he'd experienced the exhilarating side of terror for the first time at a water park in southern California.

It was the big slide, a good ten stories high, with twisting red tubes spiraling from top to bottom. Of course he had to ride the tallest attraction in the park, never mind his father's cautions and his mother's concerns. He'd been so excited as he slowly climbed the stairs with his rubber raft, so eager to take the plunge.

He'd started screaming the minute he was tipped into the dark, watery tube. His stomach bottomed out, his throat was raw with shrieking and chlorine fumes and yet—and yet—within a few feet, his terror became inextricably intermingled with the greatest thrill of his life.

This is what he remembers when Craig pauses and says, "We can talk about something else. If you like."

It could turn around right here. Alex could speak one word and they'd forget that they had strayed from their mutual, unspoken agreement to live only in the moment.

He can't remember when *no* had ceased to be a viable option.

The tea doesn't happen. Neither does the spaghetti dinner. They don't even bother to pick up bread. They are far too distracted by the radical act of actually getting to know each other.

They talk, only talk, on the walk to Craig's place, talking and talking in an endless river of questions and answers but never touching, not holding hands, though Alex knows Craig has to feel the same electricity snap between them that he does. Every revealed fact makes it crackle louder until it's almost as if the energy could consume them both.

By the time they get through the door of the apartment, Craig is all that Alex wants, needs, knows or can think about. The door has barely clicked shut behind them before Alex has dumped his bag on the floor and has Craig up against the wall with his hands on either side of Craig's face to tilt it just right.

He's watching, so he sees Craig's eyes widen for a split second before he moves in and Craig's sharp inhaled breath catches his own. He breathes it all in when their lips meet.

It's a kiss with no barriers, no boundaries, infinite possibilities and endless scope. Alex is kissing a new person, someone somehow more whole and three dimensional, someone with a family and a history and an existence beyond two days a week, dinner and sex. Someone gorgeous and kind and utterly, stunningly ridiculous, someone with no fears or insecurities, someone who will dance around a kitchen and use a frosting bag for a microphone.

Their silent agreement has been shattered to pieces and swept away. He is officially in the slide. There's no going back now.

Under his hands, pressed against the length of his body, Alex breathes Craig in, relishes the warmth of blood rushing under his skin, savors coffee and peppermint on his tongue. He catalogues all of it as if he's feeling it for the first time.

In a way, this is the absolute truth.

"What's your middle name?" The question is carried on the shortest of breaths between kisses, almost bursting out of Alex while his fingertips play over the soft twists of Craig's hair. He knows so much now, knows about parents and siblings and a pet dog named Newton in a little town called Ingatestone. He knows about countryside rambles and a first kiss named David. He knows all of this—and that there is even more to know. His fingers slip down to fumble with the buttons of Craig's shirt as he breathes his question against Craig's mouth. "Middle name? You have one?"

"Andrew." His own top shirt is pushed down his shoulders by fingers that linger and press into his skin. It falls to the floor in a puddle, leaving him in just his undershirt. "What about you?"

"Michael." If he can't get these buttons undone, he'll rip the damn thing off of Craig's body. "Did you have pets growing up?"

Warm hands slip up under his shirt and unerringly find the deliciously awful spot on his ribs that makes him weak in the knees. "Always dogs. Several dogs. Mostly spaniels, Newton's a spaniel. So did you just do football and photography in school?"

Sweet *Christ* how does something feel so sexy and ticklish all at once? And why does Alex like it so much? It should be torture. Revenge drives him to finally get the damn button-down off and attack the newly accessible and reliably hard-on-inducing expanse of Craig's collarbones with his tongue. "I play the flute, too," he mumbles between tiny licks and Craig's gasps. "Badly. You?"

Craig's hands come up to grab Alex's head and hold it still against his skin in some apparent attempt at control, but his short breath and upward-shifting hips give the lie to the effort. "Dramatics society, a writing club and swimming, which I still do a couple times a week. Do you really know how to make fake IDs?"

Alex relents and moves back up to suck another greedy kiss or five from Craig's mouth between words. "Used to. It was for fun but then it turned out I was good at it, so I sold them. It paid for my Leica. Swimming, God, no wonder this body." Yanking Craig's undershirt off, Alex lets his fingers trace over collarbone, pectoral, sternum, abdomen. "Why did you come to America for college?"

"I wanted out of England—way out—and Seattle Pacific was the only place to offer me a spot in their creative writing program that my family could afford." With a wriggle and a team effort, Alex's T-shirt is removed and tossed aside. "What was the first thing you photographed?"

"My grandmother's rose garden. What are your siblings' names?"

Craig stops, fingers tangled in the act of unbuttoning Alex's jeans. "Maybe let's not talk about my brother and sisters while you're trying to get my clothes off."

"Oh. Yeah. Okay." More kisses, never enough kisses in the world, while he works at Craig's belt buckle and thinks. "Um, why baking?"

"Because I needed a job and Theodora had an opening, and like you with the ID thing it..." Craig gasps when Alex slides a hand into his jeans. "It turned out I was all right at it after a few really hideous mistakes. Why did you get an advertising degree instead of studying photography?"

"Dad paid for school. There were stipulations." Yeah, okay, enough for now, that question is veering dangerously into really deep talk territory and... there are limits. Craig's mouth begins to form the next question and Alex leans to stop it in its tracks, closing his eyes again as he takes in the smell and taste and sound of Craig being kissed, wonders how he existed before he knew those things.

The leather of Craig's belt susurrates through the worn denim belt loops on his jeans and Alex throws it to the floor, doing his level best to never let Craig's mouth go as they kick off their shoes and peel the jeans and underwear from each other's bodies. Now free to roam, Alex's hands wander to Craig's hips and pull him away from the wall, steering him to the low bed with a firm grip.

They collapse to the mattress, and Craig presses his body upward, hands moving as if to roll them over so he's on top, but Alex catches his wrists, arrests the movement and pulls back. The surprised questions in Craig's brown eyes are as loud as if he were speaking with his voice.

"Not tonight," Alex whispers, rocking his hips down and watching in fascination as Craig's eyes fall closed when their erections slide against each other. He wants to cover Craig completely, to hold him down and make him come.

In all these months—completely at odds with his attitude toward anyone else, ever—he's allowed Craig to take charge the vast majority of the time, to top him and make him feel good. Selfish, yes, but Craig's never made any secret of the fact that he gets off on his whole body worship kink thing, on making his partner fall into a thousand pieces, and why not let him? Alex had needed that badly for a very long time...

Not tonight. Not *this* night.

"Don't lift a finger," he breathes, trailing the tip of his nose alongside Craig's. "Please."

He doesn't wait for a response before he slides down Craig's body, with his fingers trailing down Craig's arms, over his chest, along his torso. With nothing left to hide, Alex is seeing everything with new eyes, re-learning, re-memorizing.

Nothing between them, no more walls. If he's honest, he can admit they've been falling away for weeks, maybe months. Cracking and crumbling. And at some point, he'd stopped bothering to try keeping them up. In one second of alarming clarity in the bakery kitchen, he'd understood that he was perfectly okay with that.

He lets his tongue flick over warm skin, sucks in kisses he knows won't fade before morning. Craig's fingers twist into the bedding when Alex gets to his hipbones, those prominent ridges with their thin, sensitive skin. Goose bumps stipple the surface in the wake of the broad strokes of Alex's tongue, and he is flooded with satisfaction that he can do this, can make someone come undone.

Gently, ever so gently, and slowly as falling in love, he kisses his way down toward where Craig's cock strains up along his abdomen, so hard the head only barely brushes Craig's stomach. It's the work of a moment to take it into his mouth, to just hold it between his lips and let the slight hint of salt and a little bit of come overwhelm his taste buds.

"Alex, babe, please..." Fingers ruffle Alex's hair, catching his attention. He pulls off to look up, to see that Craig is gazing down at him with eyes wide open in every way, as readable as a book: desperate, wanting, needing... loving.

The half-grin that had been forming on Alex's face dies at the lightning strike of it. No one has ever looked at him like this before, yet he knows what it means as clearly as if he'd heard the words.

Knows? Feels.

Whatever he'd thought love was before—oh, and he'd had ideas, opinions—he had been vastly mistaken.

Oh. I—

It goes through him in a wave, a thrumming echo that settles warmly in the pit of his stomach when he understands.

Alex should be terrified—he is terrified, he's in the slide and there's no way out but down—but too many other emotions vie for his attention for him to focus on the one that, until today, had been his greatest defense. It is these to which he surrenders at last, to feeling and to *feeling*—

Hands that cup, curl, curve to fit the shape of his skull, fingers that thread through his hair to clutch and tug.

A mouth that opens to let out a gasp, a groan, a shuddering, whisper of a sigh, his name.

Legs that stir restlessly, calves that tighten and relax, feet that flex and toes that curl into the sheets—Alex is everything and nothing more than the sum of his parts, fully, completely and terrifyingly in love with every shaking, quaking, strung-tight and desperate, reaching inch of Craig Oliver under his hands and mouth.

IN THE DIM LIGHT OF THE MORNING AFTER, A SMALL PART OF Alex considers that it still might be a good idea to run.

The sun is beginning to filter through the sheer plum and dove gray curtains hung over the kitchen windows. Between the early hour and the muted colors of the fabric, the tiny room is still quite dark.

There's just enough light for Alex to sit up against the wall and watch Craig sleeping in peace, draped in red sheets, gray light and charcoal shadows.

You crept up on me.

He hasn't slept. Not a wink all night. If he still smoked, he'd have gone through a pack of cigarettes, and he hasn't dismissed the notion of going down to the corner shop a block away to get some. He is twitchy and amped with nerves.

What am I supposed to do with you?

The territory he's finding himself in isn't exactly uncharted, no. He's been here before.

It's just that he knows now that the first time he thought he might be in love, his map was inaccurate and his guidebook was missing several chapters. Sexual chemistry and genuine intimacy weren't the same thing; they just went hand in hand sometimes. With Jeff he'd had just one, but stupidly thought he had it all.

Making that mistake had gotten him so lost, so tightly wrapped around the ill-chosen center of his world, that when it was pulled away from him he'd gone spinning off into deep space. Risking that again fills his stomach with a nauseating terror.

But… Craig is not Jeff.

With Craig he has pancake breakfasts and slow dancing in the kitchen to Norah Jones and playful arguments and cozy dinners and laughing together in bed. He has someone who likes his photography and makes him elaborate desserts and doesn't make jellyfish-stinging backhanded compliments.

It's different this time, isn't it? All the evidence at hand tells his heart that this can be trusted, even as the back of his mind cowers from the very idea.

This is not... that.

He has to keep telling himself that. *This is not that.* One day it might even sink in.

But I can't forget... that.

That is what keeps the words locked up tight behind his teeth. *That* is why he can't sleep. *That* has never, ever left him for more than a minute or two at a time in the last several months.

He can't forget what brought him here, no matter how amazing *here* is, no matter his sudden awareness that Craig loves him, too. It keeps him on his toes, waiting for the other shoe to drop. Sometimes he thinks, *What if this becomes that?* And then he has to fight the urge to throw up.

Intellectually, he knows Craig would never... things wouldn't... *This is not that.* In a thousand ways, this is color over black and white, brightness over dark, a sunny precipice and not a deep, yawning pit. He knows, he *knows.* There is no mistaking what he saw in Craig's face last night. Having love isn't what terrifies him. It's the possibility of *losing* it that props his eyes open and sends ice through his veins. Because *this* is so much bigger than *that.*

This should be a safe place in every way. But *that* still lurks and could ruin everything, because anyone who deserves *that*—he had deserved it, hadn't he, for being so incredibly stupid?—isn't going to get to keep *this*, are they?

He's never going to get to sleep. Rolling over, Alex leans out of the bed and snags the strap of his camera bag. Long practice enables him to pull out his trusty Canon by feel and to power it on without having to turn on a lamp and wake Craig.

The low light will be tricky—the light at his place was better—but he can make it work.

Click. *This is not that.* Click. *This is not that.* Click. *This is not that.*

Alex only has the vaguest idea how any one of these photos might turn out, but he keeps going, shifting around the bed as quietly and as carefully as he can, snapping, snapping, snapping until the film runs out and he prays for luck.

If nothing else, he wants to capture one moment of *this* to have for himself no matter what happens.

Still quiet, still careful, Alex leans over Craig and places the camera on the end table with a near-silent click as plastic and metal meet wood.

This is not that.

He lets his hand fall to Craig's waist and his fingers splay half over sheet, half over warm brown skin. His first kiss falls on Craig's shoulder, pressed into the skin as if he could leave a brand behind with his lips.

The second kiss is a slow tracing of mouth from shoulder to neck; Alex brushes Craig's dreads aside and lowers himself over Craig to cover him as he touches and tastes. Craig squirms and rolls over under Alex, blinking in sleepy surprise. "Alex? What—"

Alex cuts him off with a third kiss, sliding up and over until he's nestled between Craig's thighs, fitting their hips together through the thin red jersey of the sheet. "Shh."

This is not that. If he could just not think for a little while—

The soft fabric between them provides gentle friction as Alex rolls his hips forward, groaning when Craig shifts up to meet him, half-hard and getting firmer with each slip of body against body.

The only sounds are skin on sheets, soft groans and harsh panting. Craig's hands cup Alex's face, and his leg comes up to hook behind Alex's ass, pinning them together and cocooning Alex in the stretchy give of the fabric.

He feels warm and loved and covered and surrounded and he doesn't want it to stop but he's still so—

This is not that. So scared.

Though he'd die before he willingly admitted it to anyone besides himself.

He rocks forward, his cock brushing Craig's, and he can't stop kissing Craig, it's always been his favorite thing, long kisses, sweet kisses, tiny lingering pecks and soft wet promises. Sometimes they taste like tea with milk and sugar, sometimes mint, sometimes whiskey and sometimes beer, sometimes like fresh buttercream frosting and sometimes like a middle-of-the-night spaghetti dinner.

He kisses Craig as if one day he'll wake up and never get to do it again, because he can't convince himself that isn't a distinct possibility.

Craig's hand slips down and over the sheet to wedge between their bodies and—"Fuck," Alex gasps, all he can even think when it encloses his cock. He is lost in too many sensations to count. With the first slow strokes he can't even kiss anymore, too helpless to do anything but rest his forehead against Craig's, with one hand cupping the side of Craig's head as his hips push, push and rock forward and his breath jerks out in harsh rasps.

I love—I can't —

Taut as a steel cable from fingers to toes, Alex comes hard into Craig's hand, spilling onto the sheet that separates them; his fingers curl into Craig's hair. Craig arches beneath him, too, one hand around Alex's jerking cock, the other digging short nails into the back of Alex's neck.

They collapse together, panting in a heap of soft sheets damp with sweat and come. Craig laughs softly and smacks a kiss onto Alex's forehead before flopping back down to his pillow. "Well. Good morning, babe."

"Um..." Alex is distracted by Craig's fingers brushing over his hair; the simple affection of the gesture makes his heart ache and brings all his turmoil back to the surface. It's so *easy* for Craig to be so loving and open, so fearless and generous and not locked away inside himself. "Yeah. Hey. Good morning to you, too."

"And thank you." Craig's smile is sleepy and sweet. "It's not every morning I wake up to a naked, camera-wielding photographer in my bed."

"I'm generally naked in your bed two mornings a week," Alex points out, letting light sarcasm stand in for the sincerity he can't handle. "Wait. You were awake?"

"Mmm." Craig's fingers trace back around the back of Alex's neck to tug him down, the better for kisses between words. "The camera was the new bit. And I wasn't awake, exactly. Somewhat aware for the last bit, I think. Didn't want to interrupt you with the photos." He lets out a yawn and stretches; one long leg breaks free of the sheet. "And then... well. Then I *really* didn't want to interrupt you."

No one makes him smile or laugh the way Craig can. That's got to mean something, doesn't it? Another check in the *this could never be that* column? If he counts up enough of them, can he convince himself?

Craig lets his laugh fade into a lopsided grin and runs a finger over Alex's mouth. "Feel free to wake me up like that more often. Quite enjoyable. If sticky."

"At your service." Banter is familiar. Innuendo is safe. "Maybe I'll make a game of it. You'll never know what I'll do or when I'll strike." Alex grinds against Craig just a little, just a hint, and raises an eyebrow. "I'll be a sex ninja."

Craig returns the eyebrow raise with interest. "Ooh. Something to look forward to. I like the way you think." He stops, looking thoughtful, bites his lip. "Although. Babe, those photos..."

"All mine," Alex hastens to assure. *Entirely mine.*

"Well, I didn't think you'd distribute them, of course. Just making sure they don't end up in the batch you send over to Sarita for the website." The raised eyebrow shifts into a pair of licentious, wiggling eyebrows, and Craig sticks out his tongue. "I mean, I think Theodora would probably go for it, but I'm not sure about the general dessert-buying public..."

"I don't know, a beefcake that sells cheesecake?" And when Craig laughs his big bright laugh at the ridiculous joke, it shakes the bed and runs through Alex like warm sunshine. He has to catch his breath before going on. "You might find your business increasing."

"Right, well, if times get bad, I'll bring up the idea to Theo and let her make the call." Craig stretches again. "Speaking of food. Alex, I am absolutely *starving.*"

"Starving?" The explosive laugh escapes before he can stop himself. "We got up in the middle of the night and ate all the spaghetti!"

Craig clicks his tongue in mock reproach. "*You* ate all the spaghetti. *I* was once again distracted by you sitting at my table, wrapped in nothing but my sheets." He waggles a cautioning finger. "I'm going to have to establish a dress code."

"Come on, Craig," Alex says, shifting his hips again into that lazy rolling motion that pulls a low growl from Craig's throat. "It's easier to resume fucking after dinner if neither of us had to dress for it."

Banter, distraction, sex, he knows his weapons and can use them against himself just as easily as he can anyone else. Anything to avoid the elephant only he sees.

Craig lets out a sharp gasp and arches. "You have a point... no, no, we're not doing that again. I actually am quite hungry. I think I could literally eat a horse." He shoves gently, enough to dislodge Alex and send him rolling back onto his side of the bed. "Please. Let's go get pancakes."

"Get pancakes?" Now he's as mentally off-balance as he is physically. The flipping over of their usual Sunday routine is abrupt, jarring on too many levels for Alex to handle well naked. "Like... go... out... for them?"

Okay, he sounds a little on the dumb side, but he'd rather sound dumb than let on just how quickly he filled with panic at the very idea of a Sunday pancake breakfast out.

Craig's forehead rumples into anxious creases. "I mean, I know we have a... sort of *thing* we usually do, and I feel terrible about it, but I baked a *lot* of cupcakes and muffins yesterday. Just... so many fucking cupcakes and muffins." Amazing how angelic and irresistible Craig can look just by widening his eyes and pouting. "Would you mind terribly if I outsourced our Sunday pancakes? Just this once?"

Alex goes still. They have breakfast together all the time. Well, twice a week. The difference between what they always do and what Craig is requesting is the *out* part.

Going out for Sunday breakfast... that's dangerously close to something a couple would do. It's not the same as their occasional dinners. Too much is happening, too fast and all at once. Everything he's pushed down and away and fought since January comes surging back to the surface.

Not a date.

There's a weakness in letting people in—

No, not a date, dinner. Ooh, scary, scary dinner.

It's just breakfast. Isn't it?

This is not that.

What happens if he just keeps moving forward, one step at a time?

He doesn't want to lose himself again...

One step isn't a marathon.

Craig waits, fixing Alex with a gaze that grows steadily more concerned as the seconds tick past, answerless and cavernous.

It's just breakfast.

Enough. If he can get through this and then go home and get some sleep, maybe he can get himself back under control. This doesn't even have to be a step. He's overreacting because he's tired and confused and he's making way, *way* too much of a simple request.

"No, no, let's do it, let's go get breakfast." Alex makes himself smile and stroke Craig's cheekbone with his thumb. "Absolutely. You worked hard yesterday, you deserve the break."

"Fantastic. I promise I'll make you a stack as tall as the Space Needle next week, really I will." After a quick kiss and smile, Craig rolls out of bed and heads into the bathroom. "I always make my own pancakes. Do you know anywhere we can get some decent ones?"

Alex considers as he sits up and fumbles a hand through his hair. "Maybe? There's a place I know in my neighborhood." He hasn't been there in a while, but he seems to recall the breakfast menu being relatively edible.

Clearly, being with Craig in whatever way he is with Craig has spoiled him.

The shower cuts on and Craig pokes his head out from the bathroom. "I think I can make the trek... if there's an incentive."

"More incentive than pancakes you didn't have to make?" Alex raises an eyebrow.

Craig makes a raspberry and beckons for Alex to join him in the bathroom. "Are the sheets on your bed cleaner than mine?"

"Lend me a clean T-shirt and some boxers," Alex shoots back, "and I can make that happen."

The laughter is a release, a full flood of relief, but Alex keeps the mantra running in his tired, overwhelmed mind.

This is not that… it's not, it's not…

Chapter Fourteen

"**W**ELL, IT SMELLS PROMISING, AT LEAST," CRAIG remarks as they join the crowd waiting to grab seats at the Finch. "I could absolutely murder a Danish. Just look at that display, they're the size of my head!"

"Uh huh." The sleepless night is catching up to Alex even more now, after the nearly hour-long attempt to get from Queen Anne to Capitol Hill. They'd missed the first bus, or it hadn't come at all—he can't quite remember, just knows it took far, far longer than it should have—and he wants nothing more than a seat in a booth and an entire pot of the coffee he smells brewing and, once breakfast is done, to drag Craig back to his apartment and use him as a body pillow while he sleeps the sleep of the dead.

It's highly unlikely that's what Craig had in mind when he agreed to come to Alex's neighborhood for breakfast, but honestly, that's just too bad. Good thing Craig does tend to be pretty agreeable when it comes to mutual napping. Christ, but he's tired.

There is a bonus to the exhaustion finally kicking in: Alex's turbulent emotions and circular thoughts have dissolved into an incomprehensible mush, overrun by the very clear and noisy reminder that his apartment, and by extension his bed, is just a few blocks away. All he has to do is stay awake through breakfast and then oh, sweet sleep.

He's actually starting to fantasize about it.

They had better get a shot at a booth soon. He's starting to hallucinate. He could swear that the person who just came through the door—

"Alex?"

No. Wait. Not a hallucination. *Fuck.*

Alex is caught, frozen, can't move, can't speak. His dry mouth refuses to spit out words of any stripe. Anger, courtesy, curiosity all desert him. In a moment he's wide awake again and surging with adrenaline.

He cannot react to the fact that Jeff—gorgeous, heartless Jeff—is standing in front of him for the first time in almost seven months.

Of course. *Of goddamn course.* The Finch is the one diner in Seattle he's ever gone to with any regularity, because it was once convenient to both his apartment and Jeff's. And of course he hasn't been here in months, because he's been avoiding most of the places he went with Jeff. And he's been working so hard to push everything to do with Jeff out of his life and thoughts that he'd managed to forget why he knew this place.

He'd been doing so well, until Craig's inquiry about where to get breakfast and Alex's worried exhaustion had let the Finch float to the surface of his mind. It had been the only answer Alex could have given—but it was the *worst* answer, and all of his nightmares are standing in front of him because of it.

Why did it have to be today that you wanted to go out for breakfast, Craig? We should never have left your apartment—I should have said no, should have Googled some other place; this goddamn city is full of diners. I should have volunteered to just go fucking get doughnuts, why didn't I go get doughnuts—

Alex is acutely aware that, though freshly showered and wearing clean clothes, he looks like hell because he hasn't slept in twenty-four hours. Jeff, on the other hand, is as perfectly assembled as ever: his golden skin smooth, his black hair impeccable, his facial hair neatly trimmed. He is also not alone—and his companion is just as polished and put-together, blond and blue-eyed and clean-shaven. They're like a coordinating set of expensive bookends in Ralph Lauren Casual Wear.

They both look happy and well rested, and Alex just wants to slap one of them. He's not picky about which.

He does not have the energy or the emotional fortitude to deal with this. Already, his stomach is knotting up, his heart is turning painful, slow somersaults in his chest. Hurt and anger start a slow burn low in his gut as each stinging memory resurfaces like a taunting bully.

He can't move. He absolutely cannot speak.

Jeff and his companion are exchanging uncomfortable glances when Craig breaks the long, awkward pause by extending a hand to Jeff. "Hi. Craig Oliver. Are you friends of Alex?"

"Ah..." Jeff puts on a faint smile. "I am, in a manner of speaking... I mean, it's been a while... I mean, yeah. We know each other. My name's Jeff. Jeff Arata."

Craig's eyes go wide and in his own peripheral vision, Alex sees the concerned glance Craig shoots in his direction. *Yes, Craig. That Jeff.* His jaw is beginning to ache from being so tightly clenched.

"I'm Kevin," volunteers the polished blond, extending his own hand for Craig to shake. "Kevin Henderson-Arata."

What? The hyphenated last name goes through Alex like an earthquake, almost kicking his already unsteady feet out from under him as he scrambles to process it. What the hell?

"Oh. You're... married?" Craig, no dummy, can put two and two together. His eyes are wide open, and Alex can just about see him counting back the months to January.

It's about eight, Craig. Yeah. It is a tastelessly short amount of time, given the circumstances of Jeff and Alex's split. Well, the circumstances of their entire not-quite-relationship, really.

At least Jeff has the surprising grace to blush when he drags his gaze up from his shoes to meet Alex's. *I didn't know he knew what shame was.*

"Met in December, married in March," Kevin cheerfully informs Craig, who looks like a startled owl. "My mother almost had a heart attack, it was so fast, but when you know, you know, right?"

December. How festive. Alex can't take his eyes from Jeff, who is turning redder by the moment and keeps letting his gaze slide away. *You asshole. You fucking jerk.*

Kevin is the only one who seems oblivious to the tension, going on about the apartment in Bellevue they'll be moving into next month, about his work as an accountant—"It's how we met! Jeff needed someone to get his books in order before tax season,"—about their whirlwind romance and wedding and honeymoon in Belize.

Belize. Did you rent the same cottage I fucked you in for five straight days before I caught you with a pool boy from the hotel down the beach?

When you hired a caterer for your wedding, was it that guy I found blowing you in the coatroom at that party your agent threw for your birthday?

Over and over, so many times Alex had lost count. So many other guys, and he could see them all so clearly in his memory because Jeff seemed to *like* getting caught, as if he was driving the point home: *We are not together.*

All of the fucking around had just made Alex try to hold on tighter.

All of the biting, sharp remarks about his photography—so many horrible little stings and cuts—had just made him put it away.

He'd quit smoking, resumed drinking, bought new clothes that he hated, kept his mouth shut about the seemingly endless parade of other men and, by the time a year was up, all he knew was that he didn't like himself or Jeff a whole lot, but for some unfathomable reason he still wasn't willing to let it go. He couldn't stop *trying*, tying himself into knots to be whatever Jeff was looking for.

He'd been so stupid.

"Ugh." Jeff rolled off Alex and stomped into the bathroom, coming back and tossing a bottle of mouthwash onto the bed. "Listen, babe, you're hot, but you know kissing you is like tonguefucking an ashtray, right?"

Every memory pierces with the sharpness of a needle stab in the soft crook of his elbow.

At Rave, on the dance floor, Alex shouting that he had to go in to the office in the morning. "Sure, go ahead, if you're tired. Ricky can keep me company." A sly glance from the sleek, dark-haired guy grinding up on Jeff's ass, a moment of uncertainty, a decision to stay.

Jeff went home with Ricky anyway.

He'd been like a dog that couldn't stop loving the master who beat him. Worse, he'd known it the whole time and still couldn't give up on Jeff. Jeff was like a drug, a habit he couldn't kick.

Then the habit had kicked him instead. If he hadn't stumbled, blind and shaken into exactly the right bar that night, he—

No.

Kevin finally falters to a stop in the middle of recounting their search for the new apartment and takes in Craig's horror and Jeff's difficulty meeting anyone's gaze. Alex can only imagine what he himself must look like when he snarls, "Did he ever mention me to you?"

Did he tell you he was fucking me while you were getting to know each other?

Did I even exist in your world before this moment?

Was I really nothing?

He knows the answer, of course, long before Kevin swallows, shakes his head and whispers, "I'm sorry, no."

Alex's stomach twists with the fresh reminder of harsh rejection, of not mattering.

It wasn't that he didn't want a relationship.

He just didn't want me. It didn't matter what I did.

Jeff takes a deep breath and attempts to redirect the conversation. "You have your camera bag," he comments, only the faintest shake in his voice as he keeps a wary eye on Alex and tries for amity. "Are you doing photography again? Is there anything I can see?"

But the *trying*, the *effort*, it's not a balm, it's a slap on a wound that is still too raw, too freshly patched with skin too thin to hold it together. Jeff's query tears it all open and leaves Alex rooted to the spot, with all the toxic memories burning like ammonia through his veins, erasing reason and logic and *this is not that.*

The last straw is Craig reaching to take Alex's hand. He *knows* it's meant to be supportive, meant to defuse the tension radiating from his entire body. Alex knows this.

But faced with everything that's haunted him for so long, Alex falls deep and fast into too many memories of Jeff pulling *his* hand *away*.

"We're in public. Someone could see and get the wrong idea."

When Jeff's fingers trace the strap of Alex's bag, all he hears is, *"It's all right work. It's not Leibovitz. I dunno, Alex. I don't think they'll want you to do the Urban Outfitters shoot if I show them this... it's so... it's amateur."*

And overpowering the growing mute apology in Jeff's eyes:

"So this thing's over, okay. I met someone." As if years of trying, bending, changing, hating, loving—as if it could be crumpled up and thrown away. As if *he* could be crumpled up and thrown away. A poisonous swell of panic overwhelms his mind and fills his stomach. Everything so hard-won in the last few months disintegrates under the onslaught.

I can't do this. I can't let someone do that to me again.

"I have to go," Alex chokes, and this time there's no room to wonder.

He tears his hand away, stumbles two steps—

And he runs.

⋈⋈⋈

SASHA. SASHA, COME ON, IT'S PEACH, PICK UP. PLEASE? I HAVE no idea what is going on. Craig looks like hell and isn't answering questions. I can only assume you look like hell too, and I would love to know why you aren't answering my calls or the door, oh my God. Nate and I are worried sick about both of you and we *will* get answers one way or another. Call us back or I'm going to call Aunt Marina and tell her you're sick. Do you really want to deal with your mother right now? You know she won't give up after a couple of knocks... call me.

⋈

CRAIG, IT'S SARITA. IF YOU DON'T FEEL UP TO COMING IN, YOU know that's all right, yeah? I mean, you don't look like you're sleeping enough, okay? And you're here every day, all day, so... Will and Tash and I can handle today. It's really not a big deal. Stay home. Oh—wait. You just came in. Okay. Bye, I guess.

⋈

IT'S CONNOR. IF YOU DON'T START RETURNING MY CALLS, I'M gonna start dropping in. I know something's wrong, dude. Not asking you what, but I'll be fuckin' damned if—okay, Rayna, sorry, yeah, I know Kira's starting to pick up stuff, sorry— listen, Al. I'm not letting you disappear again. Call me.

⋈

DARLING, IT'S THEO, GREETINGS FROM SOFIA! THE MOCK-UP OF the website is beautiful, perfect, exactly what I wanted. And those photos! Where did you find someone so good on our budget? I know people who would be very interested in working with him; you should remind me of his name. Oh! And I'm bringing home a sample of a Bulgarian cookie, I'll want you to add it to the shop inventory. Love and kisses, see you in a week.

꩜

A... ALEX? UM... I DIDN'T KNOW IF THIS WAS STILL YOUR number... it's Jeff. Shit. Okay. You probably knew that. Listen, you didn't look so good when you left the diner the other day. I just. I mean, I know it's rich coming from me, but I wanted to make sure you're okay. Wanted to check on you. Did your friend catch up with you? Give me a call, okay?

꩜

CRAIG, IT'S NATE. SAMMI ASKED ME TO CALL YOU AND INVITE you to dinner. She'll make anything you like. Come on, say you'll come, I bet you could use a break. Call us? We want to help, if you'll let us.

꩜

ALEX... PLEASE. PLEASE CALL ME BACK OR ANSWER THE PHONE, I don't care which. I just want to know you're all right. It's been a week since you ran off and I... please. Please call me. I don't want or need anything from you, babe, I just want to know that you'll be all right. I hope you're all right. Please.

꩜꩜꩜

Chapter Fifteen

"G ET OUT."

Craig pauses in the act of stepping over the threshold of Sucre Coeur, blinking at the greeting he's just received. "I beg your pardon?"

"Out." Theodora, back from her latest trek, does not look up from where she is perusing the account books, doesn't so much as flick a glance over the gold rims of her reading glasses before she points at the door. "Not another step, darling love, or you're fired. For a week."

"That's hardly... I didn't..." Exhaustion and confusion reduce Craig to sputtering protests. "You can't do that!"

"Can and will." Despite the threat, Theodora's gaze is soft when she does finally look up to face Craig; her smile is sympathetic. "Dear boy, any employee who falls asleep standing up while operating an electric cookie press is an employee who needs to rest."

Craig glares over the counter at Natasha, whose fair cheeks turn bright pink before she ducks her head in apology. "Sorry, Craig."

"Judas." Not that he really means it. He knows he's not himself lately, and certainly not up to par with his usual standards—waking up to Natasha's shrieks and a sprawling lake of thawing cookie dough all over himself and the center kitchen island proved that well enough yesterday. It's just...

He doesn't know what else to do to fill all the sleepless hours while he waits for a call, a text, an email, for any form of contact that just won't come.

It's been two weeks.

"Take a walk with me, Craig." Theodora picks up her purse and takes his arm. In two seconds her gentle but implacable shove propels him out of the bakery door and onto the sidewalk. "Let's chat."

With her arm tucked firmly in his, there is no way Craig can extricate himself without things becoming very awkward and possibly involving the police, so he sees little choice but to walk up the street with her, heading in the direction of their house. "I really would rather work," he tries, ignoring the urge both to yawn and to rub his eyes. "I'm fine, Theo."

"You look like hell," she replies, as casually as if she's just informed him of the time of day. "I would sincerely love to know the last time you slept through the night."

Two weeks ago. "Last night."

"For a professional storyteller, you have always been," Theodora drawls, with a shake of her blonde shag, "an absolutely atrocious liar, Craig my dear. Please do not forget that your apartment is the third floor of my home. I heard you pacing."

They stop at a crosswalk, and he takes the opportunity to level a glare at his employer, which, much to his annoyance, doesn't faze her one bit. "Is this sort of forthright meddling a Belgian trait or simply a Theodora one?"

Her only reaction is to raise one expertly groomed eyebrow. "I stand by what I say. You do look like hell. When did you last sleep a full night? Not any time recently."

Not willing to risk being caught out in another lie, he evades. "I can work."

"No, Craig. You can't." The white pedestrian light flashes; it's her signal to pull him across the street. "Everyone loves you, and they have done their very best to protect you, but they're worried, love. Will says if you're not at the shop, you're at some coffee shop or other pounding out reviews and articles. You've come in every day for two weeks, and on Saturdays you work open to close." She uncouples their arms to tick things off on her fingers. "Burned muffins, falling asleep standing up, inaccuracies in the account books... you're not in trouble, darling, but can't you please tell me what's wrong?"

He forces a smile. "I'm fine." *I'm not.* "Really, Theo. You know me, I just like to work hard."

"There's a difference between a good work ethic and driving yourself into the ground." The naked concern in Theodora's eyes is nearly too much to bear, as anyone's sympathy has been these last agonizing days. Pity is acid on his skin, worry a leaden lump in his throat. "What is going on?"

How can I possibly explain how the man I think is the love of my life literally ran away from me? Shouted at me, left me standing in the street and won't talk to me? Just thinking about it is a knife twist to the gut. Trying to talk about it has been like holding steel splinters on his tongue.

While not, generally speaking, a violent person, Craig has been entertaining images of visiting physical mayhem on Jeff Arata for two weeks. Because of course, this all goes back to Jeff. Craig doesn't know the whole story, but that part—that is crystal clear.

"Don't you get it, Craig? I'm doing you a favor. Get rid of me; you can trade up."

The story of what happened hurts like a broken bone and is full of holes. He hasn't managed to get it out yet.

Metal scrapes against flint, catching his wandering attention, and a licking tongue of flame nearly takes out a chunk of Theodora's hair as she lights a cigarette. "Do you really think I don't know a broken heart when I see it, Craig? Truly?"

He lets out a bitter laugh. Broken? Try shattered, pulverized, stomped into the sidewalk outside of a diner. *Broken* is the most basic, inadequate word he can find in his vocabulary to describe the state of his heart.

Theodora simply gazes at him sidelong as she pulls in a deep breath of cigarette smoke. "I don't think I've ever told you the story of Isabelle."

"You don't have to." His fists are tight little balls in his jeans pockets; his fingernails bite into his palms. It almost feels good, so he doesn't relax them. "It's all right, I don't need—"

"No, it's not a long story, and I tell it only so you know that I understand." The slender shoulder nearest him lifts in a shrug. "Isabelle was my first love. Sweet. Bright eyes, I remember those best. They spoke everything she felt. It's been... twenty years? Her eyes are nearly all I remember now, really. Blue as morning sky."

Craig says nothing. Theodora clearly has a piece to say, and so she shall. And then he'll go find a coffee shop and work on the slew of articles he wants to wrap up, if she's not going to let him work at the bakery.

Her eyes, though; he can still feel her eyes on him as she speaks. "We were sweethearts for a very long time. From school until we were... oh, into our twenties."

Now she stops; her gaze half on him, half on the pedestrian traffic, willing him to ask the obvious question. It's annoying, gets under his skin like barbed wire, but patience and a gimlet stare have always been Theodora's most effective weapons. He caves. "Fine, Theo, I can see where you're going with this. Why are you not with Isabelle now?"

One fine eyebrow rises high. "Put a bit of two and two together, Craig, love. Isabelle loved Theodore; she didn't think she could love Theodora. Which broke my heart into a thousand very small pieces." Her free hand swings down to pull at his, tugging it out of his pocket to give it a squeeze, the briefest fleeting pressure on his palm before she lets go. "I thought it would never stop hurting."

He doesn't want to open up, not now, maybe not ever. If he says too much it will pour out of him like gushing blood. "It never did, did it?"

Theodora rocks her head from side to side. "Yes and no. It hurts less now, so many years later. And I am secure in who I am. I have my lady friends here and there, and my bakery, and my little band of orphans and misfits taking refuge there." Her cheek dimples with her smile. "I can't tell you it never hurts, Craig, but it does become... oh, it gets to be a bit more manageable. If you don't lose yourself in hiding from it."

Annoyance flashes through him. "I'm not hiding."

"Tell it to someone who doesn't know better, darling. I did my share of hiding, and when I finally faced that Isabelle was truly gone for good, it hurt all the worse for having built up behind the wall I hid behind." She uses her cigarette butt to light another cigarette, then drops the spent butt and delicately steps on it with one gold-sandaled foot. "Obviously your problem is differently complicated, but at its root, it is the same. You have loved, and you have been hurt by this love; and Craig, you must either accept it or try to get it back. But you cannot simply bury yourself and wait for the hurt to subside. It's not practical, and besides, to the best of my ability, I won't let you."

"I just want to work, Theo." *I have to work.* The only reason Craig has been getting even the paltry, restless sleep he manages between nightmares is because he's exhausted at the end of every day from being on his feet baking endless trays of desserts or writing until he falls asleep on his laptop and wakes up to seventeen solid pages of YYYYY. The only way he can stop worrying about Alex is by throwing out all of his standard recipes and concentrating on creating a new menu of goodies while he checks the local bars for gigs he can review. All Craig has to fill the hours of aching loneliness and unhappy memories is the bakery and his writing.

Take one of those away and it can't be long before he actually goes mad.

Theo exhales in a long stream of acrid Gauloise smoke and shakes her head. "I can't, Craig. Just take a week. Rest, sleep, relax. Consider your hurts. Try to mend them, at least a little. Here." Rummaging in her purse, she pulls out a long envelope and a small box. "The cookie sample I told you about—it's a recipe called *medenki*—and your pay for the week, in advance. Do something fun."

Fun. Sure. "Theo..." he says softly. What words can he muster to make her change her mind, to shake down her surety that she understands what he needs? He knows what he needs. He needs to work.

"Not another word." She presses a finger that smells strongly of smoke over his lips. "Get home. Take care of yourself. You're quite important to me and to everyone who loves you."

For all the good it does me. Craig has to look down and swallow hard. *Don't cry in public. It's so undignified.*

It doesn't get any easier when Theodora cries out, "Oh!" and goes through her purse again to pull out another envelope. "I nearly forgot. That photographer—Alex, Sarita said? He's a friend of yours, isn't he?"

Apparently there was a limit to how much information his employees had given Theodora on his personal life. Craig doesn't know whether to laugh or have a nervous breakdown in the middle of the street. "Ah... yes?"

"I brought the check for the lovely work he did; he sent the final shots to Sarita last week. Maybe you can give it to him?" She holds out the envelope expectantly, shaking it a little when Craig doesn't take it. "If you're going to see him anytime soon, at least."

"Right, yes, of course." *I wish.* "I'll see that he gets it." *By mail, since he won't answer the phone, let alone the door.*

"I've got to get back and untangle the mess you've made of the books." Theodora plants a kiss on his cheek. "And I'll see you in a week—no sooner."

She disappears into the southward-trickling river of pedestrians, leaving Craig with an endless week ahead and no idea what to do with it.

With a sigh, he hitches his satchel more comfortably on his shoulder and resumes trudging back toward his apartment, empty silence and the least restful bed in Seattle. *I don't know what to do.* Alex won't answer his calls, Craig's forbidden to go to work, and the idea of a week alone with his thoughts spinning with helpless, unanswerable questions does not appeal.

He is so tired, and he knows so little and it hurts so much.

The street before him shifts and blurs, and he can see himself bolting out the door of the Finch after Alex. Remembers how it took a full block of running and shouting Alex's name just to get him to stop and turn around.

His eyes were what I think hell must look like.

He'd never seen anyone holding that much anger behind so fragile a barrier.

"Alex..."

A flinch, as if he'd been struck. "Go away."

Craig rocked back in surprise, as if the rebuff had been a physical shove. "What?"

"Go away. This—you and I—should never have happened."

He didn't understand—still doesn't—but he had tried, reached, pleaded —

But the walls were back up and Craig could not get through.

"Go away. Forget we met. He did."

"I'm not him—"

"I'm not fucking giving you the chance to be."

Craig's last sight of Alex was watching him turn and walk away. And that time, Craig let him go. He hadn't known what else to do or say.

He never would have let Alex go if he'd understood just how complete the break would be.

These are the memories he can't bear to spend a week playing over and over and over. Let his guard down for a minute and he will be flooded with images of gray eyes gone dark and hard, of words flung like stones.

"Did you think you could fix me, Craig?"

He can't do it. He will lose his mind if he has to try.

Craig blinks, holds his eyelids shut tight until the threatening tears recede and he can focus on his actual surroundings. *Seattle. My neighborhood. My home.*

His friendly neighborhood liquor store.

It's there on the other side of the street, dingy and small and, as he recalls, redolent of disinfectant and industrial bug spray. He's only been in a handful of times before, picking up wine for dinner parties and the like.

Now might be a good time to pay it another visit. Give himself something to do to keep the memories at bay.

Drawing back his shoulders, Craig marches across the street and into the shop. Within twenty minutes he's struggling up the stairs to his apartment with two plastic bags full of clinking glass bottles and a nebulous plan in his weary mind.

"CRAIG?"

If he could just move, unstick his feet from the sidewalk and run after Alex again, maybe this time—this time—maybe he can change the outcome—why can't he move?

"Craig!"

Craig jolts to full awareness when the shock of his elbow being shaken makes him squeeze the frosting bag clutched in his hands. "Shit!"

"Shit!" Samantha echoes, her bright red, sleeveless blouse liberally decorated with a large splat of pale beige buttercream. "This is new! I went to five vintage stores to find it."

"I'm sorry," Craig gasps. His heart races from the surprise and his fingers ache from squeezing the frosting bag so tightly. He blinks to clear his vision, startled to see that he'd drifted off while sitting at his kitchen table, in the middle of frosting a pan of cupcakes. His eyes are gritty and his neck has a crick from drooping at an awkward angle for three nightmare repetitions of that interminable sidewalk conversation, three times when he'd failed again to change what happened.

This is not his best moment.

Sarita's fingers come around to loosen Craig's fingers from the frosting bag and tug it away. "Hi there."

"You too?" The yawn escapes him before he knows it's coming. "God. How long—"

"We just got here; we ran into Sarita at the door downstairs and did the whole introduction thing. Nate was worried because you weren't picking up the phone or answering texts, and he has a key, so..." Samantha's eyes widen as she gazes around the room, noting that every available surface is covered in trays of baked goods. "I guess I see why the concern."

Craig can't stop yawning. *So tired.* "I got on a roll."

"And a muffin, and a cupcake, and a tart..." Nate, too, is wide-eyed, taking everything in from the sink, where he is dampening a cloth for Samantha. "Oh my God, Craig."

Craig stretches and lets the stretch pull him up to a standing position. He winces as his back and legs protest. He must have been out for a while. "What? I'm a baker. I bake. That's what I do."

"Yes, but your apartment has finite space, and it was approaching critical mass *before* we all arrived." Samantha walks over to meet Nate at the sink, takes the cloth from him and dabs at her blouse. "What the hell are these things?"

Ugh. He's never going to get the crick out of his neck. Craig rubs at the sore spot and squints across the room. "Ah... Black Forest cake pops soaked in kirsch and dipped in chocolate."

"Really?" She surveys the tray, picks up a pop and takes half of the confection into her mouth in one bite. "Oh, God, that's good."

As Sarita absently massages Craig's neck, her free hand waves at two trays of cupcakes frosted in the beige buttercream. "Cupcakes?"

"Dirty Girl Scout Cupcakes." At their blank looks, he elaborates. "They're made with Kahlúa, crème de menthe and Bailey's."

Nibbling at the other half of her cake pop, Samantha peeks into the fridge. "Good lord, Craig."

Craig sighs. "Brandy snaps, blueberry bourbon cheesecake tarts, rum blondies. I used the rest of the Kahlúa in the chocolate chip cookies in the jar by the toaster, and there's a lemon vodka bundt cake in the crisper drawer."

Samantha raises an eyebrow as she closes the fridge door. "Was there anything in the crisper drawer *before* your boozy cake took up residence?"

"The apples I used for the amaretto apple pie cooling on top of the fridge," Craig admits.

Sarita's hand stops its efforts to work the kink out of Craig's neck. "Holy shit, Craig."

"Did you just..." Nate waves a hand around the kitchen again. "Did you spend the entire day drowning your sorrows not in *drinking* alcohol, but in making dessert with it? As in, this is your coping mechanism?"

A glance out the window shows Craig that it's quite dark out. Huh. He'd started this morning, hadn't he? "What time is it?"

"After seven," they inform him, nearly in unison.

Craig shrugs. "Then yes, I suppose that's exactly what I did."

Sarita stares at him for a moment and then shakes her head. "Okay, that's it," she announces. "We got here just in time. Step away from the binge baking."

"Well, as it happens, I had stopped for the night already." *Only because I ran out of flour and eggs, but you don't need to know that.*

"Step away for a few days, she means." When Nate crosses his arms and lifts his chin, Craig recognizes the signs of his friend preparing for battle. He's seen them so many times—it's rather interesting to see them deployed against himself. "We're supposed to take you over to her place."

Interesting, and slightly frightening. But Craig's parents did not raise him to be a coward, thank you. He draws his shoulders up, ignoring the twinge of pain in his neck. "Ah, no, I don't think I will."

An arch giggle escapes Samantha. "Really? Because I came prepared to drug and kidnap you if—"

"Sammi, oh my God, no, I told you we're not doing that, what is wrong with you?" Nate turns to Craig with a horrified look. "I swear, I did *not* come here to drug and kidnap you, Craig. I thought the plan was to ask you *nicely*." He levels a glare at Samantha that would wither a lesser woman.

"That was before we saw him turn a five hundred square-foot studio into a... a... pastry speakeasy," Samantha protests.

"The *civilized* invitation still stands." Sighing, Nate returns his attention to Craig. "Please, Craig. You need to get out of here; seriously, you need out of this place. For a couple of days at least. We want to help."

It's too much to bear. Craig steps away and into the kitchen area, heading for the sink full of dishes he'd been counting on to keep him occupied for the rest of the night. "I very much appreciate the offer, but as you can see I have quite a lot to do here, and I have to work tomorrow—"

"No, you don't," Sarita says. Her voice is soft, but it stops Craig in his tracks, frosting-streaked mixing bowl in hand.

He forces a laugh. "Of course I do."

"No, Craig. Tomorrow's Sunday. You don't usually work on Sundays." It's Nate's turn again; his voice has gentled even further, as if he were talking to a nervous animal. "And anyway, Theodora called me. I know you're off for the next week."

All right, that's a shock. Craig turns to stare at his ex. "Theodora what?"

"Nate's your emergency contact, Craig. Remember? She called him to make sure we kept you out of the bakery and made you rest," Samantha chimes in, her sharp edges softening and game shifting from authoritative belligerence to logic, kindness and sympathy as quick as a flash. "She sent Sarita as backup, actually."

Sarita nods, one cheek dimpling as she gives Craig a tiny, sad smile. "It's true. Sorry... although I'm not, really."

Nate doesn't pipe up again; he just stands by Samantha, looking at Craig with the face of someone who knows him all too well and sees right through to the part of Craig that can't hold itself up alone much longer. Nate's desire to help is palpable.

In Craig's overworked, hurting, weary state, this is devastatingly effective. His hands drop to his sides, and the frosting bowl knocks against his leg and probably gets bits of buttercream all over his jeans. He doesn't care. There's no more fight in him, no more stoicism.

He's just so *tired* and even a bit angry, and everything hurts so much.

They're all staring. Patient. Waiting. And they outnumber him three to one. Craig shakes his head. "Yeah. Okay. That sounds good."

"Two more."

The bartender's eyebrow goes up and he stops mopping up a puddle of melted ice on the bar. "No."

With determined focus and a few bleary blinks, Alex can just about merge the bartender and his twin back into the single being he'd been three tequila slammers ago. "I want two more."

"It's nine o'clock and you've had ten tequila slammers in two hours. You should be unconscious. Forget it. I'll give you water—you can have plain, you can have sparkling, I'll put a lemon slice in it, whatever." A quick motion makes the two—four?—empty shot glasses in front of Alex disappear. "But you're cut off from alcohol."

Alex fumbles for his wallet. "I have money."

A glass of seltzer with lemon appears in front of him. "Doesn't matter, buddy. No more alcohol. Feel free to tip, though."

He wants to be angry. Wants to throw the water into the bartender's face—faces? still two of them—and get himself dragged out of Laser kicking and punching, making a scene, letting profanity rip its way out of his throat to give vent to the anger and frustration seething through his veins. He wants to hit someone, something, wants blood and scraped skin and the dull ache of bruises.

The skin he wears is too tight for everything it has to contain.

But Alex's life now is a case of the flesh crawling while the spirit is exhausted. He has no energy to *be* angry, has nothing but the motivation to sit in his own self-loathing and think of ways to numb how much everything hurts.

In two weeks of trying, he's done nothing but fail.

After leaving Craig standing shocked and speechless, Alex had gone straight to his apartment and hadn't emerged more than once for a week.

Work was taken care of by calling in sick. "Bronchitis," he'd croaked into the phone in a voice ravaged by taking up smoking again for the first time in a year. It lent a certain verisimilitude to the excuse; no one questioned him about it.

Living in one of America's larger cities meant that a steady supply of food was a mere phone call away, God bless freedom and takeout guys. Not that he felt like eating much of the time. A carton of cigarettes and three bottles of Cuervo Especial Silver purchased early in his hibernation helped see him through the better part of seven nights lying on his living room floor in the T-shirt and boxers he'd borrowed from Craig, staring at the ceiling and trying not to think.

The next Saturday he cleaned his apartment, went out and did laundry, sat at his computer to complete his work on the Sucre Coeur photographs, sent them to Sarita and—because he'd spent two hours feeling his heart contract sharply whenever a photo of Craig came up and because by now he was out of his own supply of Cuervo—went to Laser and got *astoundingly* drunk.

This last tactic he has repeated every night this week.

He could, of course, buy a fresh supply of alcohol to keep at home. He doesn't have to go out. There's a liquor store near his building; there's no real reason he has to go out except—just drinking isn't enough to erase the last look he'd seen on Craig's face.

He had tried. *Is* trying.

Hurt. Shock. Bewilderment. It's all burned on the surface of his mind and it's nothing Alex wanted to be the cause of, nothing Craig deserved. Every day is a reminder to Alex that he was nowhere near good enough for what Craig was offering, had given him. No one who causes that kind of pain out of his own selfish need could ever be good enough.

After all, he hadn't even been good enough for Jeff—to love and be loved by Craig was a fever dream, a fantasy, the sun he'd flown too near.

Pushing the memories as far away as he can manage, Alex gets up from the bar and ignores the seltzer water in favor of circling the dance floor, peering through the lasers, prowling the perimeter, skimming over the men on offer. It's a Saturday night; he can slip into his old self as easily as changing clothes, and the possibilities range before him, ripe for the picking. He could have any of them—for the night. Not even that long, if he prefers.

Temporary, transient, fleeting and anonymous. Once upon a time those had been his words to live by. Time to reclaim them—there's safety in their impermanence, and his heart never has to be on the line. Rejection isn't a weapon, as it could be in Craig's hands, as it was in Jeff's.

And it's better that way, he reminds himself, gritting his teeth against the forced sincerity of the thought and gazing with more focus at the dance floor.

His attention is caught when lights strobe off of a gleaming, shirtless stretch of golden-tanned skin. It's held when eyes like liquid night meet his gaze and a wicked little smile full of promises tilts a generous mouth.

The guy is practically glued to a sexy Latin boy with fluid hips and a tight body, but he turns away easily enough when Alex pushes through the crowd and slides a hand up his arm. Words aren't needed; Alex makes sure his body language promises where the hot Latino only teased, slipping his hands under the waistband of his dance partner's jeans, letting his fingers grip and knead an ass so tight—

"Everyone's watching, Alex."

"Like you care. Want you... we didn't finish in the shower..."

"I told Samantha we'd meet them upst—oh."

"We should go back to my place."

"It would be... ah... rude... we've hardly seen... mmm... you make it... damn it, Alex... difficult to say no..."

Alex forces his eyes open and the thought away—he's getting good at shoving memories under the surface of his consciousness since he has to do it so much. Too much. Everything reminds him of Craig.

Determined effort lets him return the smile of the stranger whose ass is literally in his hands. Alex plasters himself against the guy, running his fingers up and over the sweat-slick, well-built chest in front of him. They're so close, there's no mistaking the guy's hard-on as it grinds against Alex's, short-circuiting his pleasure receptors and wiping out everything but *want*.

It's hopeless to try for conversation with some dubstep monstrosity nearly rupturing the speakers. "Upstairs?" he mouths with a tilt of his head towards the second floor mezzanine.

A smile is the only answer he gets, but that's okay—it's also the only answer he needs. After a week of this, he is practiced once more in the pick-up, in the silent question, in reading the responses. *Like riding a bicycle*, he thinks, and ignores how this churns in his stomach with too much tequila and no dinner to speak of.

Hand in hand, they thread their way through the undulating mass of dancers and up the stairs to the second floor alcoves. Saturday means most of them are occupied—couples, trios, fucking, handjobs, nearly every possible permutation of bodies that can fit in the snug hook-up spaces are hard at work, pursuing as many illicit public acts of sexual gratification as they can in as short a time as possible.

There's one alcove available, and Alex snatches it from under the nose of a disgruntled twink who'd been about to drag what looked like a virtual clone of himself into the dark little nook. The apologetic smile Alex tosses over his shoulder as he hustles his hook-up into the alcove is far from sincere, and the twink twins look as if they want to start shit over it, but when his selected stranger pushes him down on the bench and straddles his lap, Alex doesn't really care.

The only thing that matters right now is erasing Craig.

Dark eyes glitter in the dim backlighting of the alcove as his hook-up of choice eyes him up and down, seeming to take his measure. He appears to like what he sees—he licks his lips and smiles before speaking for the first time. "Want me to blow you?"

It takes all of Alex's self-control to not wince. Not a good start. The voice is all wrong, the words crude, the offer too direct. Alex tries to ignore his distaste, tries to remember that perfunctory, meaningless sexual gratification works like this, tries to remember that there was a time he liked it and thought it was fun.

That doesn't mean that he can't have *some* standards, however. "Don't talk," Alex orders, then tilts his head back against the wall and pulls the guy's head down into a sloppy kiss. He's found it's an effective way to shut people up and get on with the fucking.

But this, too, is wrong; their mouths don't quite line up, there's too much spit, too much tongue, too much of the taste of Southern Comfort. The guy is going after Alex's tonsils with all the subtlety of a jackhammer, groaning like a D-grade porn star into Alex's mouth. It's not hot, it is not even in the general vicinity of hot. Alex's dick slowly flags and he doesn't think about the true reason why. *Clearly I did not pick the best option on the floor… fuck it, I'm not psychic. A dick is a dick is a dick. Right?*

There's got to be a way to rescue this. Tonight he is going to make this happen. Alex nudges the guy away, wriggling until he's on his knees on the bench. "Like this." He leans forward to lick up the guy's neck before biting gently down on the taut cord of muscle at the curve, making his hook-up shudder and gasp. He tries his best not to think when he wedges his hand down a stranger's jeans, tries not to flinch from what he finds there. It's *all* wrong, nothing fits, nothing's right—

"Yeah, I can do that," the guy breathes when Alex's hand closes around his cock. "You like that, I can do that—" He fumbles at Alex's fly, tucks his head into the crook of Alex's neck and starts mouthing at it—

No. He can't do this.

"Stop. Fuck." It's the wrong lips on his neck, the wrong hand trying to shove its way into his jeans, even the breathing is wrong, wrong, all of it is just fucking not what he wants and it's too much *wrong* to handle, just like it always is. "Fucking— get off me."

"What the shit, man?" The guy backs off with a shove that makes Alex's head thump against the fabric-covered wall, and for a second he sees stars. "You don't want this? You brought me in here, you dick."

"It's not—no—" Between the tequila and the bump to the head, his thoughts are choppy waters, impossible to navigate. He shifts back down to a sitting position, his knees aching. "I thought—I can't—"

The guy squares his shoulders and rolls his head to crack his neck. "So we're not fucking doing this? Are you kidding me?"

His heart's in his throat, but Alex presses on. "Get out," he chokes, cupping the back of his head in his palm and blinking away tears that cover every type of pain he's felt in the last week. If he lets them fall, they could flood the building.

"Fine, whatever. I don't have time for this. Bye, asshole." Shoving his way out of the alcove, the stranger is gone, mumbling, "Fucking cocktease," and disappearing into the crowd before the curtains swing shut. Alex closes his eyes and leans his head against the alcove wall; pain swirls in bright colors against the dark of his eyelids.

He keeps failing. Over and over and over, he tries so hard to erase Craig, and he fails.

It's not just Craig's face he wants to erase. It's every touch, every golden, warm memory, every gentle word and generous gesture he needs gone. He wants the toxic acid of excess and carelessness to eat away at every bright moment of the last eight months until there's nothing left that makes him want to go running back.

But alcohol isn't wiping out the memories, and whenever someone touches him it's as if they're only covering Craig's handprints—they can't get through, their touch doesn't sink in. He feels only Craig's touch; the hands of strangers are out of place on the stretched-thin surface of his skin. Lips don't fit, no one sounds right, and it's too much to bear to think about how wrong all of them have tasted...

He wants Craig, and only Craig, but he can't, he just can't, there's too much to risk. If just thinking he was in love could tear him into pieces, he doesn't want to know the damage real love could do.

He doesn't know if he could survive it going wrong.

Opening his eyes, Alex winces away from the strobes flashing in through the cracks of the curtains. He'd hit the back wall harder than he thought when his spurned hook-up shoved him; he's going to have the mother of all hangovers in the morning.

And yet—it still won't hurt worse than not having Craig.

Alex staggers to his feet and pushes through the curtains, stumbles out of the alcove into the upstairs crowd. Cheers and jeering ring out around him, but he ignores all of it and focuses on getting himself down the stairs and out the door into the humid night.

Some shade of this has gone down every single awful night this week—a couple of the guys took his failure with grace, squeezing his hand and making him think they might understand everything going wrong in his life. Others were slightly less charitable, glaring at him and scoffing as they shoved out of the alcove as if they couldn't get away fast enough. One kept trying to turn his choked out *no* into a *yes*, offering drinks with a slimy persuasion that finally sent him fleeing for home to huddle under the steaming hot spray of his shower for over an hour.

And then there was tonight.

This isn't working. Can he do nothing right? He used to be so good at fucking up, at letting himself fall into his bad decisions and enjoy the ride, and it didn't matter who got hurt because none of it was permanent, right?

He wonders now, with no little sense of self-loathing, what sort of wreckage he'd left in his wake. It had to have been substantial to earn him the karmic bitch-slap that was Jeffrey Arata. And then the extra bonus of being unable to let go of Craig, having to carry around all the good memories and the one final, heart-wrenching image of Craig's face—so hurt, so confused, and yet somehow still completely loving and full of worry for Alex despite all of the horrible words tumbling from Alex's mouth.

Alex groans and all but collapses under the weight of the memory; he sits on the curb with his swimming head cradled in his hands. Seattle heaves and breathes all around him, lights and car horns and the murmurs of passing pedestrians, a city that is alive nearly every hour of every day. Right now, he would give his entire world for it to fall silent for one second so he could find one clear thought in his aching head.

Any thought other than, *If I weren't such a coward, I could go back to him.*

"Too bad I am a coward," he grumbles, pressing the heels of his hands against eyes that seem to have developed a slow, damp leak. Because it doesn't matter, now, that he's found both the time and the desire for love, does it? His fingers are too clumsy to hold it; his heart is too walled up behind fear to let it in; his entire existence is completely undeserving of it. He'd taken the leap, jumped as hard as he could and missed the other side of the canyon by *that* much.

Alex struggles back to his feet, brushes off his jeans and lights a cigarette as he resumes his stumble homeward. His apartment will be dark, his bed empty, his heart aching around its hollowed-out center. He tries for the millionth time to convince himself that it's best that way, that pancakes and mellow blues and laughter and warm, sweet, slow sex on a Sunday morning are nothing but stepping stones paving the way to his own ruin.

This is not that...

But *this* could become *that.*

Love is just a weakness.

But God help him, part of him has never wanted to give in to weakness so much in his entire life; it's shouting louder all the time and he can't seem to drown it out.

Chapter Sixteen

*T*HIS IS RUDE.

Craig glares from his perch on a severely overstuffed and flower-festooned sofa, where he's been since he was unceremoniously dragged from his apartment. In Sarita's kitchen, his friends are chatting and laughing with no cares in the world: Samantha stirs a large pot of chicken cacciatore she's thrown together. Nate pops open a bottle of wine. Sarita puts away the last of the desserts they hauled over from his apartment. They're all getting along like the proverbial house afire.

And he is abandoned on the sofa. They haven't even offered him a glass of wine. He's been sitting here for at least an hour, watching them, and nothing. Granted, he hasn't volunteered a word in all that time. He was in shock for a good long while after their arrival, and it took a while to pull himself together. Then he kept himself busy putting his thoughts in order, sorting his priorities.

Oh, were his priorities ever sorted. They weren't going to know what hit them.

His friends seem oblivious to any impending storm. "I'm going to be popular at the faculty in-service on Monday with those Kahlúa cookies," Samantha remarks as she at last wanders over to hand Craig a plate of the chicken cacciatore and a glass of white wine. "I don't know how much planning we'll get done for the school year, but boy, will people be happy about it."

"Uh huh. Just leave me some of those cheesecake tarts." Nate flops down next to Craig with his own food and wine. "Ooh, comfortable couch. Hey, maybe we can put in a movie, Sarita? What do you have?"

"Oh, shut up. Have either of you heard from him at all?" Craig snaps, slapping priority number one on the table before they can get started with another round of tedious small talk. He is wide awake. Leaving his apartment hasn't meant leaving behind the elephant in the room, and he is tired of pretending not to notice it.

They all stare at him for a moment, and then—"Oh thank *God* you finally brought it up, I was going out of my mind," Sarita breathes. "Craig, what the hell happened? You two were fine when I left the bakery for my grandfather's party? And that was just two weeks ago."

He ignores her for the moment—he'll ask the questions, thank you, and she won't have answers—and turns to Samantha, not even trying to hide his naked desperation. "I need to know." Setting down his plate, he grabs her free hand. "Samantha, please. If he'd talk to anyone, it's you; you're his cousin, his closest friend."

But Samantha shakes her head so that the heavy fall of her hair drops around her face to hide her expression. "Not a word. I mean, I'm not too worried, since I'm *his* In Case Of Emergency person and we haven't heard anything from the police or Aunt Marina. Which is good, since I don't think we have bail money—"

"But he won't talk to you either. No wonder you're with me and not him." Craig drains half a glass of Chardonnay in a long gulp. "Fantastic. I really thought…"

Samantha and Nate exchange glances. "I'm sure you know we've tried," Nate begins, fidgeting with his fork. "Sammi's gone every other day to bang on his door. I've called. We both have."

"And he's not answering anything. Yeah. I know." Despite Samantha's assurances about not hearing from the police, Craig feels no better. He misses Alex, and he's worried about him, and there is nothing at all reassuring about any of this. "Fuck, I hate this, I hate all of it."

"What *happened*, Craig?" Sarita tries again, leaning forward to touch Craig's knee. "All we know is that something is going on, and we only know that because you look like you've been dragged through a hedge backwards, and you have for the last two weeks." She sits back up and hesitates. "I mean, you baked two dozen strawberry cupcakes for the Jensen birthday party three days ago, you know?"

He glares. "Yeah? It's my job? What?"

She bites down on her lip. "Craig… Sarah Jensen is, like, amazingly, deathly allergic to strawberries. They ordered chocolate cupcakes. We really had to scramble to fix that—we didn't tell Theodora about it, though."

All he can do is stare. Christ, he really has lost the plot, hasn't he? But where can he begin? Even he doesn't know the whole story.

What he does know is bad enough. And as much as this will hurt…

What if his friends can help him make any sense of it, as they seem to believe they can? Certainly holding it so close to himself has helped nothing. And if he's to break his silence with anyone, these three are the most fitting choices.

One day he'll think about how very peculiar it is that they are the best candidates to help him work out this problem. One day.

In the meantime, Craig closes his eyes and dives in. "Well. The last time I saw or spoke to Alex... we had an amazing night together, and the next morning we went out to breakfast... and we ran into Jeff and his husband."

"Husband!" The generous mouthful of Chardonnay that Samantha has just taken into her mouth only narrowly misses being spat across the room. At the last second she swallows it and instantly launches into a red-faced coughing fit. Nate scrambles to rub her back until she can breathe again. Cheeks still pink, she stares at Craig with gray eyes as wide as dinner plates. "Say that again?"

"Husband." Craig can only shrug, which probably looks a lot more casual than he feels, especially facing those eyes that look too much like Alex's. "We ran into them at this diner, and Alex just... he froze. He just froze and he looked so *awful*, and it *was* really awful, and... and then he ran out."

"And you went after him, right?" Samantha's eyes are still huge over the rim of her wine glass as she raises it for another, more moderate sip. Nate is staring with his mouth open, oblivious to the fact that he's shaking his head in tiny, disbelieving increments.

"Of course I went after him." It comes out as more of an angry bark than Craig had intended, but he's been reliving the worst morning of his life over and over without relief for two weeks and now he has to re-enact it. Yes, this could be helpful and cathartic, and maybe they'll all have some good advice or insight, but that doesn't make it hurt any less at fucking all. "I went after him and…"

"And…" Nate and Samantha look as if they're both bracing themselves for the worst. Well, they are probably well acquainted with the worst Alex can dish out. Right now, Craig wishes they'd given him a little warning. It wouldn't have changed a single thing he's done, but at least he might have been prepared.

He is a prize idiot. Hindsight is twenty-twenty in the most unwelcome of ways.

"And… he let me have it. Told me to get lost, basically. That he was doing me a favor, that we should never have happened…" His stomach is full of rusty nails and tinfoil. "Well. Essentially, he panicked, and he trampled right over me."

Samantha's face falls. "I should have told you he could be so…"

"Too bad you didn't." Craig pours the rest of his wine down his throat. "I should've paid better attention anyway, as it turns out."

From her perch in a nearby chair, Sarita clears her throat. "Um… I'm so sorry. I don't mean to bother you, really I don't. It's just I'm still in the dark here, a bit? I mean, I get that you and Alex had a fight," she clarifies, cupping her wineglass in her hands. "And I hate to twist the knife in the wound, but, um, without me being too nosy, can anyone fill me in on who Jeff is?"

Though she doesn't mean to twist the knife, Sarita's question does exactly that. Craig can't speak. There's not another word he can say, not about Jeff. All he really knows is that this is all Jeff's fault, and he would dearly love to strangle the bastard for it.

Samantha picks up the conversation with a peal of bitter laughter. "Who is Jeff," she sniffs, pouring herself another glass of wine. "Fucking Jeff. Jeff the Jerk. Jeff the *Married* Jerk, apparently, that undeserving son of a bitch. I could shoot him right now, I really think I could."

"Yeah, Sammi, they don't allow curling irons and vintage-style heels in prison; let's not, okay?" Nate rubs Samantha's back again and turns to face Sarita. "Jeff is... he's kind of Alex's ex. And nobody likes him. Well, I guess his husband does. Okay, I don't get that." He shifts again to face Craig. "Someone liked him enough to marry him? How does that work?"

"I'm supposed to know? I just met the guy!" Craig dumps the rest of the wine into his glass and drinks it down. "I don't like him, tell you that much. I didn't before, but I might hate him now."

Nate shakes his head and looks back at Sarita. "Anyway. Jeff is a jerk, and he really treated Alex like shit, but Alex had a massive thing for him for years. And then... I guess he didn't, and he met Craig, here."

Sarita still looks a little lost, but she nods. "I think I understand enough. God, Craig. I'm so sorry."

All Craig can do is shrug. He's sorry, too. Sorry for all of it, all the way back to the beginning. What good does that do?

They sit in silence, refilling their glasses from a new bottle of wine and resuming dinner. Samantha seems to be ticking through thoughts. And sure enough, when the silence is broken, Samantha's is the first voice heard. "It's weird, though," she mutters through a mouthful of pasta.

"What is?" Craig's not really eating, just poking at his plate.

"Eat," Samantha demands, all schoolteacher, pointing with her fork as if prepared to use it offensively. She chews the last of her bite and goes on. "This whole thing. It's just so weird. It has always *been* weird, from the first day Alex met Jeff." She pauses, clearly searching for words, swaying her fork back and forth like a pendulum while she thinks. "Honestly, Craig. Truth time. We've never told you, but... this Alex? Your Alex? He's not the same Alex I grew up with. He's not even the same Alex that Nate met when Nate and I got together, and that was, what, baby, five years ago?"

It looks as if Craig might get some of the insight he'd hoped for, but so far it doesn't make much sense. "What do you mean?"

"Don't get us wrong." Nate leans forward, painfully earnest. "This Alex—your Alex—when he's being, you know, sane, I like him a lot. Not that I ever didn't like him—"

"What is this *my* Alex business?" He'd laugh if it weren't so frustrating. "Are you saying he's like Dr. Jekyll and Mr. Hyde?"

Nate wobbles his hands as if he's balancing objects in them and makes a face. "It's not that far off—sort of."

Okay, now Craig does laugh. "That's ludicrous."

"You are literally the second relationship he has ever had in his life," Samantha says bluntly.

What? Craig is stunned. "I... but... no. He's twenty-five years old, for the love of God." He knows age is a ridiculous argument but... well, really. Really?

"And Jeff, wonderful Jeff whom we all loved just like crazy—" Samantha's gritted teeth give the lie to the sentiment, "Jeff was his first boyfriend. If you can call whatever they had a relationship—if you can call Jeff a boyfriend. Which, no, I'm not going to dignify it by calling him that. But Jeff was definitely the first long-term thing Alex's ever, ever been in."

Her face is as sober and solemn as Craig has ever seen it, all traces of pixie-ish mischief flown quite entirely away; oh, God, she means it.

Samantha looks at him carefully before going on. "Before Jeff, before you... okay. Bluntly speaking? He started college at the University of Oregon and slept his way through half of Portland's gay male population. Probably a lot of the straight ones, too—he was that confident. Charming, when he wanted or needed to be."

"No one ever knew what hit them," Nate adds. "We'd go visit him in Oregon and go with him to parties, and it was like watching a series of surgical strikes. He never, ever slept alone and never with the same guy twice. Same thing when he came back to visit, he rarely slept on our couch because he'd just about always find someone."

"When he transferred back here, he calmed down, kind of—I think the workload of adjusting to the new school helped with that." Samantha looks as though she regrets helping to open this Pandora's box, and Craig almost wishes they hadn't, too. Nothing he's hearing squares with what he knows of the Alex he loves. But he can't help but listen, almost spellbound, as Sammi goes on. "And of course, by then, he'd met Jeff on one of those weekends he didn't spend on our couch. Which is why he moved back here in the first place, and let me tell you how *so very happy* Uncle Dieter—his dad, I mean—was about *that*."

Craig isn't entirely surprised by any of these facts, but the scope of the revelations is a bit of a shock. "Why didn't you tell me any of this?"

"Because he was happy with you," Samantha says, very simply. "And him actually being happy is a lot better than the manic, fake happy we saw a lot of the time when he was with Jeff, so we didn't... there didn't seem to be much point in telling you that he used to be a serial one-night stand kind of guy and, frankly, a douchebag. I love him, you know he's like my brother, but seriously. He could be a real jerk."

Okay. This is a lot. Craig gets up to go in search of another bottle of wine, trying to ignore the feeling of everyone's eyes on his back. *I hadn't expected this.*

He doesn't mind it at all—he's not a virgin, he's had his share of one-night stands, of course, that's how he's spent his own twenties—but it's still not completely slotting into place. Although... sometimes... certain mannerisms and memories... Craig can see how it might have been a thing. He can match traces of this devil-may-care Alex with the closed-off, cautious Alex he knows. Only traces, but they help to make Alex's behavior a little less incomprehensible.

What they don't do is explain their current situation. Craig locates a fresh bottle of Chardonnay in the refrigerator, pops the cork and refills his glass. He has to take a nerve-calming swallow before he can breathe in and face the peanut gallery in the living room. "Then what?"

"Then things got weird," Sammi finishes, getting up to put her plate and Nate's into the sink. She reaches for the wine, but Craig keeps a death grip on the neck of the bottle. Stepping back, she raises her hands in a gesture of surrender and goes for another bottle.

Samantha fiddles around with the new bottle, uncorking it, refilling her glass and puttering over to refill Nate's and Sarita's. When she ducks into the refrigerator to pull out the amaretto apple pie, Craig loses patience. "Weird how, dammit?"

Pausing in the act of setting the pie down on the counter, Samantha looks surprised. "Well, Jeff was around all the time even more when Sasha moved back here. Which was new. Very, very new."

"So?"

"I mean *all* of the time," she emphasizes. "If Sasha wasn't talking about him, he was with him. All the time. At first we just assumed the sex was that amazing."

"But it went on. And on. And there was no one else, Craig." Nate chimes in. "You really, really have no idea how unusual that was for Alex at the time."

"You've repeated it enough, I think I can guess," Craig says through gritted teeth.

Nate smiles helplessly. "Sorry. I mean—here's the biggest thing. Alex had a lot of job offers when he graduated; he could have left Seattle for good, but he picked the agency he's at now just because it's here, and… well." He exchanges glances with Samantha. "Let's say we don't think family and friendship were the only or even the main reasons for that choice."

"And you didn't like it." Craig waves away the plate of pie Samantha offers him. Food is still not high on his list of priorities this evening. "Right?"

Nate looks at him as if he's crazy. "Well, of course we didn't like it. Jeff's a *dick*. Man, we *hated* Jeff."

Give me strength. "I guessed that he was a dick from the first night Alex and I were together. Is there a point to this very long story?" Maybe he wasn't going to get as much insight as he'd hoped.

Samantha's knuckles whiten around the handle of the pie server in her hand. "The entire story *is* the point. Have you not been listening?"

At the sound of the edge that has entered Samantha's voice, Nate jumps up from the couch and comes to interpose himself between the two of them, an island of calm. He rubs his girlfriend's arm and keeps his steady gaze on Craig. "Sammi's saying, Alex changed while he was with Jeff. Just... we had to sit there and watch him get obsessed. We still don't know why—he wouldn't talk about it. But it was confusing for everyone who knew him, because honestly, when they were together, they didn't even seem to *like* each other much."

"I'm pretty sure they were hate-fucking by the end. And after a while... he disappeared." Samantha's fingers relax and she sets the pie server aside. "Craig, until that day he ran into me at Sucre Coeur, we hadn't seen Alex in months. As near as we can tell, no one had. Except for you."

"Last we saw him, Samantha was trying to talk to him about Jeff, but..." Nate shrugs, helpless. "Well, they've always been really good at pushing each others' buttons. Family, right? No one does it better. Alex exploded, and Alex walked. It was a very merry Christmas."

"Yeah, he's good at that." Craig has to squeeze his eyes shut against the endlessly repeating memory of Alex walking away from *him*. "So that much, at least, hasn't changed."

Samantha catches the falling wineglass as Craig's fingers loosen around it, but Craig doesn't open his eyes. In the next instant, the glass is replaced by the comforting warm squeeze of her hand. "Craig. What did he *say* to you?"

"I told you."

"No." Her hand squeezes again. "The part you aren't telling us."

The part I'll never not hear again, you mean. "I'd rather not."

Since Samantha's already holding Craig's right hand, he assumes it's Nate who takes the wine bottle out of his left and replaces it with his own hand. "Craig."

Glass on my tongue. "He asked me if I had thought I could fix him."

He hears Sarita's soft gasp, and a sharp ache goes through his right hand when Samantha squeezes it; her nails dig into the soft skin on the back of his hand. "Which of course you never did."

Laughable. "Actually, I *did* think I could, in a way, that's the hell of it." Craig manages to pry his eyes open against the hurt. "Bloody fucking arrogant of me, right?" Hell is hindsight and clarity. He looks at Sarita and can't help but snort out an ironic laugh, even as his heart aches at the stricken expression on her face. "You told me to go rescue someone else... well. There you go."

He looks around at all of them, how wide-eyed, startled and lost they are. He can only laugh bitterly again as he goes on, untangling his fingers from Samantha's so he can reclaim his glass and take a long swallow of wine.

"I never asked if he *wanted* me to help. Not once. Just thought that, with time, we could work together to heal whatever had been broken. But of course I had no idea how deep the wound really went—and maybe I didn't want to." Into his glass goes the last of the bottle. How many bottles have they had? Does it matter? "And maybe it was really bloody selfish of me to think I was being magnanimous and generous and helpful to this poor broken guy, don't you think?"

"Stop it." Samantha tries to take the glass, but Craig pulls back, startled, and then stumbles back a step, two steps, and crashes to the linoleum in a heap. *Fuck.*

In a flash they're all down with him, surrounding him with embracing arms and non-judgmental love while he rests his head on Nate's shoulder and squeezes his eyes shut again, still determined not to let a single tear fall. "This is so stupid, so completely dumb; I was so wrong."

"You weren't, it's not," Nate whispers into his ear. "You love him. You weren't arrogant or selfish—you were *you*, you were generous and loving and exactly what he needed—remember, I know you, okay, man? I know what it's like to be loved by you."

They get the wineglass out of his hand and just hold him while he shakes and listens to their reassurances, their warm whispers and warmer embraces wrapping him in caring and support, soothing his hurt and anger.

It doesn't go far. All three of them don't add up to the one and only Alex that he really, really wants; it can't be helped. But they hold him tight and give all they can while he shakes like a leaf.

I miss you, Alex. I miss you so much...

He'd never known anything to hurt like this, to flay him so raw and leave him flailing.

When the trembling finally stops, he opens his eyes to see Sarita kneeling in front of him, her slender hands wrapped around his, less stricken but sadder, now. "Hi there."

"Hi." He's still held by Nate and Samantha, the two of them wrapped around him like kittens. "And hello again to the pair of you."

Samantha's soft curls tickle the nape of his neck. "Hello. You smell really nice, Craig. Like cookies and pine trees. Are you feeling a little better?"

"The floor is cold and I think I am very, very drunk." His eyes and jaw ache from the effort of holding back tears, but he's pleased to have done it—he sees only a faint hint of damp darkness on a tiny patch of Nate's T-shirt. It's sad that he's so pleased, but he'll cling to every little victory right at this moment. "Tired."

"I'm going to offer you an Ambien—" Samantha begins. Craig can't help but chuckle while he struggles to his feet.

"And I am going to turn it down." He gives her hand a squeeze before hauling her, then Nate, up to their feet. "Chamomile tea will suffice."

"Which I can get." Sarita had come up with him. Now she grabs an electric kettle and starts filling it. "I've got a kettle and a fresh box of the stuff. Anyone else want any?"

A yawn overtakes Samantha as she shakes her head. "No, thank you. I think Nate and I just need to go home. Long drive. Craig?"

The counter is all that's holding him up. Craig focuses on Samantha with vision gone soft-focus. "Mmm?"

"We're going to go now. We can come back whenever you want. School doesn't start for another couple of weeks." She steps carefully across the tiles and touches his cheek. "Will you be all right?"

Unlikely. "For the moment."

Nate's arms slip around his waist in a hug. "Try to sleep."

It's good that they're leaving, because the mother-henning is getting to be a bit much. He wants his tea; he wants to stretch out on Sarita's couch. Craig's fingers curl under the countertop to brace himself as he watches the ballet of departure—the presentation of pasta leftovers, one more refused offer of tea, the gathering up of discarded sandals and running shoes. Samantha and Nate are out the door with one last blown kiss that Craig can only return with a nod, and then, with the click of a lock, it's just him and Sarita and mutually contemplative silence.

For the first time in two weeks, silence is not as loud as a scream. It's still a dull roar, but Craig will take that and call it progress.

"If you'll trudge yourself over to the sofa," Sarita advises from where she leans against the front door, "I'll have that tea for you."

He nods.

"You have to actually move."

"Getting to it." Trying to see is like peering through an aquarium He's fairly certain Sarita has sprouted a second couch. Huh. This flat isn't so big, how'd she fit it in here?

And how did she get herself tucked under his arm like this? "Right, you're six feet tall, I'm... absolutely not. This ought to be fun. One foot forward at a time, Craig." Her hand tugs at his. "Come on. One foot... slide it... there you go. Good."

They creep and slide their way to the original couch, Craig trying very hard not to look at how it and the second couch are merging. Oh, regret in the morning; it won't be new, but it's going to hurt a little more this time.

When Sarita ducks out from under his arm and gives him a gentle push, Craig topples right into the sofa cushions. But because she doesn't untangle her fingers in time, she goes with him, landing on his chest with a screech right in his ear that sets his head spinning. "Ow," he manages, and the aquarium goes yellowish around the edges.

"Sorry, fuck." She scrambles to slide off of him, not quite managing to avoid getting him in the ribs with one pointy elbow. "Oh, damn it. Sorry, Craig. Please don't fire me."

"I'm too tired to fire anyone; ask me about it again tomorrow," he says, squinting as red threads of pain shoot through the yellow edges of his vision. "Oh God, can I please have my tea now, before you throw me out the window or a wrecking ball comes through here or something?"

"Aye aye, captain. It's ready. I set it steeping before Nate and Sam left." She disappears, returning to press a warm, fragrant mug of tea into his hand. When she flops down on the couch next to him, he sees she's got one of her own. "Not chamomile, actually. It's spice tea. I thought it would do you more good after the wine. Two sugars, milk for you?"

"Works for me. Cheers." Irony tips his mouth up in a grim smile as he hoists his mug toward her. He notices she doesn't return the salute, just sits curled up in the corner of the sofa watching him with dark eyes more solemn than usual. "Sarita, only room for one sad sack in this flat, and I've had my claim staked for hours now."

She pulls her ponytail over her shoulder and plays with it, keeping her eyes on him with a thoughtful expression. "Not a sad sack," she says eventually, as she twists a lock of hair around her finger. "Just a concerned one. But I admit I am about ten pounds of concern in a five-pound sack."

"Right. I think we've carried the sack metaphor about as far as it will go." It does make him smile a little, another little victory to... well. Sack away. As it were. Craig takes deep gulps of his tea before he can start laughing, because if he starts laughing he might not be able to stop, and there's not much that's funny right now.

"Well, I'm not the writer, Mr. Oliver, I leave that to you and your eloquent pen." A small spark of merriment sparks to briefest life before her shoulders drop with the heave of her sigh. "I'm sorry, Craig. About the rescue thing."

He'd thought he had nothing left to talk about—thought he'd shaken it all out on the kitchen floor—but that momentary twinkle of good cheer in Sarita's eyes jolts something loose in Craig. "You didn't mean it literally. And even if you had, you couldn't have known I'd actually try to do it."

"I don't think you meant to." Her fingers pluck at the wide collar of her loose blue shirt. "I think it just happened."

"No, I meant to." When he takes a deep breath, the room swims. Right. No more of that. "Just like I meant to do something to prove I wasn't a slave to routine..."

Her breath catches in a sigh. "Oh. Oh, Craig. Damn."

Tears threaten at the corners of his eyes again. He squeezes them more tightly shut. "Forget it." His tea smells good. He takes another warm, comforting swallow. "You're always so smart. I wish you could tell me why this is happening. Is there a philosophical theory that can help me out here?"

Not much has the capacity to ruffle Sarita's composure. It's one of her best qualities, one used to great effect on busy early morning shifts at the bakery and in many of their recent stints as wedding bakers. Craig sees that it fails her now, though she does not drop her tea, but merely twitches and widens her eyes. "Oh, I don't know if that's a wise conversation to have right now, Craig."

"Have my actions struck you as particularly wise, lately?" Craig's view out of the corner of his bleary eye is of drained wine bottles, a stack of wrappers from the Dirty Girl Scout Cupcakes and an uneaten slice of amaretto apple pie. "Think for a moment. I haven't been sleeping, I'm rather drunk; I spent my entire day baking dozens and dozens of alcoholic desserts..." He tries to shrug carelessly, but limbs and reflexes made awkward with wine nearly send his tea flying, and they both have to scramble to keep it from spilling all over the sofa.

By the time they settle into the spatter-free cushions once more, the mad rush has cleared Craig's thinking a bit, and shaking his head doesn't make things swim quite as much. "Point is, Sarita, I fell in love and it blew up in my face. How can one more stupid thing make any of this worse?"

"It might make you *feel* worse," she points out. "That wasn't what I had in mind when I asked if you had more to discuss."

"I'm just trying to make sense of it. Trying to convince myself I'd feel better if I could understand why it's happening. Cosmically, or something."

Sarita chuckles, just a little, very softly. "Determinism."

This might as well be Greek. "Hmm?"

She twists her head a little and her neck cracks with the motion. "Determinism. The idea that everything in the universe is predetermined, and we only *think* we have free will and choices."

His eyes widen. "God, that sounds horrifying."

"You wanted some kind of cosmic explanation," she reminds him. "Well, there you are. That's one. God exists, and he's got it all figured out for you. Whether you like it or not."

"Yeah..." He thinks it over, drinking his tea and scratching his head. "That's a little more bleak than I think I was looking for."

"Understandable." Sarita's sad little smile is back. "I'm not really down with it either: the idea that maybe everything is predetermined and some great big dude in the sky is just letting us *think* we're making our own choices... it doesn't seem entirely healthy."

Craig rolls his head along the back of the sofa to look at her. "Not so much. Can you think of anything better?"

"I don't know, Craig. I'm not studying philosophy because I'm trying to work out what I believe in. I'm studying it because it's interesting to see all the reasons humans come up with to justify the way we exist in the world, why we do what we do." But she does smile as she snuggles back into her corner of the couch. "I mean, sometimes, when things are going well, yeah, all right, it's nice to think that maybe someone moved the chess pieces around specifically to let me have a good day... which isn't strictly deterministic, but whatever."

When she doesn't go on, he leans over to give her a poke in the leg. "Was that it?"

"No..." She draws it out, ending her sentence with a low whistle. "See, when things are going badly, I *resent* that idea. I don't want to be a pawn in a cosmic game, Craig. I don't want things planned for me, good or bad. I mean, if I meet someone, I don't want it to be someone picked out for me! I think life might be a mixture of serendipity and your own force of will. That's what I'm comfortable with, anyway." A tilt of her head, a narrowing of her eyes, and he gets the uncanny feeling she's looking right into his core. "Maybe instead of wondering why all this happened, you could just go with the fact that it happened, and work out where you'll go now."

Unflappable, intuitive and direct. He knew there was a reason he liked being around Sarita. "It's always the simplest path for you, isn't it? Like when you told me to enjoy just being with Alex."

"And you did enjoy being with Alex," she points out. "Regardless of what's happening now, you did, and it was good for a while."

She does have a point. Maybe he can entertain the idea of moving forward, in that case. "Smart girl."

"It's good for my ego that you think so. I only got a B on my determinism paper back in the day." She drains her tea mug and sets it aside. "Now. I have some suggestions."

"Fire away."

Sarita leans forward. "For tonight, I say finish your tea and go to sleep. It's been a long day, and my personal opinion is that for the last couple of weeks, you've been thinking too much and trying too hard. So first, sleep."

Craig manages a limp salute before finishing off the tea as directed. "Aye aye, captain."

"And tomorrow, I suggest we go visit my brother. You remember Devesh." Twining her fingers together, Sarita braces her elbows on her knees and rests her chin on her hands, her smile brightening. "Not being a cosmic chess god, I leave you to make your own choice in the matter, but I do highly recommend it."

Craig remembers through the lingering fog of intoxication that Devesh is also gay. His heart twists in his chest as he skirts the edges of his emotional pit once more. "I think it's too soon to set me up with anyone, Sarita."

"Um, I agree, which is why I'm not suggesting *that*. Well, that and his husband might object?" She tilts her head and blows a raspberry. "Devesh *and* Sunil, remember? The Yorkie breeders? They've got a litter that's old enough to adopt, I thought we might go visit the puppies." Even with her head tilted nearly sideways, she manages to nod. "Puppies make everything better."

As much as part of him wants to think along these lines, remembering all his efforts, remembering the look on Alex's face when they ran into Jeff—no. "Nothing makes everything better."

Guilt shades Sarita's face as she slides off of the sofa and moves toward a closet in the corner. "Fair enough. But even you have to admit that puppies might be a distraction you could use right now."

"And then what?" Craig stretches out over the sofa cushions, hoping sleep hits him like a brick. That would be the most welcome distraction, at this moment.

A blanket snowdrifts over him, followed by Sarita's hand, which gently lifts his head to slip a soft pillow beneath it. "Then by serendipity and force of will, we find the next distraction— and the next, Craig. It's all we can do."

As the lights in the apartment are switched off one by one, leaving sleep a lurking presence, Craig wonders how something can sound so bleak and yet so hopeful all at once.

Chapter Seventeen

"**D**ESPERATE TIMES," CONNOR ANNOUNCES TO HIS BIG-eyed infant daughter, "call for desperate measures. Right, dimples?"

Kira's only reply is a shrill peal of giggles when he tickles her feet, but Connor is willing to take it as agreement as he eyeballs the building before him and considers his best course of action for getting through Alex's apartment door. "You don't know this yet, but your Uncle Alex can be a real pain in the aaaaa... bacus."

One day he will get a better handle on his language in front of his daughter. He will. He's improving all the time. Really. This time he's actually managed to *find* a substitute for the word he was about to utter.

Anyway. "He's not gonna just answer the door," Connor muses, considering the last time something like this happened. "He hasn't answered his phone, so he isn't gonna answer the door without a fight. But the rest of this isn't gonna work if I can't get *through* the door, hey?"

Kira squeals again, and blows a wad of spit bubbles. Connor finds this encouraging.

"I think the key is, I gotta be persistent enough he lets me in, right, but not so big a jerk that the neighbors call the cops."

Alex's neighborhood is not exactly a rough-and-tumble part of the city, but it does see enough disturbance to mean its nervous residents are never too far from their phones and the 911 function. The last thing Connor needs is to get hauled off by Seattle's boys in blue and hit with a public nuisance charge. Rayna would never let him hear the end of it.

So he just has to work fast, right?

"God fu... reakin' bless," he mutters, yanking open the building door while Kira kicks and flails excitedly in the baby carrier he's wearing.

Connor has no issues with Alex's apartment building, generally. Today he does. He had to park several blocks away, and Alex lives on the second floor of a building with no elevator. Weighed down by his daughter, her diaper bag and his camera bag, Connor's mood is not entirely sanguine, and his ability to find appropriate substitutes for his swearing was wearing thin before he even started the trudge up the courtyard steps.

"Open your go... sh darn door, Scheff," he yells when he finally arrives, his patience held together by a thread. Any mild concern he may have felt, about things so trivial as *neighbors* and *the police,* melts away as he pounds on the door. "I know you're in there."

Actually, he doesn't know this for *sure,* and he's going to feel pretty dumb if Alex is not home and the cops are called, but hey, it's worth the stab in the dark. An Alex who is not answering his phone or emails is, in Connor's experience, an Alex who is not leaving the apartment much.

And Connor would not be here if he didn't give a shit about his friend—kid brother, really, even if the ties that initially bound them together had been composed of stop bath and fixer rather than blood. Doesn't matter. A brother is a brother is a brother, and brothers take care of their own.

It's been two weeks since he last saw or heard from Alex. And sure, part of his brain says *only* two weeks, but after the whole last fucking mess with Jeff, Connor's more attuned to signs of trouble. He'd seen Alex happy with Craig at the bakery—and then Alex missed the time they'd scheduled to look over photos and pick the best ones for the bakery site.

Alex doesn't miss appointments. Alex is punctual to a degree that most people find alarming—well, Connor does, it's sick, who's on time like that all of the time?—and if he is going to be late or miss something, which is rarer than an intact, mint-condition vintage Hasselblad, he calls or texts.

But then, he missed a Labor Day barbecue with the entire Monaghan clan last time, a party they'd set up months before, a party that Connor's entire family spent worrying about their adopted extra. It had taken Connor that long, too many months, to realize there had been a problem.

Connor Monaghan does not take the same chances twice. *Something is wrong, and I'd bet my life it's got something to do with Craig.*

"Open up, man," he calls, thumping his fist on the door in rhythm with Kira's kicks. "Seriously. Don't make me resort to drastic measures."

If he has to resort to drastic measures, he is almost *certainly* going to get hauled off by the police.

Footsteps thump across the floor on the other side of the door, and Connor waits, holding his breath, for the door to be opened. But no, the steps veer off—into the kitchen, if he remembers the floor plan correctly—and he hears cabinets being opened, water running and steps thumping back in what he's pretty sure is the direction of the bedroom. The door remains impenetrable.

He takes a step back and stares. "He's ignoring me," he informs Kira, mouth agape and hand still raised to knock. "Do you even believe that son of a bi… lly goat is ignoring me?"

"Ooo," Kira says, craning her head to look at him with big brown eyes.

"Ooo is fu… nking right, dimples. Jesus, I gotta get a handle on myself. Okay." He eyeballs the door. "Drastic measures are called for."

Once upon a time, when he was younger, drastic measures would have involved ramming his body into the door until it came down. He's still not entirely over the fact that this can no longer be a solution—it's so direct and efficient—but sadly, boxing injuries, the knowledge that his homeowner's insurance probably won't cover damage to someone else's apartment and the fact that he's got his nine-month-old daughter strapped to his chest like a bomb puts a damper on that kind of fun.

However, there is still plenty of fun to be had when you've memorized the entirety of AC/DC's musical catalog. Taking in a deep breath, he channels his not-very-inner Bon Scott, throws back his head and starts to sing.

Belatedly, it occurs to Connor that the lyrics to "If You Want Blood" are probably one of those things to which Rayna does not want their daughter exposed. He covers Kira's ears with his hands and carries on, hoping for the best. Maybe she won't talk about this in therapy one day.

No sign of the neighbors as he wraps up: good luck for him. It's good luck that doesn't hold as he launches into the next song, however. One by one, doors down the hall pop open and astonished residents poke their heads out as Connor, hands still covering Kira's ears and a fresh nervousness in his voice, struts up and down the hall singing about big balls.

And, much to his boundless fury, the door to apartment fifteen stays firmly shut.

Fucking enough of this. Two songs is probably already pushing the boundaries of his audience's tolerance. "I'm not leaving until you open the door, Al," he shouts, pretending to ignore the neighbors but keeping a peripheral eye on them in case they do decide to go for their phones. "I know a lot of songs and I don't have any shame whatsoever, and you know it, so either answer the door or I'll be billing you for my bail money."

Nothing.

"You asked for it," he mutters. Time for the nukes. He just hopes that having Kira attached to his chest is a guaranteed deterrent to an Alex who will almost certainly want to beat the shit out of him. Connor shakes his head, shakes it again and finally cracks his neck.

"I got your mom on the phone, and if you don't get out here and tell her you're not dead, she's coming over with the cops," he calls, not even bothering to hammer on the door.

The door swings open to reveal Alex, hair standing on end and murder in his eyes.

"Fuck you," he snarls, right before he spots Kira and his eyes get huge. "Oh, shit—I didn't know you had—I mean, damn it—fuck! Sorry!"

"Uk uk uk," Kira volunteers cheerfully, and Connor grins, holding up his hands to show that he doesn't actually have his phone out or Marina Scheff on it.

"I take it you know Kira doesn't actually mean *uk*, right?" he asks.

The anger in Alex's eyes is joined by no small amount of sheepish embarrassment. "Yeah."

"And that Rayna is probably going to kill you, because I'm sure as sh… ugar not taking the fall for it?"

Alex presses his mouth into a line and nods. "Yeah."

Silence falls, and Connor keeps an eye on Alex, waiting for him to say more or to slam the door in their faces. Alex just stands in his doorway and stares at them, clearly waiting for Connor to lead the conversation wherever it's going to go.

Okay, then. "So… you look like shhhhiii… hungover," Connor says, trying to hide his shock. He's being kind. Alex actually looks as if he was strapped to the back end of a Metro bus and dragged at least four stops.

"I am hungover." Alex leans against the doorjamb, eyes bloodshot and dark-circled.

"Well. I hope you're up for company; we came all this way." Connor unzips his camera bag and pulls out a package. "I brought sandwiches. Roast beef. Horseradish."

Alex shakes his head and backs up; his hand reaches for the door. "Now's not a good time, Connor—"

"And I brought Kira. You're her godfather, you should spend more time with her. " He tickles Kira's foot with his free hand to make her giggle. "No time like the present! It's great, babies are the perfect remedy for a hangover."

"I'm pretty sure that's not true," Alex begins, alarmed, but Connor is not taking no for an answer. Before Alex can stop him, Connor has installed Kira in Alex's arms and is pushing through the door to dump their bags onto the floor. Once unburdened, he's in the kitchen, pulling down plates for the sandwiches and taking a pair of soft drinks out of the refrigerator, pretending to ignore the fact that Alex is still standing in the doorway holding Kira and looking like someone's just smacked him upside the head.

Good. Getting and *keeping* Alex off-balance is pretty much the only way Connor's going to get information out of him. He slaps the plates down on the kitchen table and waves his friend over. "So. I was just in the neighborhood."

"Bull... uh, bullpoop." Alex slumps down in one of the pipe-and-canvas chairs he calls kitchen furniture and glares. "You're never just in the neighborhood. You don't leave *your* neighborhood. You don't have to."

"What, I can't drive? I don't know how to leave home? This is what you're saying? When I have visited you in this very apartment on multiple occasions?" Connor scoffs. He slides over a plate and soda. "Shut up and eat something. You look like... well, you know what you look like."

"Such diplomacy." It seems to take Alex a moment to figure out how to hold Kira with one hand and pick up his sandwich with the other. It takes a lot for Connor not to laugh at the spectacle; poor guy's clearly been through enough lately. Although a lot of it is probably his own doing, really.

But Connor can still feel sympathy. "So." He picks up his own sandwich, keeping himself casual as hell. "Things going a little rough for you these days?"

A shrug. "Seen better ones."

Oh, good. I love playing dentist. Jesus, can you never just talk? He wouldn't have to play dirty if Alex weren't so difficult. He doesn't take it personally—he's seen Alex be coy and opaque and downright buttheaded with lots of people. But it's infuriating all the same. And while it makes most folks give up and walk off, it just encourages Connor to be a dick. "How's Craig?"

The question surprises Alex mid-bite; all he can do is glare while he chews and swallows, and Connor regrets nothing. He just waits and works on his own sandwich until Alex finally says, "None of your business."

"I dunno. You and I had a date to work on the photos we took of him and the gang at the bakery, and you bailed on me without notice, so in a very, uh, *circuitous* sorta way, yeah, it's my business." Ooh, that was a little edgier than he meant it to be. Well, he's still pissed, and he's concerned, and if he gets a little gruff, who the fuck's it gonna hurt? The important thing is, he was right: this has totally got something to do with Craig.

Alex's arm tightens more securely around Kira as he begins to pay very careful attention to an invisible spot on the kitchen wall. "Sorry."

"Alex." *Pulling teeth, pulling teeth, pulling teeth, I swear to fucking God...*

"Look," Alex snarls, snapping his head around to level another of his poisonous glares across the table. "I don't have to—"

"Remember when I said I wasn't gonna let you disappear on me again?" Connor interrupts, setting his sandwich aside so he can lean across the table. "This is me following through on that. Got it?"

It looks as if Alex is going to punch Connor in the nose, but—"Yeah. Got it," he mutters, hugging Kira close and resuming work on his lunch.

Connor lets things rest. Not a skill he's used to using— Rayna's had to hammer it into his head over the years. If he had his way all the time, he'd push and push and push until he got shit done; that's how he's done it all his life and it worked okay. But he's learning, see. *Sometimes you gotta be subtle. You gotta do an end run instead of just plowing through the line. Gotta use your teammates to your advantage.*

Which is, after all, why Kira is with him today.

They finish their sandwiches in silence—broken only by Kira, babbling aimlessly at her feet—and therefore without further incident. Seems like a good time to put phase two of his plan into effect. "Say, listen, I gotta borrow your little darkroom setup."

The look this produces on Alex's face is truly comical. "You own a *photography-related* business. You have a *darkroom*. An actual, professional darkroom that two people can be in at once without the threat of drowning on the wet table or suffocating from chemical fumes."

"Yeah, but I can't take Kira in there." His excuse is both air- and watertight. "And Rayna's at the gallery setting up for their big show, my dad and stepmom are on a cruise and my brothers took their kids to the Mariners game."

Alex cocks a skeptical eyebrow. "And you didn't want to go with them?"

"Hey, I'm all for watching the home team get creamed by the Yankees, you know that, but Kira's kinda young for that kinda thing, so, you know, here I am." He shrugs and hopes his grin looks innocent enough. "I got some photos I need to develop and no one to watch Kira. I figured since you weren't answering my calls, I had no hope of getting you over to my place. So..." He shrugs one more time. "You kinda brought this on yourself, bucko."

"You could develop them later," Alex points out, eyes narrowed. "Is there really that big a rush?"

"Eh. I wanted to get it done today. Come on," Connor coaxes, pulling out his most winning grin. "I'm only developing to negative and I'm already here. Might as well let me do it."

Alex's face doesn't relax. "You're up to something."

"Yeah," Connor admits. He is, no hiding that, and he'd be a dumb-ass to try. But he doesn't have to tell everything, right? "I'm up to making sure you're still alive and that you're not gonna disappear, and in the meantime if I get to develop some photos, bonus."

He leans back in his chair with his soda and waits. Of course, he's only nominally leaving this up to Alex. If Alex demands they leave, Connor's just going to lock himself in the bathroom and refuse to come out.

He's on a mission and he isn't leaving till he gets it done.

Alex finally sighs and rolls his eyes. "Fine. Develop your sh... stuff."

"Thanks, buddy. Nah, don't get up." Connor pats Alex on the shoulder and pushes him back down into his chair. "I'll set up the room. I know where you keep the necessaries."

Not that he's going to need them.

Still, he drags the table into the bathroom and wedges it into the shower, gets out the tubs and sets them up. He does feel slightly guilty pouring out chemicals he has no intention of using, but Alex has to believe this is why he's here, and shit, it's not as if he's taking that much.

His last step is replacing the regular light bulb with the darkroom one and he's ready. "Okay," he calls to the kitchen, where Alex is still holding Kira on his knee and looking slightly panicked. "I'll see you both in a couple of hours."

"Wait," Alex sputters, his panic escalating visibly. "What if she cries?"

Connor shrugs. "Check her diaper."

"Oh, God."

"There's spares in her bag," Connor says, shutting the bathroom door and turning on the extractor fan before Alex can find him about to explode laughing. He slides to the floor, holding in his howls of mirth until it hurts.

He reaches into his bag and extracts his iPad. He's been stuck on level 97 in Candy Crush for about a month now, with no time to focus on figuring it out. This time alone is just another bonus for being a clever, meddling asshole; for this kind of priceless benefit, he resolves to be a clever, meddling asshole way more often.

It doesn't take long for him to sink deep into his game, tapping and sliding his finger over rows of sweets and jellies, always keeping an ear out for anything going horribly wrong. Not that he expects anything too bad—he and Rayna had been truly blessed with the world's most adorable and happy baby. Kira could not be easier to tend. Alex could play peekaboo with her for hours and she would still be amazingly content.

Judging from the pitch and decibel level of the shrieks Connor hears from the living room, that's exactly what's happening. Occasionally he hears Alex say, astonishment plain in his voice, "Again? Really?" But he must keep doing it, because Kira's shrieking giggles go on and on and on.

Kira is not, however, immune to discomforts like hunger and wet diapers. Connor's Dad Ear allows him to translate the giggles as they shift into fretful fussing before Alex registers them, and he has to hold himself back from zipping out to take care of his daughter. The jig will be up in a heartbeat if he emerges from the bathroom before a reasonable time for processing passes.

The bliss of free time is now the agony of forced inaction.

Kira's fussing morphs into tiny hiccupping sobs that Connor knows will ramp up into a full-on tantrum if Alex can't figure out the issue soon. And it kills him, but still he waits while

Alex begins to panic. "What? Oh, God, was that last face too scary? I'm sorry, okay, please, don't cry."

Which of course does not work, and Connor nearly claws the palms of his hands off.

"Okay. I'm... I'm checking this..." A deep breath. "Okay. Checking the—nope, thank God, everything's dry and clean. Okay. So... okay. Do I rock you to sleep or something?" A full-lunged, angry scream is the answer Alex gets to that. "No. No sleep then. Oh, God, Kira, please, I'm sorry, your dad's an idiot and I'm an idiot and I don't speak baby."

There's a sudden jingling and rummaging sound. Good. He finally had the sense to check the diaper bag. "Do you want a toy? I—oh, no, okay, please—please stop hitting me with that." Zippers and snaps click and whirr in quick succession. "How about a pacifier? You want a—wow. Wow, you can really spit."

Connor muffles his snort into his hand. "Let's see..." Rummage, rummage, rummage. "Oh, hey, there's a bottle in—oh. Is that what you were looking for?" Kira is babbling now, impatient for her lunch, probably stretching to reach for it. "Got it. Wait, though, let me shake it up. And not think about how this has to be fresh from your mom. Oh, my God."

Connor is impressed with how Alex can be both not entirely helpless and totally squeamish at the same time.

The couch creaks as Alex settles down into it, and Connor can just barely make out the sound of Kira sucking away at her bottle. "There you go. Yeah. That's better. I mean, I have no idea how you're finding that enjoyable, but more power to you, small fry."

Kira's soft suckling sounds are the only noise for a long, long time, and then—

"Your Uncle Craig would be better at this."

The utterance is low and dark, and the pain in it makes it sound tight, like the skin over a bruised cheekbone. Connor winces. He thought Alex might be more inclined to confess his woes to someone who can't repeat them; and as much as this hurts, he's glad to be right.

"I miss him." Silence. A sigh. "I keep finding things I miss him doing. His cookies are better than the ones at the bakery near work. He makes better spaghetti. Better tea, I never get the tea right. I drink tea voluntarily, what even?" There's a ragged edge of hysteria in Alex's chuckle. "And now babies. He's handled babies before, I never have; he probably would have known right away you were hungry."

The next laugh is a half-sob. "I messed up. I *am* messed up. He made things better, but I don't deserve it. But I still miss it. That's messed up. Not fair."

Silence, again, except for Kira's little humming noises as she eats and Alex's long, slow, deep breaths. Connor's iPad sits abandoned in his lap while he listens and hurts for his friend. *This is Jeff's fault*, he thinks, as certain of this as he has ever been of anything. No way does Alex think that about himself because of anything Craig did. Not that Connor's really been around Craig a whole lot, but—he knows.

He knows, and the proof is in his bag right now. It's a huge part of why he's here.

But it is not time for that yet. Connor presses his ear to the door and keeps listening. Alex isn't saying a whole lot— who would, to a baby?—but what he does say is informative enough.

"It was a mistake to leave him but he's better off without anyone who would make that kind of mistake, right? Nobody needs that kind of fu.... screw-up in their lives."

Ouch. *This is definitely Jeff's fault, and I better remember I promised Rayna no more fighting.* It's difficult, though. While pre-Jeff Alex would have been unlikely to date Craig, pre-Jeff Alex was never this hard on himself, never hated himself like this. Pre-Jeff Alex had swagger and attitude and thought he was God's gift to the Earth and okay, that had been annoying as shit, but Connor would do just about anything to have any semblance of that Alex back right now. That guy was a jerk, but he wasn't a giant, sucking black hole of self-hatred. *Nobody deserves to feel like that. Nobody.* Except maybe Jeff.

Connor slumps back against the door to think. Something's got to be done about this. Therapy, for one thing, but that's not up to him or anything he can make happen. So, okay. Next best thing, getting Alex and Craig back together. Maybe he can't make that happen, but he can try to help facilitate it, right? He knows for sure now that there is something to facilitate, so he might as well give it a shot. Alex would never initiate; he thinks he's too much in the wrong.

No, the bulk of the work's gonna have to come from the other side. If Craig wants it. And Connor has excellent reason to believe that he will.

Not that he won't *try* to encourage Alex a little, now that he's concrete-solid in his certainty that he should.

Connor gets so absorbed in considering his options that it takes a while for him to realize that it's been very silent in the living room for some time. With mild concern, he opens the bathroom door and peers out to see what's going on.

Aw. That's fucking adorable.

Alex has fallen sound asleep on the sofa with Kira on his chest and just as deeply asleep, her tiny body rising gently with every breath Alex takes. One of Alex's hands holds Kira firmly in place; the other dangles towards the floor. A half-empty bottle, pointed nipple down, leaks into the nondescript carpet.

If Connor had his camera with him, he'd get a picture; it's that perfect a moment. That's all right, though. He has just as perfect a moment at hand, and better for his purposes.

Dipping a hand into his camera bag, Connor pulls out a small, expertly framed and matted photo and tiptoes into Alex's bedroom. He places it next to Alex's glasses and alarm clock on the bedside table and steps back to survey his work.

Perfect. If Connor were to *tell* Alex he needed to sack up and get back together with Craig, it would go over like a lead balloon. But a little subtle encouragement can't hurt. Right?

It's one moment, one second Connor happened to capture, that's all. Nothing massive. Except—

Except that there's so much in this second: a breathtaking connection, a moment of intimacy snatched in a tiny, crowded bakery kitchen. Connor almost hadn't taken it; his breath had caught in his chest when he saw such a pure moment of quiet love between two people.

It had made him think of his father and mother—not his stepmother, but his birth mother. Before she died in a car accident when Connor was ten, he remembers his mother and father being around each other in just the same spirit as Alex and Craig in this photograph.

That's what had gotten him to press the button, to freeze the moment forever.

The day Alex hadn't shown up to work on the bakery photos, Connor developed this in black and white, made it a stark moment that might almost come to life and let you hear the sound of Alex whispering in Craig's ear, catch Craig's soft chuckle as he squeezes frosting onto a cupcake, actually see

Alex's arms tighten around Craig's waist and link them so closely together you couldn't fit a sigh between their bodies.

It's love in a concentrated, frozen second of time, and he hopes it lights a fire under Alex. *This is worth fighting for.* Sentimental, Connor is not. But his heart burns fiercely and he can love and identify love; and if he can, then Alex can too, whether he wants to admit it or not.

Connor backs out of the bedroom and into the living room and crouches down by the couch. He shakes Alex's shoulder with a gentle hand. "Wake up, sleeping beauty."

"Ugh... uh..." Alex blinks, focuses on Connor. "Sh... oot. Um. Sorry. Did you get your stuff done?"

"Um. Sure." No need to admit that it's been less than an hour. Connor is grateful; he had been prepared to spend the full two hours here, but thank God for sleepy people and sleepy babies, right? "Go back to sleep. Kira and I will leave you alone now."

"Okay." He does seem to fall back to sleep almost immediately, and barely twitches as Connor extracts Kira from his grip and gets her strapped into her carrier, facing in so she can nod back off herself.

Alex's quiet snores and mumbles follow them out the door.

He's so tired. And hurting. And that's no way for anyone to live.

Kira grumbles as they emerge into the sun, rubbing her face against Connor's chest. He chuckles softly. "One more stop, dimples?" He rubs her soft hair, enjoying her drowsy burble. "Can you be good for me a little longer while we make one more visit?"

"Buh," Kira puffs with a tiny pop of her lips. Her head droops sleepily sideways. Connor heads for his car. *Works for me.*

Chapter Eighteen

W HEN ALEX COMES TO, IT'S NOT UNLIKE SWIMMING UP through a fog.

Slowly, he blinks gritty eyes and becomes aware of himself in stages: his back hurts from sleeping on the couch. His head still aches from last night's overindulgence. His stomach is not really thrilled with the amount of horseradish the deli put on that sandwich Connor brought him.

He swings his legs down and sits slumped at the edge of the couch, trying to rub away the sensation of sand in his eyes. A squinting glance at his phone tells him he's slept well past three o'clock, almost to four. Great. Not that he had plans for the day, but he's annoyed that he's slept through half of it. Plus he's never going to get to sleep before dawn, now, and tomorrow is a workday.

Not that he's entirely sure he gives any number of shits about that.

Or much of anything.

Is this my life from now on? Alex wonders, shoving himself to his feet and shambling into the kitchen for a drink of water. No light, no color, no laughter, an endless trudge of days that blend one into the other except when he lets Connor or Sammi barge in?

It doesn't have to be, whispers a hopeful little voice—a hopeful little voice that he instantly tunes out.

It doesn't matter how much he misses Craig—*so much*—that'll pass. It will. He'll make it pass, damn it; he made the only sensible decision that could be made for both of them, so this whole thing where his chest aches around the place where his heart would be if it were whole and healthy and worth a damn, well, that will pass too; it is going, goddamn it, to pass. He will, oh yes he will, make it pass.

Coming back by the kitchen table, he spots a pair of files he brought home Friday, information on some potential clients that is supposed to help him craft Clio-winning ad campaigns for whatever crap they're trying to sell. As a distraction, an aid on the path to getting over things, work is not the most fun option in the world, but without leaving his apartment it's the option he's got. With a sigh, he scoops up the files and heads into the bedroom to grab his glasses.

He doesn't notice the new addition to his nightstand, not at first.

It hits him when he reaches the living room, knocks his feet out from under him and sends him sprawling on the couch, hand over his mouth, glasses and files dropped forgotten on the floor.

Did I just see that?

Had he, in fact, imagined a framed black and white photograph of him and Craig in the kitchen at Sucre Coeur, a photograph that had to have been taken two weeks ago and without them noticing?

Was it real, that forever-trapped moment when he held Craig in his arms and watched him pipe white frosting clouds onto cupcakes? He remembers his breaths syncing with Craig's slow, steady ones as Craig resumed his work, that silly paper hat all of the Sucre Coeur staff had to wear only barely covering the thick twists of his dreads. He whispered in Craig's ear—he doesn't remember what he said, but remembers it made Craig smile.

He'd loved it when he could be the one to make Craig smile. Craig was so cheerful all the time, but it was a special moment when Alex could make Craig happy the way Craig made him happy...

Alex stumbles to his feet and back to the door of his bedroom, where he blinks at his nightstand. There it is. Next to his alarm clock, solidly framed in black wood and white matte. In a few lurching steps, he's got it in his hand and is sliding down next to his bed, eyes fixed on it, drinking in every detail.

Connor. Of course it had to be Connor. Connor taking the picture and Connor leaving it here. Alex's fingers trace the lines of Craig's arms—*I loved being in them*—and his face—*his smile is better than sunlight*—and shoulders—*I never did develop those pictures I took of him sleeping*—and he wishes he could feel the real, living flesh and blood Craig under his fingertips.

It hurts, it hurts like fire where his heart should be, but he can't help smiling through the tears gathering in his eyes—a knock on the door startles him out of it.

Connor. It has to be him. He must have forgotten something. *I will choke him for this.*

The edges of the frame bite into Alex's fingers as he strides to the door and jerks it open. "Connor, I fucking—"

Except—it's not Connor.

"Can I come in?" Jeff asks quietly, his fingers knotted together and white at the knuckles.

"Wh... buh..." And now Alex's other hand starts to ache as it tightens around the doorknob; the skin over his knuckles thins and whitens while blood drains away. *I need to improve my diet*, he thinks inanely, stifling a giggle. *Another day like this might actually kill me. What does a heart attack feel like?*

Jeff tilts his head, eyes searching. "Alex?"

Stepping back, Alex shakes his head, unsure whether he is trying to snap out of his shock or make the illusion—it has to be an illusion—disappear.

But Jeff doesn't disappear, just stands there looking nervous—amazing, Jeff has nervous in him; Alex would never have guessed—and waiting and, shit, fine, Alex takes another step back, braces himself and opens his mouth. "Come in."

"Thanks." Jeff steps inside, but only two steps, and hovers around the doorway as if he wants to bolt and run. It's so confusing that Alex feels some of his own tension melt away, his stomach unknot, while he tries to reconcile his ex-lover Jeff—beautiful Jeff of the vile, poisonous remarks and fucking around and cold, hard arrogance—with this Jeff, who is visibly nervous and awkward for what has got to be the first time in his life.

Nope. Can't. "It's not even four o'clock, I know," he says, "but the sight of you makes me need a drink. Want one?"

Jeff stares at him for a moment and then lets out the smallest chuckle. "Desperately."

The liquor cabinet hasn't been replenished, so Alex gets a pair of wine glasses and locates a bottle of Pinot Grigio in the crisper drawer of his refrigerator. He'd had to put the photo down—it's a nasty shock to turn around and see Jeff sitting at the kitchen table with it in his hands. Anger floods Alex.

"This guy," Jeff says, pointing to the picture. "This is that guy you were with that day. At the diner. He bakes? Are you two—"

"Put it down." *Before I smash this bottle over your head.* "Put it—don't touch—why the *fuck* are you here?"

Jeff inhales, sets down the picture frame and says in a burst, "That's a fair question."

"Then fucking answer it." Alex shakes with all-consuming anger. He gets the wine glasses onto the table without making them clatter against the wooden surface, but he hands Jeff the corkscrew and bottle. "And open this."

"Absolutely. Yes. Sure." But oddly, Jeff's hands don't seem to be any steadier than Alex's. The corkscrew slips and clicks against the neck of the bottle before he can finally jab the point into the cork. "Um. Let's get some of this stuff down—"

"No," Alex snaps, clenching his fingers into and out of fists. "Talk and uncork at the same time. You're not going to stay long, so if you want any of that wine, you'll fucking multitask."

"Okay." Jeff takes a couple more breaths, shoulders heaving, He gets the bottle open and starts pouring. "Um. So, I came to apologize."

This is the very last thing Alex expects. "You came to apologize." He makes no effort to bottle up his hysterical laughter, the whole thing is so ludicrous. *Why didn't I just slam the damn door in Jeff's face, why?* "Apologize! Why? Are you in some twelve-step program?"

Jeff's concentration is focused like a laser on pouring out the wine. "Not exactly."

Not exactly. Alex snorts. "So what are you apologizing for? For being a complete sociopath? For all those dick, backhanded 'compliments' you threw at me? For treating me like shit? For fuck—"

"For all of it. Everything." Jeff hands him a glass. "Hey. Don't drop that."

Moving to the North Pole is sounding very good right now. Isolated, nearly impossible to get a cell phone signal, great photography opportunities. But mostly, isolated. Alex takes the wine glass and falls into a chair. "Okay. Fine. Explain."

"Well." Jeff's fingers flex and flutter around the bulb of his glass, but he does not drink. "I mean, it's just.... look. This is hard."

"No, being with you was hard." Alex drains half his glass in one go. "Spitting out an apology you won't mean ought to be easy; it's just stringing words together. You've always been good at that."

"You think I wouldn't mean it?" That's rich: Jeff actually is wide-eyed with something that looks like surprise—and hurt. "You think I'd come here, knowing how much you have to hate me, and make a *fake* apology?"

Alex snorts. "Well, you were always pretty good at saying whatever you needed to say to justify the shit you pulled and make yourself feel better."

"All right, I earned that."

"I'm holding back on what you've earned." It's a sneer; he can't help it and he is very fucking okay with it. Down goes another quarter of the wine in his glass, and he's only just now starting to stop shaking. "Okay. Fine. Let's assume you really do mean this, or think you do. What would you say?"

"I would say I'm sorry, for starters," Jeff informs him; it's a definite effort for him to keep his voice as even as it is, Alex can tell. "I'd work backwards, starting with the really fucking shitty way I ended things with you. That was... it was uncalled for. I should have explained things to you, I should have been a decent fucking human being."

"Yeah, well, I don't think you've ever been within slapping distance of decency; don't be too surprised you couldn't pull it off." Alex leans back, then forward, twitching, restless and hating that he can't be calm and reasonable.

Although—why should he be? He shoves his glass aside. "Let's not go into a laundry list. We'll be here way too long, and I'm not about to spend a week explaining every shit thing you did, because I am *positive* you don't have a full list." It's his turn now to breathe, to settle his nerves so that he can get through this. "I don't really need an apology. You know what I need? I need to know *why*."

"Why?" Jeff blinks and shakes his head. "Why?"

"Yeah. Why. Why you did it. Why you were such a raging asshole." He has to close his eyes. "I mean, you know, I thought I was in love with you."

A long exhalation. "That's why," Jeff finally says.

Alex's eyes snap open. "What the fuck?"

"I'm not saying it's a good excuse. It is beyond not." At last, Jeff takes a substantial swallow of his wine. "But that's why. I mean, I didn't know for sure you were, because you never talk about stuff like that. I was just, you know, after a while I started to realize there were feelings there and, okay, I freaked out."

Alex laughs again; it seems as if he'll never run out of hysteria. "You were a dick from day *one*."

"Well, let's be honest. We're both kind of jerks sometimes. We know our own kind." Eyebrows up, Jeff leans his chin on his hand. "It's sort of what brought us together—right?"

Not that Alex has any interest in being fair, but—"Yeah, all right. That's fair."

"Okay. So." Jeff pauses and swirls his glass in his free hand, seemingly mesmerized by the moving liquid. "This is going to keep sounding shitty. You want me to keep going?"

"To be honest, my opinion of you has no further beneath the floor to go," Alex tells him.

"It's not that." Jeff shakes his head. "Think what you want of me, it doesn't matter; I've earned anything you think about me. I just... I hurt you without thinking for so long, I'm not interested in consciously saying things that will hurt you now."

Down goes the last of Alex's wine, and he shuts his eyes tight. "Then don't think about it. Just... just get it out. Please. Just say it."

At least this time he can brace himself, knowing something's coming.

"We had an agreement, Alex. Remember? From the beginning. We said we weren't going to let it mean anything."

"Friends with benefits." He's not sure he likes where this is going.

"Right." It's quiet except for the tiny, tinkling chime of Jeff's fingernail against his glass. "You... you were breaking the agreement."

"You have to be fucking kidding me." Alex's mouth and eyes fly open and it is hard, oh so hard, to resist the urge to wring Jeff's neck. "Are you blaming *me* for your inability to not be a complete fucking asshole?"

"Yes! No... no! Well." As if he knows he's in danger of being strangled, Jeff scoots his chair back and holds his hands out in a gesture of surrender. "No. I'm just telling you what led me to do it. Okay? I mean, I should have ended it. I should have just ended it."

"Then why didn't you?" Alex's throat clogs up, dry and scratchy as if he's swallowed a ball of aluminum foil, or knives, or glass. "Why?"

"The friends part." Jeff's skin flushes a dull red. "*Friends with benefits.* I didn't want to lose my friend. I just wanted him to stop having feelings for me."

All Alex can do for way, way too long is stare. "Okay. Jeff? That's fucked. You know that's fucked, and stupid, and wow, no. Did you seriously think that treating me like shit was going to be a great way to keep me as a friend?"

"I'm a male model," Jeff says, letting a nervous laugh escape. "The common wisdom is that we're not the brightest of the species."

"You model to pay off your student loans. You have an anthropology degree from UDub; you're not a complete idiot," Alex says without thinking.

It's the smallest gesture of unintentional amity, but it breaks the tension and sends them both into silence, just looking at each other across the table: no anger, no fear, only resignation.

Alex is just... tired. Tired of so, so much. Of hurting, of resisting, of hating himself.

"You..." The words stick in his throat, along with the ball of whatever is grating its tender insides. "You made me feel like I was worthless. And the sick thing is, by the end I thought I deserved it... I still kind of do think I earned it."

"Why—" Jeff's eyes are huge and confused. Alex waves him into silence.

"Just... long story, my life before I met you, the me being a jerk thing... just. Yeah." He swallows, and swallows some more, and pours another half glass of wine to try to wash the harshness down his throat. "Karma. I'm not a great person."

"No one is."

Craig is. "Some people are."

"Well." Jeff reaches for the bottle to top off his own glass. "That doesn't matter. You didn't deserve me being that kind of a shit to you, I promise. You aren't worthless. You weren't what I wanted in a boyfriend, but that's not a crime of high treason." He starts to sip at the fresh pour, and stops. "But... listen. Alex... you resented me so much by the end. Why would you have wanted to stay with me?"

"I was hoping you'd stop treating me like crap," Alex tells him, and the honesty feels as if hooks are being ripped from his skin. "I just thought it might turn around—if it could turn around and you could be decent to me, maybe it would prove I was worth something. I needed that to happen, and it didn't, it never did."

Jeff's face is a study in pain. "I'm sorry. Alex, I—"

"No. Don't. I..." He's shaking again. Why is he shaking? "I've got more issues than just you, trust me. I probably need therapy."

"Well, join the club." Alex guesses his face must be a mask of shock, because his ex laughs and shakes his head. "Yeah. I'm in therapy. You're not actually surprised?"

"A little," Alex admits. "I wouldn't have credited you with that kind of self-awareness."

"Meeting Kevin and falling for him... he's Episcopalian." Jeff waits, and when Alex can't indicate comprehension, he goes on. "We had to get counseling with the bishop before the church would do this blessing thing they do for gay marriages. And let me tell you, it shed light on me as a person, and what I saw was pretty horrible." He sips his wine. "I'm a little surprised Kevin still agreed to marry me, to be honest. I mean, seriously, what he sees in me, I have no idea, but I love him. And he *did* make therapy one of the conditions of going through with it."

Alex goes with the simplest of the confusing matters surrounding him. "I still can't believe you did go through with it. Kevin and Jeffrey Henderson-Arata," he says aloud and grimaces. "Could you be any more white picket fence? You have *two last names*."

"Oh, and you with a cupcake-baking Englishman—I heard that accent at the diner, don't even try to deny it. Like that isn't basically the most adorable thing in the world." Jeff picks up the photo of Alex and Craig at Sucre Coeur and waves it. "Listen, if I'd met this one first, I *might* have fought you for him. I clearly would have lost, but I would have been tempted to fight."

He can't. He can't say that it's over, can't tell Jeff the extent of the damage done. Can't admit it out loud. "He's an amazing guy," Alex mumbles into his glass, unable to look at Jeff or the picture or anywhere but the grain of the wood tabletop or the white plaster of the walls.

"I can see that. Anyone can. You're lucky." Jeff sets the photo down. "I'm happy for you, Alex. This—" His finger taps the glass covering the picture. "This is something worth having. Better than anything I could have given you."

The words are true in a way that makes Alex's stomach twist with hurt and steals his breath. *You didn't need to be such a fucking shit about proving it to me. I don't care if you're getting therapy...* His stretched-thin patience is at the breaking point. "Can you go now, Jeff? I just... I need to not have you here."

Jeff pushes away from the table, his chair squeaking across the linoleum. "Ah... yeah. Everything all right?"

"I'm not particularly feeling like that's a question you have the right to ask." He's being careful, so careful, holding everything together with threads worn too thin. "I appreciate you coming by."

"Okay... " Jeff is back to uncertainty, as if Alex has thrown him off-balance, as if he expects a different response. *Not fun, is it?* But Alex feels no satisfaction in being able to unnerve Jeff. It's just a drop in the bucket of vengeance Jeff deserves, for one thing, but most of all it just doesn't feel good.

Alex reaches the door first and opens it. "Maybe I'll see you around."

"Alex." Jeff's hand covers his, and the last iron shreds of Alex's control are exerted in not flinching. "I meant what I said. I am sorry."

"And I do appreciate that." Alex waits, the nerves under his skin crawling, until Jeff lets him go and wanders out of the apartment, face still clouded with confusion.

Alex manages to stay upright until he can't hear Jeff's footsteps; only then does he allow himself to slide down the door, cradling his head in his hands when he hits the floor.

For long, slow minutes he considers this unexpected, unasked-for encounter, tumbling thoughts and impressions end over end. *I can't forgive him. I can't ever forgive him. He probably wanted that, but I can't.*

His head thumps against the door once, twice, one more time before a dull throb begins to radiate through his skull. *He doesn't deserve forgiveness. He's happy and married and in love and he wants me to say it's okay that he did that to me? It's fucking unfair that he gets to be so happy after what he did. After he fucked me up and fucked me over, I don't...*

Alex reaches for the doorknob and pulls himself to his feet. There's still a swallow or two of white wine in his glass on the table; he snatches it up and pours it down his acid-raw throat.

The picture is still on the table, too. Alex's free hand strokes the wood of the frame before he realizes what he's doing and then he snatches his fingers away as if burned, squeezes his eyes shut so he can't see it and falls into his chair again.

Craig isn't Jeff. Craig was never Jeff, would never have been. And I fucked up, I ran away because of what Jeff did, I let him ruin the best thing I ever had. His eyes open, his gaze strays back down, almost as if pulled to look at the way Craig was smiling—smiling at him, leaning into him.

I didn't deserve what Jeff did, but after all that, maybe I do deserve...?

They'd been the only two people in the world, in that moment.

Two people. Together. Happy. Just as Jeff and Kevin had been in the brief moment before everything exploded that day in the Finch.

If I know I didn't deserve what Jeff did, why don't I let myself...?

If Jeff, of all people, somehow deserves to end up happy like that...

Alex shoves his chair back, not noticing how it clatters to the floor as he bolts out of it and races for his bedroom.

"Craig," Sarita says with a rueful shake of her head as she steers through the streets. "When I said my brother had puppies, you know that wasn't a veiled pitch for you to let him extort money from you for one of them. You know that, right?"

Craig lifts the pet carrier sitting in his lap and pokes a finger through the bars. "Shush. She's being silly, eh, Fitz?"

The tiny, bright-eyed mop of caramel-brownie-striped fur in the carrier lets out the smallest of puppy barks as if he agrees with Craig. His little Yorkie tail goes ninety miles an hour as he licks at Craig's finger. Craig tilts his head at Sarita. "Even he agrees."

"He's twelve weeks old, he's a dog, he'll 'agree' with anything you say." But she's smiling—maybe a touch ruefully, but it is a smile. "He's cute, though. I just think it's a lot of money to drop, and I think my brother took advantage of the fact that you're a soft touch and extra vulnerable right now."

"Tsk. If anyone took advantage, it's Fitz." He strokes the puppy's tiny muzzle. "As if I could resist the tiniest puppy in Seattle, could I; just look at him."

"Hopeless," is all Sarita says, but she has a smile in her voice.

No, he hadn't planned to go home just yet, and definitely not with a puppy. He'd barely played with the first pair of Yorkshire terrier pups that Devesh and his husband Sunil had brought out. Oh, they'd been lively and healthy and as adorable as a pair of dust mops with eyes could be, but he'd just gone through the motions of playing with them.

Then Sunil had brought out the runt of the litter, a little cuddler he and Devesh had improbably saddled with the glorious name of Sir Roderick Fitzhugh, Mighty Scourge of Yorkshire, and the next thing Craig knew, he and Sarita were at a pet store with Fitz and a cart full of puppy supplies.

Retail therapy. It's helping. A little. It's less fattening than lemon vodka bundt cake, at any rate.

He'd have stayed at Sarita's a couple more days, but her landlord doesn't allow pets, even visiting, so the purchase of Fitz had put the kibosh on their sleepover. "I can stay here, if you want," she offers as they get through the door to his place with a considerable mountain of his belongings in precarious tow. "I know you don't have a couch, but I don't mind sharing a bed with you. I know you won't grope and I promise I don't snore."

It's tempting, oddly enough. Apparently there was something to Theodora's insistence that he not hide from his hurt. He feels a little better after last night—mild hangover aside— after letting friends take care of him, after getting out of this oppressive little apartment of his. It might be nice to have Sarita here for a night, watching movies on his laptop and playing with Fitz.

On the other hand, even the thought is exhausting. Maybe it's better to confine emotional breakdowns and expensive purchases to a more spaced-out schedule. "Maybe tomorrow?

Come back here after you close up, and we'll order pizza. See what's on Netflix."

Conflict flits through her eyes. "You sure?"

"Yeah, I think so." He sets the carrier down and opens it to let Fitz scrabble out and nose around the apartment. "I mean, maybe Fitz and I should have a night to bond or something."

The look on her face lets him know she sees right through him, but she doesn't protest. "Tomorrow for sure, though," she warns, in a tone that brooks no argument.

"Without fail. I'll see you after seven."

"Yes, you will," she says, nodding firmly even as he closes the door after her. He leans on it to settle himself and catch his breath.

A tiny yip catches his attention. Fitz has trotted to the door as if to help see Sarita off and is now perched on his fuzzy haunches, cocking his little head as if he's actually listening. Craig can't help but smile at the idea, not to mention the sheer adorableness of his new pet. "Have you had a good look 'round?" he asks. "Might as well, this is your home."

Fitz does nothing to dispel the illusion that he understands English when he snuffles off to inspect the baseboards and furniture.

Craig slumps at his kitchen table and breathes a sigh he's been holding back for the last hour. There's a stack of dessert carriers he should clean and put away, as well as several bags of toys and supplies and a puppy bed for Fitz he should sort out. His overnight bag probably ought to be emptied and the several days' worth of unworn clothing returned to the closet. A very small studio apartment can become extremely cluttered with alarming swiftness.

But he sits, and he watches his pet and he thinks about Alex.

He misses Alex so much. Bravado aside, he doesn't really think Fitz is going to be a foolproof distraction.

Tea, he decides, pushing away from the table. It's after five, and he hasn't had anything all day except some croissants he'd eaten at Devesh and Sunil's. As if reminded, his stomach growls. *Tea, and food, then thinking. Or I can multitask. Food and thinking.*

After a cupboard scramble, he's got a plan for tomato soup and a tuna salad sandwich on toast for himself, has a bowl of organic puppy mash down on the floor for Fitz and is filling the kettle when he hears a knock at the door. Craig blinks and looks at Fitz. "You expecting anyone?"

Fitz lets out a yippy little bark and cocks his head.

"I'll take that as a no." Craig plugs in the kettle and turns it on before heading for the door. "But I'm not, either, so I do wonder—hello, Connor?"

And it is indeed Alex's best friend, complete with adorable baby strapped to his chest. "Hiya," Connor says, grinning as he holds up a bag. "Good to see you, too. Cinnamon pretzel?"

Well, this is unexpected.

"Ah, sure... come in..." Bemused, Craig ushers the pair of Monaghans into his apartment, helping Connor to divest himself of a diaper bag, a satchel and, of course, Kira. "This is a lot of stuff to haul up to the third floor."

"Twice, even. You weren't home the first time I knocked, so I went across the street. I've been watching for you to get home for a long while." Connor points to Craig's bed. "Mind if I put Kira down? The coffee shop was playing all this soft indie rock stuff and we've had a big day already; it knocked her right out."

"No, of course, absolutely." Waiting for him to get home? Thank goodness, Craig supposes, for innate British politeness even in the face of situations that make no sense whatsoever. *Well. I suppose there's a reason we're the ones who gave the world Monty Python...* He helps Connor pile pillows around Kira and wonders what, exactly, is going on. "Would you like some tea? Or dinner, even? I was about to throw something together."

Connor flings himself into a chair. "Yeah to the tea, nah to the dinner. You got company?"

Craig frowns. "Company?"

"I heard you talking to someone."

"Oh, no, I see. No." He points down to where Fitz is making whuffing noises into his food. "I... I sort of acquired a dog. Today. Which is why I'm home now, actually. I wasn't supposed to be..." *He waited for me. Why?*

"That's a dog?" When Connor cocks his head to get a better look at Fitz, it's a little unnerving how much he *resembles* the puppy. "Huh. That is definitely a dog. And you were talking to him."

Craig draws himself upright, stopping short of sticking his nose into the air. *I have dignity, thank you.* "Many people talk to their pets."

"Uh huh." Connor sits back upright with a slow grin. "So. How ya doin', Craig?"

"Um..." Well, there's a question, isn't there? Craig is really not sure what answer Connor might be seeking. Or what answer might be appropriate to give. How do you answer this question coming from your ex-lover's best friend—who surely must be aware of what's going on—without coming off as desperate or needy?

Which, frankly... that particular horse might be shot in the foot before it even gets to running. Connor did hear him talking to his dog, after all.

No. Lots of people talk to their pets. I didn't make that up.

Oh, he might just be losing the plot here a little bit.

Also, why is Connor here?

Fine. Executive decision. *Pretend everything is completely under control.* Also, evade Connor's question, since he has no good answer. "I'll get the tea, shall I?"

A shrug. Connor, obviously, does not have any need to pretend control. It's very annoying. "Sure."

Very, very annoying.

Still full of questions and worries and wonderings, Craig gets a pair of mugs and the tea things and puts on his best face when he turns to face his guest. He doesn't like feeling tipped off balance. He really doesn't like the smirk on Connor's face that tells him that this is a fellow who is very good at doing the tipping.

Craig is pretty sure he's the one who will come out on the losing side of this—but he's not going down without a struggle. He at least wants answers. "So," he begins, bringing the milk and sugar to the table. "It's not usual for you to wander up this way on a Sunday, I think. A bit far for you, isn't it?"

Connor wobbles his hand as if to say it was no big deal. "Eh, well, we're meeting Rayna soon, she's not far from here today." He flashes a big, big smile of pride. "She's working on the new exhibition at the Fountainhead."

Well. That's airtight. Craig seems to recall Rayna mentioning the show when she came to pick Connor up at Sucre Coeur two weeks ago. "The Color and Mood series? Oh, that's got to be a fun job. I've seen the flyers; the show looks really interesting." Still, something isn't sitting quite right. Craig carries on, pouring boiling water and arranging the sugar spoons until he works out what. "Ah, but, the Fountainhead, that's quite a few blocks away."

"A few, sure." Connor shrugs and fiddles with the bag of pretzels. "But it's sort of in the neighborhood, so I figured hey, why not come see you and all? It's only a few stops extra."

And I'm Princess Anne. Craig raises an eyebrow. Something is definitely up. He doesn't even know Connor and he can spot it. "Are we on drop-in terms just yet?"

The smile doesn't falter. "I figure now's as good a time as any for us to get on 'em."

Oh, nothing rattles you, does it? Clearly a more direct line of questioning is in order, never mind that it goes against everything in Craig's very English nature. "But you were waiting for hours." Keeping cool, keeping casual, smiling away, he puts their mugs on the table next to the milk and sugar. "So then it's not really a drop-in."

"You implying I maybe got ulterior motives?"

"Oh, no." Craig beams. "I'm saying it outright."

Connor's fingers keep plucking at the pretzel bag and he chuckles. "We got people in common, you seem cool, no reason not to be friends."

"But hours—" The crinkle of the paper catches Craig's attention at last and he takes a closer look at the bag. He knows that logo, doesn't he? It's tugging at the back of his mind, something familiar, something—he's bought pretzels at that same shop, yes? Several times. Right? Best pretzels in Seattle, Alex always said—

That's by Alex's place. It clicks into place like the flip of a switch. "You were at his flat. You've seen him. Today."

Connor flops an arm over the back of his chair, lopsided grin in full effect. "Nice deduction, Holmes."

Dear God. "Tell me how he is." So much for cool, calm and neither desperate nor needy. He's not entirely surprised to find that he's lunged across the table and grabbed Connor's hand.

Not, perhaps, his most dignified moment, but he hasn't got a pair of fucks to rub together.

"He's been better." Connor calmly extracts his hand from Craig's grip. "But he's mostly okay. Clearly drinking like a fish and the apartment smells like an ashtray—to be blunt."

"I expect you are blunt quite a lot of the time," Craig says, perhaps with obvious impatience; which is very rude, he knows, but again, he is completely lacking in fucks.

Connor snickers. "Yeah. It's a gift."

"You've seen him. My God, you've seen him." He can't decide if he wants to scream, laugh or run the miles to Alex's apartment and demand one last time to be allowed entrance. "I don't know—how did you—I want—" But finishing a thought, let alone a spoken sentence, is suddenly impossible. He's pulled in too many directions.

"You wanna know what I think, is what you want." It's not a question.

"I don't think that's actually where I was going with that," Craig shoots back. He adds milk and sugar to his tea. "But do go on."

Connor shrugs one shoulder nonchalantly, irritating as hell. "You need to get your"—he stops and glances at his daughter, who is still sound asleep—"ass down there and get him back."

For a moment, all Craig can do is sit, frozen, with his spoon in mid-stir. *Really. Really? That's what you have to offer?* "Just... go down there and get him back."

"Yeah."

"Oh!" Craig throws his spoon down on the table and his hands in the air, letting a bark of laughter escape him. "Oh yes! Because that's so easy. I never once thought of that! Good heavens, how stupid of me."

"Aw, come on—" Connor reaches out his hand, but Craig ignores him.

"No, no, because when someone refuses to answer your calls, emails, text messages or even his *door* when you knock on it, it really paves the way for reconciliation." He chokes down the hysterical laughter bubbling up from his stomach. "No, no, I haven't spent the last two weeks trying to figure out how to make him *listen* to me for a minute so I can try to get him back, oh, no, I haven't at all—"

"Well, I got *my* ass in the door."

At this almost lazy interruption, Craig shuts up and glares across the table at Connor, who, with care that appears extreme for the task, pulls the tea bags from his mug and adds sugar, stirring with a slow and maddening precision. He takes a long, long drink; his eyes twinkle over his mug, and he doesn't say another word.

It's impolite to strangle one's guests. His mother would be very disappointed that he even had the urge. "Fine," Craig snaps. "How exactly did you manage that?"

"I stood outside his apartment and told him his mother was on her way with the cops. When you meet his mom, you'll get why that's scary."

Craig's jaw drops. "I think you may be a genuinely awful person."

"Maybe." Connor tilts his head. "But I'm the one who got in the door."

Well, fine. The man does have an *exquisite* point.

Craig's irritation drains away, and he slumps against the back of his chair, back to where he'd been before Connor knocked on his door. Fitz is nosing around his feet and whining; Craig picks up the puppy and scratches his little neck. "The thing is... I... I mean, even if he'd let me in the door, the plain fact is I have no idea what to say to him. I don't know what to ask him, if I should apologize, what words are the right ones... I mean..." Words slip through the fingers of his mind like sand, and he gropes to find anything comprehensible. "I didn't even get to know what happened to him before it came back and absolutely destroyed our relationship."

Connor watches him, assessing, measuring as always. "You know now, though?"

"Yeah. Enough." But it scratches at him, chafes and rubs from the inside out until he can't hold it in any longer. "No. Not enough. Well, enough about that, but—this is ridiculous. I'm in love with someone I hardly even know. Did you know that?" A hysterical giggle slips past his disintegrating control. "Literally. I didn't know his middle name until two weeks ago. We just... we never talked about ourselves because he clearly didn't trust me and I was too afraid to push him. I fell in love with Alex and I can't tell you what his favorite color is."

"Green."

Craig's fingers stop in the act of rubbing Fitz's ears. "Sorry?"

"His favorite color. It's green." Connor taps his spoon against his mug. "What the hell does that matter?"

"Well, I mean—" Off-balance and flailing again, Craig makes his own assessment of just how much he likes Connor. At this moment, the numbers aren't looking so good. "I mean, it's no wonder I don't know what to say to him. I don't even know him."

"Yeah, okay, but it's not like saying, 'So your favorite color is green, let's get back together,' is the way to go, I gotta tell you." Connor is snickering, which does not help his case. "That's the kind of shit that's only useful when you gotta buy somebody presents. Forget the details. I bet you know enough of what's actually important."

"More easy answers from the great Connor Monaghan." Craig can practically feel his mother clocking him upside the head for the unbridled lack of manners, but he's tired of Connor being so unflappable and of himself feeling so dumb. "Do you really think that if it were so very easy, I wouldn't have already done it?"

The mask slips for one swift second as Connor leans across the table. "It is actually that easy, dumb-ass."

"Oh, now we're name-calling."

"Well, you're kind of being a superior jerk for someone who doesn't know how to get his boyfriend or whatever you two are back," Connor snaps. "Fuck the details, Oliver, okay? Go with what you *know*. You said you love him. That true?"

"Well, of course, but—"

Connor draws his finger across his throat and waits for Craig to shut up. "Do you love him?" His voice demands no answer but the most simple and sincere that Craig can give.

So he does. "More than anything."

A nod. "What do you love about him?"

"Everything." Simple, yet... well, yes. It's a bit complicated.

With another nod, Connor sits back. "All righty. Elaborate."

Craig knows he looks like a pie-eyed idiot. "Sorry?"

"Yeah, just..." Connor waves a hand, nonchalance in his every line. "Tell me what you love."

"I love everything," Craig snaps. "I love all of Alex, not just this part or that."

"I don't mind if it's a long list." Still smiling with infuriating casualness, Connor settles more comfortably into his chair and waits. He is obviously not going to be of any further help, however dubious, until Craig does this ridiculous thing.

Fine. "I told you. Everything." But Craig stops to think, to take stock when Connor's eyes don't lose their expectant look, their demand for more. "Right. So... he's funny—sarcastic funny, dark sarcastic. I love that."

Connor just nods.

"I love that he's never, ever at rest even when he's sitting still—he just has this energy?" Craig has to set Fitz down so he can talk with his hands, sketching in the air as if he could bring Alex into the room just by describing him. "I love the way his eyes light up when he laughs. I love how he doesn't know how to do anything in the kitchen but wants to help anyway. I love the fact that he has the most absolutely hilarious little grumbles and snores I have ever heard."

"The snoring is definitely funny," Connor concedes, cracking a smile.

"I love that I met him in a bar, like, it's the most amazing cliché in the world and we all know it, but I love it anyway. I love that he is always, *always* humming and tapping pencils on things." Now he almost can't stop. "I love that when he's asleep after a bad day, he... he finds me. Just... in his sleep, he finds me. He did it the first night we met."

I still wonder if you felt me kiss you that night.

"I love that there's more to know, for me to find out. But... I even love the parts that are harder to handle than others. Even whatever part of him led him to literally run away from me." Craig stops to breathe, to swallow the lump in his throat. "I think that part must need quite a lot more love than the rest, really."

Connor stares again for a very long time before nodding. "Okay. That's it."

"That's what?"

"That's what you say. All of that. But you have to, you know, actually say it. You should try that."

"He won't even open his door." Craig's tea tastes like his exasperation.

"If that's the only thing stopping you at this point, I got incentive." Getting to his feet, Connor pulls a picture frame from his bag and slides it across the table, face down. "Don't—" He raises a finger in clear warning. "Don't look at that until after we're gone."

Craig looks up at him, astonished, hand outstretched over the picture frame. "That's it? Just go to his place and tell him how I feel, that's your grand solution?"

"Well, I mean..." It can't be easy to shrug while strapping on a Baby Bjorn, but Connor manages it. "Yeah, I'm serious. Go to his place and tell Alex what you just told me, even if you have to do it through the door. Just tell him, 'cause he needs to know. Is sitting on your ass really a better idea?"

"But I—"

Connor waves his hand. "Just... just look at that photo. No, I said after I leave."

With heroic effort, Craig resists the urge to snatch up the frame and take a good long look at whatever is in it. "What is it?"

"The swift kick in the ass you seem to be looking for, I hope." Bags are retrieved, a sleeping baby cradled in her father's arms, a door opened. "For what it's worth, I'm behind you a hundred percent, Craig."

Before Craig can say anything more, Connor has smiled at him and disappeared down the stairs. Craig waits for his footsteps to clatter into silence before snatching up the photo and turning it over.

His heart slams to a stop.

Oh. He can't breathe. *I remember this.* Everything hurts. *I didn't see him take this.* He reaches forward, as if he could get through the glass and make the picture real. *Why isn't it real?*

He can feel Alex's arms encircling him, an anchor, a safe place, a harbor. Hear the warmth of Alex's tickling whisper in his ear. Remember leaning into the embrace, moving on with his work, as if it were natural and everyday—and it *was* like that, it was, *goddamn* it, and he sits and shakes, holding the photo, trying to remind himself of what it's like to be able to breathe and think without it hurting.

Fitz nudges at Craig's foot, head cocked with puppy questions as he whines and whuffles, while Craig's hands clutch tight around the framed photograph, pressing it to his chest, where his heart still doesn't feel as though it's resumed normal activity. Craig wants to comfort the little dog and knows he should, but he can't get his fingers to uncurl from around the sharp-cornered wood that holds everything he wants in one frozen moment.

I have to get him back.

He can't move.

Tonight. I have to do this tonight. Somehow.

Just as soon as he can move.

Not another minute, I can't do this any longer.

There's a knock at the door.

Chapter Nineteen

THE KNOCK SEEMS TO ECHO THROUGH THE APARTMENT. *Boom. Boom. Boom.*

No. Wait. Stop.

That's not knocking.

It takes Craig's brain a minute to catch up—there had been knocking, that was real, it had happened. But it had been short, the knock itself only a tense, hesitant rapping.

The echoing boom in his ears is his heartbeat, or at least what he imagines is his heartbeat. The rush of blood through his veins is moving double-time *because* of the knocking that had startled adrenaline into flooding his body; it's racing through him and pounding in his ears and no wonder he thinks someone is banging his door down. He closes his eyes and pulls in a long breath.

Another, even more hesitant knock comes—a real knock, no confusion this time—and Craig pries his eyes open to look at Fitz, still perched at his feet with a look of puppy concern on his furry little face. "Still not for you, I take it."

The only response he gets is a cold, wet nose pressed firmly into his ankle, as if Fitz is trying with all the might of his not-quite two pounds to shove Craig toward the door. "All right, all right, I can take a hint."

He's slow to uncurl his fingers from their pale-knuckled grip on the photo frame, to carry it over to the nightstand and place it next to his laptop and lamp. He casts it one last look that wrenches his heart out of place before he picks up Fitz and trudges to the door.

"I don't know who it could be now," he says to Fitz, scratching the fuzzmonster under his chin. "Connor coming back? Perhaps he forgot something." He almost hopes it is Connor, having to haul his belongings up the stairs a third time. *Serve him right for that dirty trick with the photograph.*

Just as his hand closes around the doorknob, "I'm not Connor," a familiar, ragged, tired voice informs him through the thin wood.

No. Craig stops in his tracks. *No, you are not.*

And then he can't get the door open fast enough, scrambling to undo the locks and pull it wide. What he sees—all he can do is blink, stunned stupid, unsure that what he's seeing is real.

"Alex," he breathes, and his mind just... stops.

The man standing in the doorway, clinging to the door frame for dear life, is red-eyed and damp-haired under a green knit cap, rumpled and at least one day unshaven. A plain red T-shirt and blue jeans hang from the frame that, in only two weeks, seems to have lost weight it couldn't spare. It's the scruffiest Craig has seen Alex in the months they've known each other.

He's the best thing Craig's ever laid eyes on.

"Hello, you," he manages at last, knowing he must look quite the idiot with his shocked face trying to smile and stay stoic all at once. He's nearly afraid to breathe; Alex looks as if he'll turn and fly away if Craig so much as sneezes. "Been a bit."

"Yeah, kind of." Alex's gaze bounces around like a rubber ball, never landing on anything for more than a second or two. "Is that a dog?"

"Oh, ah, yes." Craig holds up the puppy. "Fitz."

"Fitz." Alex nods, still restless and strung so visibly tight. "He looks like a Fitz."

"Doesn't he just." He wants to smile, to laugh, to think that just the fact that Alex is here means everything is put right again, but he knows that wish, no matter how fervent, can't be trusted as true. Not yet. Craig pulls Fitz close to his chest and takes a step back. "Ah, would you like—"

"Here," Alex blurts out, as his hand comes from behind his back to shove a plastic box at Craig. His gaze still bounces and wanders until he lowers his head, hand extended and shaking so that whatever is in the box rattles against the sides.

Craig starts back another step and fumbles for the box with his free hand. He sets Fitz down and scoots him gently off toward the back of the apartment.

What he finds in the box is a surprise.

Cookies.

He thinks. Maybe.

Plain, ordinary chocolate chip cookies, clearly and obviously not from a bakery—they're not pretty. Misshapen, blackened lumps fill the container, not an edible-looking one in the lot. Puzzled, Craig looks back up to see Alex watching him steadily at last, eyes wary, body tense and still poised for flight. "I don't…"

"They're a fucking metaphor. Apparently." As he shoves his hands into his pockets Alex laughs, but it's a shaky laugh edged in nerves. "They weren't supposed to be. They were just supposed to be cookies. I thought I shouldn't show up empty-handed, and cookies seemed appropriate."

"Right…" He won't let himself get his hopes up. Well, not much. Well, not too much. But this means something, doesn't it? It could, couldn't it?

Craig's heart is in his throat.

"But I can't even make cookies without you. And they were *tube* cookies." Alex laughs again and pulls his hands out of his pockets to rub his temples. "Who fucks up tube cookies? Slice and bake! It says it on the package!"

"Babe..." Craig begins, but his hesitant attempt is promptly run over by Alex's continuing rant.

"I forgot to set the timer, and I went to take a shower before I came here, but I had to clean out my bathroom because fucking Connor set up the darkroom and didn't even use it and next thing I know I'm pulling burned cookies out of my oven and my entire apartment stinks and the smoke detector is going fucking crazy and all I can think is, *Craig would have remembered the timer.* But you weren't there and I couldn't wait anymore so I didn't try again, I just threw them in a box and came here and I'm so sor—"

Craig can see only one way to stop the breathless ramble, a calculated risk and possible disaster: tossing the box of cookies aside, he grabs Alex by the front of his shirt.

He hopes that kisses will always and forever be a spectacular, wonderful, brain-meltingly effective way to shut Alex up.

A heady rush of sweet relief and *yes this* washes through Craig at the moment their lips meet, from his tingling toes up through his head. Under his curled-up fist, through the soft cotton clenched tight in his fingers, the boom of a heartbeat resounds like a knock on a door, not a flutter but a thump.

He kisses Alex as if it could give him life, as if he'd been drowning and this was the only source of breath that could save him. He holds on and holds on and holds on and lets it go to his head, taking every breath and gasp and heartbeat into his mouth and memory.

This is everything that has ever been right.

And Alex doesn't pull away. Shaking hands grip at Craig's waist, pulling him tight—close and holding firm, they give his sparking, trembling hope a catalyst for ignition.

Craig has to be the one to break it off. He doesn't want to, but he has to breathe, and he has so many questions. Slowly, never letting go his grip on Alex's shirt, Craig pulls away to look at him, really look into his eyes. "Why," he asks in a whisper, "are you here? Please?"

Alex's mouth works, opens and closes in silence until—"I," he begins, falters, and then he just folds down and forward in a boneless heap that Craig's arms reach for and catch without sparing a thought.

I can't hold us both. I can't hold us both up—

They sink to the floor, a desperate clutched-together pile in the doorway; Alex shakes so hard in Craig's embrace it feels as if he might fly to pieces if Craig doesn't hold on for all he is worth. which of course Craig is so, so very willing to do, for as long as he's needed and beyond.

Alex can't stop shaking—*why?*—and Craig's shoulder is growing damp with tears shed in determined silence—*what happened?*—and he's so mired in and torn between being ecstatic—*you're here*—and worried as hell—*you're hurting*—he doesn't even know where to begin.

"Shhh," he whispers, feeling so helpless. At least it's a start. "Shh. I've got you."

He buries his face in the taut, warm and familiar curve of Alex's neck; his own stinging tears pepper the skin alongside tiny constellations of freckles he knows and loves so well. Alex squeezes him so tightly he can't breathe in more than shallow little catches of air, it hurts, it *hurts*, but the ache is a drop in the bucket next to the thought of letting go and risking the chance of Alex panicking and running again.

So Craig holds tight, and Craig breathes in the tiniest quiet breaths, and Craig hopes so, so desperately, with every ounce of wishing in his bottomless soul, that Alex has chosen to come back to him.

The shaking ebbs from shaking to trembling to shivering to tremors to stillness and silence. A thousand questions surround them and press in thicker than fog, but Craig waits, still squeezed tight and holding on for dear life.

Don't go, don't go, don't go, not again; I'll stop breathing if you go; don't ever go again.

He can't make the first move; it's not his to make.

Please, please...

"I'm sorry."

The words are muffled in Craig's shoulder, so that he feels them more than hears them; the sound vibrates through his skin.

"I'm sorry," Alex repeats, and lifts his head, hauling in a huge gulp of air and *no*, he's going to try to go, Craig can see it, *no*. "I'm sorry, I'm so—I'm such a fuckup—I shouldn't have—the things I said—"

He starts to push Craig away, to squirm out of the tight grip, but *no*, Craig isn't doing this, not again. "I'm not letting go," he tells Alex as panic races through him, and winds his fingers into the fabric of Alex's T-shirt to hold him in place. "I am not ever, ever letting you go, not now that you're here again. No."

"You don't understand, Craig, I made a mistake—" Alex works his arms free, only to stare with wild eyes when Craig seizes his wrists. "You don't need me, you don't deserve to have to put up—"

"Stop it, please, Alex, just stop." Craig disentangles himself just long enough to swing up onto his knees and climb into Alex's lap and straddle him to pin him down. "Don't leave me again, please don't," he whispers, sliding his fingers to the nape of Alex's neck and pressing in just enough to be firm and tilt his head back, to hold him still but not to hurt. Leaning down, he takes kiss after kiss, begging between breaths. "Never again. Stay with me, please, please stay."

"I'm not going anywhere, but Craig, I'm a mess," Alex gasps, but his hands grip Craig's waist, holding on for dear life as he snatches his own kisses as if enough of them will save him. "I'm not good, I'm fucked up, I'm—"

"Everything I want, shut it." He hears the shaking in the desperate laugh that escapes his mouth and he presses his forehead to Alex's. They're both trembling now, thighs to shoulders to fingers to toes, they'll take the building down if they can't stop. "I'll say it until you believe it, but you can't leave if you want to hear it."

"Why?" Pulling back, Alex doesn't let go of Craig but still looks as if he could pull free and flee at any second. "Why? What could you need to say to me? I should be apologizing from now until I die."

I have to say it now, don't I? I have to tell him, like Connor said. I have to at least say that I...

Now that he has all the room in the world to breathe, Craig still can't. This is it. Maybe the last chance he'll get. And is there any point in hiding it any longer? The worst thing already happened when he was too scared to say it.

He closes his eyes and lets out the last of the air in his lungs before he takes the leap. "I love you."

The reasons can wait—he hopes.

Alex jerks under Craig's hands. "You what?"

"I love you," Craig says again, quite simply, quite honestly, with his full heart trembling in every word. "I was too afraid to tell you before. I thought you would leave me if I did."

When he opens his eyes again, Alex is looking at him with wide eyes gone dark, all bewilderment and fear. "But I did leave."

"So I have nothing to lose, and now you know." They're not out of the woods, but he's told the truth and Alex isn't moving an inch. The world didn't end. "What about you?"

Alex's breath shudders out in a puzzled laugh. "What *about* me?"

The half-shrug Craig pulls is far, far more casual than he's feeling. "Alex. You didn't just come over here to bring me cookies. I hope."

Conflict flickers behind Alex's eyes, painful to watch yet almost, oddly, heartening. He's still holding up his walls with both hands, but Craig can almost see them coming down, maybe... or is that wishful thinking?

"Did you mean it?" Alex finally asks, the words coming out as if he's pushing them with all his might. "What you... that you want...?"

"Not just want. Love. That I love you," Craig corrects, letting his fingers run down over Alex's temple and trace the line of his jaw, allowing his thumb to stroke Alex's cheek. His throat fills as he keeps taking in the sight of Alex's beloved, confused, apprehensive, overwhelmed face, the face he wants to wake up to every morning as long as they've got life in them. "I've loved you quite a lot for quite a little while now. Don't reduce it."

Alex just stares at him, so still and quiet for so, so long and then—blur, rush, grab, he's got Craig in that breath-stealing grip again and his face buried in Craig's chest, saying, "I love you, I love you, fuck, I love you, fuck, fuck, fuck, fuck."

There is no other way this moment could go that Craig could accept as absolutely, perfectly authentic. He holds onto it and to Alex with everything he's got in him; he wants to laugh and to cry and most of all to never, ever let go ever again.

Fitz scrabbles, yapping, across the hardwood floor to the commotion and tries to climb up between them. Alex hiccups and laughs as he pulls away from Craig to pick up the puppy, hugging him close and scratching the furry little head. His eyes are damp but shining when his gaze meets Craig's, and whatever has kept Craig's heart tethered to the ground lets go, loosening the strings and letting him fly at last. No, *this* is everything that's right.

"I accept both your love and your apology," Craig says, not even trying to stop himself from smiling like a great big goony idiot. "You can't take that back now. Not a single fuck of it."

Alex keeps hiccupping and laughing; his face flushes dull red. He buries it in Fitz's fur for a moment. "Oh, God, that was—"

"Pretty fucking perfect," Craig says, grinning and grinning and grinning. "When you tell the story, and you will, you are absolutely not allowed to change a single word. I want you to swear you won't."

When Alex looks up, his face wears a faint ghost of the playful half-smile that Craig hasn't seen in far too long. "Never. Not ever. Not after the day I've had just talking myself into coming here... "

"Hmm?" He shifts and settles into Alex's lap. "Do tell."

"It's been weird..." A breath puffs out Alex's cheeks and he rolls his eyes to the ceiling. "So, Jeff came by my apartment."

And that's nearly enough to dislodge Craig from his seat. "He what?"

Alex waves his hand and rolls his eyes again. "Long story—
I'll explain the rest of it later, but seriously I have had a long
day—"

"Sounds like we have stories to trade, then."

"You thought I was Connor; I bet we do." When Alex tucks
his face into Fitz's fur again, he seems to be pausing to gather
his thoughts. A long moment passes before he speaks again.
"Anyway, Jeff came by, and we had this *excruciating* talk, he
apologized and it was bizarre, I just... I made him go. And I
started to think that maybe... maybe if he got to find love,
if he somehow deserved it after everything... then I didn't
deserve the way he treated me, even if I was kind of a jerk
before I met you. So if he gets to be loved by someone, then
damn it, so do I."

"Oh." Craig takes a moment to imagine that conversation,
pictures Alex rattled and indecisive in the wake of it, and his
heart aches. "Alex, good lord, of course you deserve to be
loved. I have an absolutely enormous list of reasons why, if you
want them."

Alex laughs—full-on, outright laughs this time—and oh,
it's sweet to hear. "You can say that. Keep saying it, like you
said. One day I'll all the way believe it." He buries his nose in
the puppy fur at Fitz's neck and scratches the fluff with a long
finger before looking up at Craig again, more solemn but not
guarded, which is just as sweet as the laughter. "I mean. If we
get back together. I do get you. Right?"

Oh, boy, do you ever. "You get me," Craig nods. "That is, if
you'll have me." He pokes at the top of Alex's head, the close
proximity finally letting him recognize the hat covering it. "Or
if I'll have *you*, maybe. You stole my cap."

"This coming from the man who is sitting on me and making
my legs fall asleep. I think I have more to put up with." Alex

raises an eyebrow. "I found this hat at my apartment, where you left it and obviously haven't missed it. But I'd be happy to give it back to you."

Craig leans forward to press a kiss through the knitted wool, deciding he's not ready to get up from Alex's lap just yet. "Nah. It looks too good on you."

"Trade it to you for the puppy."

"Absolutely not."

"I'm wearing your boxers, too," Alex offers, assuming an expression of patently false innocence. "And your T-shirt. Maybe you want those back? Boxers and the hat for the puppy?"

Tilting his head, Craig pretends to seriously consider the offer. "No, I expect I can manage to get those back from you later. So it's still a no on Fitz. He'll be staying here."

"Hmm." The mock innocence vanishes, leaving Alex biting his lip in uncertainty. "Can... maybe I can stay here too? With you?"

Bringing his hands up, Craig cups Alex's face and holds it still, carefully avoiding squishing Fitz as he kisses Alex, long and slow and sweet.

It's everything.

But it's still missing something. He knows exactly what.

"Would you like to come in," Craig asks, sitting back and smiling so wide his cheeks ache, "and have some tea?"

ॐ THE END ॐ

Acknowledgments

IT IS FAIR TO SAY THAT THIS BOOK WOULD NEVER HAVE SEEN the light of day were it not for the encouragement of dozens of people stretching back decades. I owe so much in the way of gratitude and thanks.

To Alana—for lighting the spark of this story, for pushing and cheering me through writing it, for sending me pictures of Mr. Floof Rockmonster to keep me going. I could not have done this without you.

To Mimsy—for every late-night conversation, every screech of joy, every little Britpick and, most especially, for every kick up the backside when I began to flag. No way could I have survived this without you.

To Kat, Nadia and Samantha—for pre-reading and helping, for all the wonderful encouragement and virtual hand-holding. I would have collapsed in a weeping heap so many times were it not for the time you all took to help me out. I am, however, sorry about the Jeff thing, Nadia.

To Alice—for telling me I could do this, and for your incomparable, delightful way with puns. Bless you and your fuzzy cats! One day you and I are going to hang out and drink wine and watch trashy movies together and it's going to be the best thing, I can't wait. Thank you for being a rock.

To Wow—for being wonderful and smart and helpful and a fantastic source of reason and calm when I needed it most.

To Annie, Candy and Lex—for taking a chance on me and for telling me to calm the heck down and trust myself.

To Mom—for that one time you didn't believe I wrote a poem that I had given you, so I sat down and immediately wrote another one out of spite, and you said, "Huh. I guess you can actually write." And for really believing I could from that point on and just waiting for me to get on with it.

To Jessica—for being my sounding board, virtual sister and one of my best, dearest friends for twenty years, and for all of the support and belief you gave to me even during your worst struggles. Your generous spirit is a gift beyond compare.

To Angela, Aaron and the entire Thomas clan—for being happy for me and believing I could do this. You have all been wonderful and the best spiritual relatives a girl could ask for.

To Gladys—for all of the beautiful artwork you gave me, for being your delightful, inspirational self and for being my favorite fellow tea enthusiast.

To Mrs. Parker—for always believing that I would write something big one day; that has kept me going for longer than I can tell you. Thank you for being the best English teacher in the world.

To Fandom—for being you. It all started with you. There's not a sentence in this book that didn't get its start because you were behind me. You are a force to be reckoned with and I will never regret falling headfirst into the crazy joy of it all. Thank you for helping me find focus, discipline and the will to go on. For every kind word and every piece of criticism—you helped me grow. I can't ever forget it. ❧

About the Author

LISSA REED IS A WRITER OF FICTION, BLOGS AND BAWDY Renaissance song parodies. She traces her first interest in becoming a writer to the fourth grade, when her teacher gave her the gift of her first composition book. A former college newspaper editor, Reed shifted her focus to romance and literary fiction early in her writing career. She lives in the Dallas-Fort Worth area and is currently working on her new novel, *Certainly, Possibly, You*, the sequel to *Definitely, Maybe, Yours*.

Questions for Discussion

1. Craig was not looking for a boyfriend, nor did he think of Alex as good boyfriend material when he met him. What made him change his thinking? What was it about Alex and about them together that caused Craig to fall?

2. Tea plays an important role in the early part of Craig and Alex's relationship, but it means something different for each of them. What does tea mean to Craig? To Alex?

3. How did the offer of tea change a typical one night stand into something different for Alex?

4. How did it change the course of their connection and their relationship as it grew?

5. Baked goods also play an important role in Craig and Alex's relationship, from the first rum cookie to the blackened tube cookies. What symbolism can you find in their gifts to each other?

6. In the beginning of the story, Craig has substituted routine for something missing from his life. What was missing and how did he find it?

7. What does Craig bring to Alex's life that Alex was previously missing?

8. Jeff's behavior toward Alex during their relationship and Alex's response to it end up affecting far more people than just Jeff and Alex. Discuss who is affected by their

dysfunctional relationship and how it permeated into all of Alex's relationships with family and friends.

9. At the end of chapter ten, Sarita tells Craig that love is as simple as spending time with someone, talking to them, and enjoying it, as long as you let it be. Is that true? Why, then, do we make love so complex?

10. How did Connor remind Alex of what was important? Why was Connor such an important figure in the story?

11. Could Craig and Alex have a future together had Jeff not come to Alex's apartment? How did Jeff and Alex's conversation change the course of the story?

—AC Holloway

Also from
interlude  press™

The Luckiest by Mila McWarren

When New York-based memoirist Aaron Wilkinson gathers with his high school friends to marry off two of their own, he is forced to spend a week with Nik, the boy who broke his heart.

As they settle into the Texas beach house where the nuptials will be performed, Nik quickly makes his intentions clear: he wants Aaron back. "He's coming hard, baby," a friend warns, setting the tone for a week of transition where Aaron and Nik must decide if they are playing for keeps.

ISBN 978-1-941530-39-9 | Available July 2015

Spice by Lilah Suzanne

As writer of the popular "Ask Eros" advice column, Simon Beck has an answer to every relationship question his readers can throw at him. When it comes to his own life, the answers are a little more elusive—until computer troubles introduce him to the newest and cutest member of his company's IT support team. Simon may be charmed by Benji's sweet and unassuming manner, but will he find the answer to the one relationship question he has never been able to solve: how to know when he's met Mr. Right?

ISBN 978-1-941530-25-2 | Available March 2015

One **story** can change **everything**.
www.interlude**press**.com

Now available from

interlude 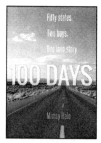 press™

100 Days by Mimsy Hale

Jake and Aiden have been best friends—and nothing more—since the age of six. Now college graduates, they take a road trip around the USA, visiting every state in 100 days.

As they start their cross-country odyssey, Jake and Aiden think they have their journey and their futures mapped out. But the road has a funny way of changing course.

ISBN 978-1-941530-23-8 | Available April 2015

Chef's Table by Lynn Charles

Chef Evan Sandford steadily climbed the ladder to become one of New York City's culinary elite. But in his quest to build his reputation, he forgot what got him there: the lessons on food and life from a loving hometown neighbor. Patrick Sullivan is contented keeping the memory of his grandmother's Irish cooking alive through his work at a Brooklyn diner, but when Evan walks in for a meal, Patrick is swept up by his drive—forcing him to consider if a contented life is a fulfilled one. The two men begin a journey forging a friendship through their culinary histories. But even with the excitement of their burgeoning romance, can they tap into that secret recipe of great love, great food and transcendent joy?

ISBN 978-1-941530-17-7

Forever Man by A.J. DeWall

Ren and Cole never acted on that thing that always bubbled beneath the surface of their friendship, not until a chance encounter in a Santa Fe bar and a song that would tip the scales forced them to confront their feelings. Will the influence of a music superstar, a New York socialite and a mystical property manager finally bring them together, or will a history of missed opportunities, their own fears and an impending wedding keep them apart? Can they just have one night, and then walk away?

ISBN 978-1-941530-00-9

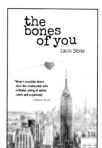

The Bones of You by Laura Stone

Oliver Andrews is focused on his final months at Cambridge University when his life is up-ended with a simple email attachment: a clip from a U.S. morning new show. The moment he watches the video of his one-time love Seth Larsen, now a Broadway star, Oliver must begin making choices that could lead him back to love—or break his heart. The Bones of You is full of laughter and tears, with a collection of irritable Hungarians, flirtatious Irishwomen, and actors abusing Shakespeare coloring Oliver and Seth's attempts at reconciliation.

ISBN 978-1-941530-16-0

One **story** can change **everything**.

www.interlude**press**.com